Praise for  by Claire McFall:

NOMINATED FOR THE CARNEGIE MEDAL.

'... a touching, often funny and sometimes harrowing
first novel about first love.'
The Guardian

'A strong and moving love story that
unfurls like the most beautiful flower. It is a beautifully
written book – poignant and moving.
I couldn't put it down.'
Birmingham Post

'... happy, sad, gripping, beautiful, heart-wrenching and
everything in between.'
Read and Repeat

'... will touch your heart and make you believe that
there is more to life than what we can see. A stunning
original debut from an author we will need to watch out
for in the future.'
Serendipity Reviews

'It was amazing – gorgeous, epic, addictive...
A stunning, stunning debut that left me
absolutely breathless.'
The Book Addicted Girl

'A beautiful take on the afterlife.'
Death, Books and Tea

'*Ferryman* is an addictive read which will tear your heart out and rip it to shreds, but carry on reading because this story needs to be told!'
Readaraptor

'I loved it. Could not put it down! McFall has created great characters, a romance I loved and a landscape that is fresh. Highly recommend!'
Readingawaythedays

'... a fantastic book, a real breath of fresh air.'
Bookapoet

'This book is a must-read and the only question you will want to ask at the end is: When does the author release another book?'
Eloise, 16

'... probably one of the best Young Adult romance books I have ever read.'
Harriet, 13

'... a great choice for young adult readers. It's a book that gives you a wonderful warm feeling.'
Emer, 13

First published in the UK in 2014 by Templar Publishing,
an imprint of The Templar Company Limited,
Deepdene Lodge, Deepdene Avenue,
Dorking, Surrey, RH5 4AT, UK
www.templarco.co.uk

Copyright © Claire McFall 2014
Title lettering by blacksheep-uk.com
Cover design by Will Steele

1 3 5 7 9 10 8 6 4 2

ISBN 978-1-84877-767-5
Printed and bound by CPI Group (UK) Ltd, Croydon, CR0 4YY

CLAIRE McFALL

templar

To Ruth, for buttons and doors...

CHAPTER ONE

My lips were dry, the moisture sucked out of them by the ragged gasping of my breathing as it struggled to keep up with the frantic pounding of my heart. I didn't lick them, impeded by the flashlight clenched tightly between my teeth, held there because both my hands were busy. In my right hand I gripped a block of putty the size of a pack of playing cards; in my left, a blue wire, the gleaming copper ends glinting like flame in the narrow beam of the torch. Carefully, hesitantly, I eased the sharpened points deep into the block of explosive, then I raised my fingers three inches and gripped the tiny switch. Offering up a prayer to no one, I flicked the lever from left to right. A red light blinked on.

I sighed, feeling relief wash through me.

As delicately as I could manage, I lifted the device and slotted it neatly beneath a jumble of motherboards and hard drives. Then I checked each connection, each wire, each switch. Everything had to be perfect; everything had to be right. As a last touch, I pushed a discreet button, and the tiny black box emitted a single shrill beep. I looked at my watch. 11.27 p.m.

Job done, I lifted the heavy metal panel door of the servers unit and slotted it back into place. The sharp edges made a loud grating sound as they slid into position and I froze, listening. Only the whirring of the air conditioning unit kept me company. Satisfied my presence was still unnoticed, I quickly screwed the bolts back in, hiding my handiwork within the depths of the computer. The red light was just visible through the vent near the base, but nobody was going to be looking that closely. Not tonight. Not in the next twenty minutes. I snapped off the flashlight and plunged myself into darkness before I got off my knees.

Now to get out without attracting attention. CCTV cameras were fitted in every room, the overhead lights set with motion detectors. Even the most inept security guard couldn't fail to notice if a hallway suddenly lit up when nobody was supposed to be there. There was an alarm on every window and every exterior door. A bit of a pickle for someone working alone. Luckily I was not.

I flipped out my mobile and dialled the only stored number. Someone answered after just one ring.

"Hello?" A detached male voice spoke, the crackling of the line didn't quite mask his thick Welsh accent.

"I'm done."

"Give me a minute and a half."

The dial tone rang in my ear before the last word had fully formed.

Snapping the clamshell closed, I eased the phone back into my pocket and counted slowly to ninety in my head. Then I lifted the hood of my jumper and eased it over my hair, pulling it forward until it hung low, half concealing my face. I walked straight out of the door and along the corridor towards the lift.

The overhead fluorescents buzzed into life, banishing the shadows of the darkened building and lighting my way. I ignored the waiting lift and took the stairwell, jogging lightly down several floors until I reached ground level. A heavy fire door spat me out into a foyer, cavernous and sparkling white. Strolling forward, I jumped over the low turnstiles where daytime workers swiped their government IDs, letting the long sleeves of my top cover my fingers as I leaned on the pillars to leapfrog; then I marched past the empty security reception, out through the front door.

A car was waiting for me at the roadside, gleaming black in the pool of light from the wide open entranceway. I opened the passenger door, pausing to look at a noisy kerfuffle happening a little way along the street. Several security guards were struggling to contain a group of youths armed with spray cans and baseball bats. I smiled. How convenient for me.

"Get in," a low voice ordered from within the vehicle.

I did as the man said, and as soon as I closed the door the car ghosted away. I fastened my seat belt as we turned left at the end of the road, joining a steady stream of traffic. Even at this time of night the city centre remained congested, providing plenty of cover for us to disappear, should any prying eyes be watching.

"Any problems?"

In the yellow glare of the streetlights I stared at the silhouette of my driver, Samuel. He looked straight ahead, his eyes darting from vehicle to vehicle, hunting for the red and black markings of a GE patrol.

"No," I said, my voice hushed.

"How long have we got?"

I twisted my wrist to squint at my watch, the tiny luminous dials winking at me through the darkness.

"About five minutes."

"Plenty of time to clear the scene."

I nodded, but he wasn't paying attention to me. He was on high alert, the same way he always was whenever Alexander made him travel within the Central Zone. He didn't like it here; it was too tightly controlled, too penned in. We were silent as we wound slowly through the maze of gridlocked cars. I wanted to turn on the radio, but Samuel hadn't given me permission and I didn't want to ask. Instead I stared at my watch, following the second hand as it rotated in jerking circles, counting the minutes as they ticked past. I didn't feel it when the clock struck 11.47 p.m., but the sky behind me flashed white then orange in the rear-view mirror.

"Good work, Lizzie," Samuel muttered to me as he passed by the bollards marking the edge of the Zone. "Alex will be pleased."

I didn't say anything. I hoped the security guards

were still outside, dealing with the hired yobs.

We sped up as we crossed the river and made our way into the East End. Traffic was lighter here. Most people didn't have the money for cars or, more specifically, petrol. Besides, it wasn't the sort of area where it was safe to be out after dark. Stop-and-grabs were widespread, and it was common for drivers to ignore red lights at junctions. No one was likely to interfere with our car, however. They knew better.

Samuel pulled up outside a large tenement building. It had been a block of flats, but Alexander had bought them all and then converted the place into one huge four-storey mansion. On the outside it was as tatty and rundown as any of the other buildings on the street, but inside it was the central hub of his empire, testament to how his business had grown. And he was doing very well.

We got out of the car and a young lackey appeared immediately to take the keys from Samuel.

"Wipe it, strip it, sell it," Samuel told him.

Then he clapped me on the shoulder and guided me inside. I felt a familiar knot tie itself in my stomach. We were going to see Alexander.

The door was opened for us before we reached it, a great hulking figure nodding curtly to Samuel, one hand on a bulge in his leather jacket. He was the gatekeeper, the man who decided whether or not you got in; and if you did, whether you went up, down or straight ahead. Business transactions happened on the ground floor, dodgy dealings in the basement. Only 'family' went upstairs.

Those special few who made it into Alexander's inner circle.

We headed straight for the staircase, making for the first floor where Alexander kept his private office. It wasn't so much an office as a vast open space housing everything a gangster might need, and quite a few things he probably never would. There was a stainless steel, state-of-the-art kitchen area, which housed more booze than food; a pool table; a giant flat screen attached to the wall; several luxurious white leather sofas; a corner bedecked with office furniture and, half hidden behind a screen, a king-sized bed. The whole room was opulent and decadent, and I hated the place.

"You made the news," Alexander said as soon as we entered, pressing a button on the remote so that the television sprang to life. "A special broadcast. It interrupted _Detective Plum._"

I looked at the screen, trying hard to keep my face impassive. A female reporter stood to the left of the shot, mouthing silently into the camera. Over her right shoulder, flames and smoke billowed from a grand stone building, the government logo just visible beneath the flashing blue lights of the emergency services. Ticker tape running along the bottom of the screen announced that police suspected terrorists were involved in the bombing of the Home Office Information building.

They were right to suspect.

"I knew I could trust my Elizabeth," he said softly, rolling off the sofa and crossing the room towards us. His walk was like a cat, stealthy and lithe. He came right up to me and placed his hands on either side of my face. "Clever girl," he kissed me full on the lips. My mouth tingled at the same time as my stomach clenched with fear.

Then he dropped his hands and turned to his brother, dismissing me. I stared at the two of them: so similar, so very, very different. The Evans brothers. Both were on the short side of average, both had green eyes and brown hair, both spoke with lilting Welsh accents. But, whereas Samuel was lean and wiry in a tough way, Alexander, mindful of the fact that his brother was a full inch taller, had worked his muscles till they bulked out, and the broadness of his chest and shoulders was clear beneath the designer-cut suit he wore. Alexander also had the first hint of lines etching into the corners of his mouth; at twenty-eight he was four years older than his brother. But the main difference was that Samuel had the intricate, symmetrical knot tattooed on his left cheek, whereas Alexander's cheek was beautifully smooth, lasered clean.

Alexander was also a hell of a lot meaner.

"Any problems?"

Samuel shook his head. "She went in; all the stuff was there, where it should have been; she set up the bomb; then we created a distraction to get her out. Simple. And it all went like clockwork."

Alexander nodded, twisting one side of his mouth up into a satisfied smile. He liked it when things went like clockwork. So did I; because when they didn't, someone invariably ended up visiting Zane in the basement and they were never seen again. Zane was Alexander's personal bodyguard, but he also dealt with employees who had to be 'despatched' from the payroll. He was here now, lingering discreetly on one of the sofas, alert blue eyes watching everything that went on. His posture was relaxed, but I knew that if I raised my hand to take a swing at Alexander, he'd be across the room and I'd be face down in the thick shag of the carpet, my arm dislocated up my back, before my palm made contact with Alexander's cheek. That, or he'd just shoot me. But then Alexander would be annoyed; he didn't like blood in his office.

"And the car?"

"We'll get rid of it, after it's been cleaned down. Nobody saw us, but that doesn't mean the police won't go through the CCTV for the street. We'll probably have to take a loss on it."

Alexander made a face. He didn't like making losses either.

"We should have used something older, a cheap car." Samuel shook his head.

"Bad idea, Alex. It would have looked out of place in that part of town. We'd have been stopped by a GE patrol before we got anywhere near."

I tried not to smile as Alexander nodded in rueful agreement. Samuel was the only one who dared to argue with his brother, he was also the only person who could get away with calling him Alex. Alexander didn't shorten names. That's why I was Elizabeth to him, and Lizzie to everyone else.

"You're sure there will be nothing to tie this to us?"

Samuel nodded.

"Lizzie kept her face out of the cameras; no one will be able to identify her."

"Gloves?"

Both brothers looked to me. I paled. Samuel had told me to wear gloves, had made a point of handing them to me. And I'd deliberately left them in the car. Samuel wasn't going to tell on me, but he wasn't going to take the heat for it either.

"I can't work with gloves on," I said, my strangled whisper barely audible above the sound of four people quietly breathing. "My fingers slip."

Alexander's face darkened.

"If you've left fingerprints..."

"I haven't!" I stammered. "I didn't touch anything, only the gear. I swear. Even when I was taking the panel on and off, I covered my hands with my sleeves." I held up my arms, hidden beneath the overlong fabric of my hoodie, as proof.

"I sincerely hope so," Alexander said softly.

My pulse broke into a sprint, dewy sweat forming at the base of my back. Alexander didn't shout, ever. Someone who had to bellow and bawl had lost control, and Alexander never, ever lost control. In any case, there was never any need for him to raise his voice, because whenever he opened his mouth to speak, everyone shut the hell up and listened. But when he was quiet, when his voice dropped to the low murmur of a lover, that was when he was most dangerous. That was when your life hung in the balance. I knew if my name cropped up in the police investigation – and if it did, even if it was only mentioned once, in passing, Alexander would know about it – then I would be taking a trip with Zane. I saw him now, out of the corner of my eye, smiling at me.

Three sharp raps sounded. I jumped, and we all turned towards the door. We waited, but the door didn't open. Whoever was outside knew well enough that entry to Alexander's office was strictly by invitation only – unless you were Samuel.

"Zane."

Though Alexander was only feet from the door, he turned and looked at his bodyguard. It was part of the charade, after all. What sort of gangster opened his own door?

Zane got up and breezed past us, shielding the room with his body as he opened the door. No bullet was getting through the thickness of his bulk to take his boss by surprise.

I tried to listen to his low conversation, but nothing audible drifted my way. After a few seconds, Zane clicked the door quietly closed and crossed to where we stood. He leaned close, whispered a few words in Alexander's ear. I saw Alexander's eyes narrow, then widen in warning and reproach as he caught me watching, unduly interested.

"I see," he said, still staring at me.

Raising his right hand to my face, his fingers traced lightly around the tattoo on my cheek. I forced myself to hold his gaze.

"I have some business to take care of downstairs. Elizabeth, why don't you go and make yourself comfortable."

It wasn't a suggestion.

I stared at him, mutinous. I knew exactly what he wanted me to do, but Zane and Samuel were still in the room. It was a test, a vindictive game; just one more opportunity for Alexander to remind me that I belonged to him.

I did belong to him.

Turning on my heel, I made my way slowly towards the bed. Mindful of three pairs of eyes on me, my cheeks burned as I stripped off my hoodie and T-shirt as I walked. The rest of my clothes I shrugged off behind the screen. Then I crawled into his bed to wait.

CHAPTER TWO

Lying on my back, I stared at myself. Two cold grey eyes stared back. They were framed by thick, dark lashes, and stood out in a pinched, snowy-white face. My hair was a mess, the short pixie cut ruffled and sticking up at odd angles. In my nose and running up the sides of both ears, silver and diamanté studs glittered in the spotlights Alexander's interior designer had installed along with the mirrored ceiling. The lights lit up every angle of my androgynous frame; and my face, with its set, hardened expression that was much too worldly-wise for my eighteen years. It was a hard face to look at.

Trailing my eyes down, I gazed at the arm flung across my stomach. Against my pallid skin it looked tanned, the muscles huge, the bicep almost as thick as my waist. It was heavy, pinning me down. At first glance it might have seemed the embrace of a lover, but it wasn't. Alexander lay on his front, his face turned away from me. His arm around me was nothing more than a possessive gesture: I was not allowed to move until he said so.

I was his. Not his wife, or his girlfriend. I was something he owned, like the building, or the sleek silver Jaguar he drove, or the collection of expensive watches laid out on a shelf in the dressing room, cleverly concealed behind the bed. In fact, I was less than that, because he cared a great deal more for his fancy toys than he did for me. But he had total and utter control over every aspect of my life. He dictated where I went, what I did, who I spoke to. I did nothing without permission, and I knew with total certainty that it would be up to him to decide when it was time for me to die.

Because if it wasn't for him, I would be dead already.

When the global economy collapsed, the world as we knew it changed overnight. China and the USA were at each other's throats, with Europe caught in the crossfire. Germany and France were pushing hard for laws and policies that would reel Britain in, make her a slave. So we left the EU. We'd been persuaded, in desperation, into taking the Euro, but we soon came out of it again, and tried to go it alone. It didn't work very well. After just five years the country was bankrupt, the people starving. The government in London made the decision to dissolve the United Kingdom, to make it every Englishman for himself. They cut off Scotland, Northern Ireland and Wales – built great cement and steel structures that put the Berlin Wall to shame. And they cast out the Celts – sent us back to our hills and our heather and our empty pockets. The law was simple: any Celt caught in England without a visa was tattooed – a Celtic knot, on the left cheek where it was impossible to hide – and then sent back home. Any Celt caught in England without a visa and with a tattoo, was shot. No trial, no mercy.

I was caught by the GE, the Government Enforcers, for the first time when I was sixteen. I wasn't homeless, but I was sleeping on the street, just for that night. I had a job, working in a little café, but I'd run out of cash and I couldn't pay the rent on the cupboard-sized bedsit I was living in, so I was out. But only for one night – one single night. I'd get my wages the next day, pay what I owed, and have a roof back over my head, even if it was a leaky one. All I had to do was survive a few hours of darkness. I found myself a semi-dry doorway, spread my jacket out over my knees, and prepared to try to sleep, the rucksack containing all my important possessions hugged tight to my chest.

I didn't even have time to get uncomfortable.

"What's this then? You can't sleep here, love. Come on, up you get."

A strong hand hooked under my arm and pulled me up onto my feet. A middle-aged man with a bushy grey moustache and a GE uniform looked at me, not unkindly, as I dusted myself off. His partner, however, was scowling at me, like I was a rat that had crawled out of a drain.

"Where's your ID card?" he snapped.

I didn't have one.

"I haven't got all day. Where's your ID card?"

I just stared at him, eyes begging for mercy. The one with the moustache sighed sadly. His partner crowed with unconcealed delight.

"Well, well, well. I think we've got ourselves a Celt!"

He slapped cuffs on me, hustled me out of the alleyway and forced me into the back of a waiting GE van. From there I was taken to a police station, where an officer swabbed the inside of my cheek and ran me through the database. No hits. Not English.

"Where are you from?" she asked.

"Glasgow," I muttered. There was no point lying, not now.

"So why didn't you leave?"

We'd all been told to get out, given ninety days to make our way back to our 'homelands'. You could apply for a visa, if you'd lived in England long enough, but I hadn't, and I wouldn't have had the money or the skills to pass the Home Office's twenty checks anyway. There were no appeals, there was no asylum.

I shrugged.

"You know, the people in this country can't afford to pay for everyone," she went on.

I stared at her. She was one of *them*: the people who thought the government had got it right. The people who were quite happy to cut off millions and see them living in poverty and squalor like some Third World country.

She frowned, annoyed that I wouldn't respond, wouldn't apologise for my existence.

"How old are you?"

I glowered at her, then answered the question she was really asking.

"Old enough."

Twelve. That was the age limit they'd set, the age at which you were deemed old enough to be responsible for the fact you were standing in a country that no longer wanted you. The age at which you could be scarred for life. Just twelve.

She grunted in response.

"Come with me. You're lucky, you'll not have to wait long today."

I didn't have to wait at all. Tattoo Room 3 was empty. I was escorted in, handcuffed to the chair, and a thick leather strap was tied across my forehead to keep my head still. A pointless exercise: who was going to weave their head about when a man was coming at their face with a needle?

It was the most painful thing I had experienced, up until that point at least. The design was intricate, beautiful really. A Celtic knot. It was something I wouldn't have minded having on my hip or my shoulder, something to remind me of home. If I'd had a choice. I would *not* have chosen to have it burned into my face.

They left me to cry myself to sleep in a police cell overnight, then in the morning I was put on a bus with about thirty others and we were driven back up north. Soldiers at the border conducted us through a tunnel, then simply let us go. Like animals released into the wild, we were expected just to survive. Never mind that there was little in the way of government in Scotland any more, and absolutely no welfare state. There were no jobs, no money, no food. No chances.

As soon as I could, I got myself back down to England, buying my way with my looks, my smile and my body, catching a lift with a rich businessman with no morals and a big boot. Once we got to London he went his way and I went mine, and I survived. I slept rough, I tried to get a job, but it was harder this time. I'd been marked. Nobody wanted the GE raiding their business, so they wouldn't take the risk. Without money, there were few places indoors to hide. It was only a matter of time before they caught me; and this time, when they did, I was dead.

It was raining on the night that should have been my last. Raining hard, the drops bounced off the concrete, driven faster by the strong wind. I was walking; not going anywhere, just walking. It was too wet to bunk down, and by keeping moving I could at least stay warm. Trouble was, seventeen-year-old girls on the street, at night, on their own, attracted things. Like men: driving past in cars, spilling out of pubs. They'd erupt from the gutter to catcall and paw, grabbing a handful if they thought they could get away with it. The seedier the area, the worse it got. You could head for the safety of the Central Zone, for the GE, but it was a balancing act. Too far out from the city centre and you were walking into trouble, too close and you were walking into worse.

I was definitely flirting with danger, weaving my way through the bollards that marked out the Zone, but I'd had a bad night. A man had actually stopped, got out of his car and tried to drag me inside. I'd screamed for help, but no one wanted so much as to look out of their windows, so I'd had to defend myself. I'd kicked him, hard, and then I'd run. I was fine, but I was shaken, and I was in no hurry to repeat the experience. So I moved towards the lights and the CCTV of the Central Zone.

They probably saw me on one of the cameras positioned at every corner. I had my hood up, to keep off the rain, but more importantly to hide my face. It must have looked suspicious, because the next street I turned into, the GE patrol car was waiting for me. Two doors opened, two officers stepped out. One spoke into the radio pinned to his chest.

"We've got her. Yeah, I can see it from here. Going to be a Code Six. Send round a van."

I could guess easily enough what that meant. It was time to do some more running.

All GE officers carry guns. They claim it's for protection, but in reality it's so that they can dish out the swift, final judgement and sentence on any Celts they catch, so there's no time for pleas or trials or true justice. I knew as soon as I tried to run they were allowed to gun me down in the street, they didn't have to take me to the station and put me down in the sanitary, humane way. I was dead either way, but if I bolted, there was the smallest chance I could outrun a bullet.

"Don't!" one of them warned, seeing the thought on my face as if it were written on my forehead. He stepped forward, right hand reaching to his side, fingers fumbling with the catch of his holster. I glimpsed a flash of dark grey, the shining length of a barrel, and then I was gone.

I sprinted back the way I'd come, weaving and dancing, keeping myself close to expensive cars or large windows, knowing they wouldn't want to shoot, miss, and risk causing major damage to something belonging to somebody important. It was that sort of neighbourhood. But even uptown has its alleyways, its narrow back lanes where rats scuttle and dodgy deals are done, and that's where I was heading. Somewhere dark; somewhere someone small could disappear.

I kicked down just such an alleyway as one of the GEs decided he had a clear shot. The bullet whipped past me, slamming into the brick wall. Dust flew up in a cloud to my right, sending my already pounding heart into overdrive. I panicked, willing my legs to move faster, willing my lungs to keep working. I was barely looking where I was going, just concentrating on putting one foot in front of the other, as quickly as possible. So when I hit the man standing in the darkest depths of the passage, I took him down.

We sprawled on the ground, limbs entwining, his back scraping along the concrete floor for several feet. The impact knocked my breath from my lungs and snapped my neck, sending a jolt down my back like I'd broken my spine. Two arms, his, grabbed me, held me there, while both of us tried to work out what had just happened.

That wasn't Alexander. Alexander was standing in the

shadow of a doorway, right where I'd fallen, halfway through concluding a drug deal with the stranger I'd inadvertently attacked. His sharp eyes quickly took in the tattoo, clearly visible on my cheek now that my hood had fallen down, and the two GE officers chasing me. Without hesitating, he stepped out into their path, lifted his hand, and shot both men in the chest. There was no explosion, no crack of gunfire, just two hollow pops as the bullets burst out of his silencer. I watched them drop, astounded.

Then I turned to him just as he turned to me.

If I thought I'd met my saviour, I was sadly mistaken. Alexander had been protecting himself, the wad of money for the bag of cocaine he'd just handed over was burning a hole in his pocket. If the GE had caught him, he'd have been tattooed, jailed, maybe even executed. No, he wasn't rescuing me; he was looking out for his own interests. And making sure I never opened my mouth about this was definitely in his interest. He considered me for the length of a heartbeat, then lifted the gun again.

"No!" I managed to find my voice. "No, please. Please."

I was staring into death.

"Christ, shoot her, Alex. I think she's broken my wrist."

So he fired. He pulled the trigger, sent a bullet flying through the air at a thousand miles an hour.

But he didn't shoot me.

The low-ranking dealer should have known better than to shorten his boss's name.

Alexander picked me up, dragged me down the lane away from the three corpses lying in puddles of rainwater and their own blood, and stuck me in the passenger seat of his car. Then he drove off, taking me out of danger. Into hell.

From that minute on, he owned me.

I sighed and closed my eyes, wondering if there was any chance of more sleep, but the clock inlaid into the wall said 7.57 a.m., and Alexander always woke up at eight, without an alarm and without fail. I had to get up then, too. By nine, we'd be joined by Zane and any other business associates Alexander was trying to smarm by inviting them to his private office. A buxom blonde in his bed might send off the right signals; but me, I was just untidy.

"Elizabeth."

I opened my eyes, and he was staring at me. He didn't smile; Alexander rarely smiled, unless he was about to punish someone. He just stared – green eyes seeing right through me – as if he could see my soul. He was a very hard man to lie to, that was one of the reasons he was so successful. He knew when people weren't telling the truth, or when they were feeling guilty. If someone was on the take, or trying to play both sides, trying to get one over on him, Alexander would be onto them like lightning. And they'd be dead.

"I need you to make a few deliveries today," he said.

Deliveries. That was how I'd started out my career working for Alexander. Dropping off and picking up. I'd been good at it, too. I asked no questions and I did what

I was told. I didn't do drugs, so I was never tempted to open up the mysterious brown packages handed to me and help myself to a sample, and I wasn't the average drug runner. The police weren't looking for a girl who looked like she should still be in school. I was able to slip in unnoticed where big, mean men would set alarm bells ringing. More importantly, I knew I had to do well, or he'd decide I wasn't useful any more.

"Okay," I replied. I hesitated. "Are they daylight deliveries?"

"Yes."

I didn't wince, but my heart sank. I hated going out in the daylight. The tattoo was impossible to hide; that was, after all, the whole point of it.

I bit my lip and decided that, since it was the morning and he seemed to be in a reasonable mood, I would push my luck.

"Can I take someone with me?"

He shook his head before I'd even got half my question out.

"No, I want you to keep a low profile."

I nodded, accepting that. I had learned from experience not to argue.

"See Zane. He'll tell you what I need you to do."

Alexander rolled off the bed, leaving me to make a face to myself in the ceiling. Zane would be deliberately difficult. He worshipped Alexander, and although he wasn't a homosexual, sometimes I was sure he wished he could take my place in his master's bed. I would have happily swapped. He didn't like to speak to me, and he made no secret of that fact that he couldn't understand why Alexander kept me around – though he said nothing to his face of course.

I was right. An hour later, Zane took me downstairs, *way* downstairs, into the basement. He stomped around, his expression making it crystal clear that he thought dealing with me was beneath him.

"Mr Alexander has a very specific job for you," he glowered at me out of the corner of his eye. "He needs you to make a drop off, then you're on cash collection."

"Cash collection?" I echoed, dubious.

"Yes. Cash collection," Zane snapped.

I was surprised. Usually Alexander sent muscle to pick up payments. But more than that, he very rarely sent me out alone any more, and never with any money in my pocket. He didn't want me to get any ideas in my head about disappearing. Perhaps, at last, he'd started to trust me. Or, more likely, this was another of his little tests, upping the ante until he found the one I'd fail.

"Where?"

"The drop off is St Paul's." My breath sucked in: the Central Zone. Zane ignored me. "And the collection is out at Kensington. There's a proper address in the bag, and a change of clothes. Don't use it till you've done the drop off."

Zane dumped a small rucksack on the table in front of me. It was pink and blue, more girlie than anything else I owned. It looked like something a schoolgirl would wear. I sighed, guessing that was the role I was playing. My eyes flitted to the left, where Zane was unlocking a steel cabinet with a large, jangling collection of keys. Inside was my package.

"This," he said, turning round and holding up a small brown parcel about the size of a brick, "has been weighed accurate to a milligram."

So don't steal any.

Not that I would.

"Who's picking it up?"

He gave an evil grin, and I felt unease bubbling in my stomach.

"It's a man called Riley."

"How will I know him? ID?"

"You'll know." He was smirking like the cat that got the cream. Warning sirens were firing in my brain.

"Zane—"

"He's GE." He dropped the bombshell, then watched my face, waiting to see it fall. I refused to give him the satisfaction, but inside I was quaking. I knew that Alexander had several high-ranking officers from the police and the GE in his pocket; it was how he kept them away from his premises, how most of his deals went unnoticed, unpunished. I'd never met any of them before, or at least, I didn't know if I had. They terrified me. They could shoot me on the spot, my inky cheek the only warrant they would need.

"Fine," I said, forcing my voice not to tremble. "Is there a list for the collections?"

Zane gave me a long look, disappointed in my lack of reaction, then thumped a large book down on the table. He shuffled through until he found the right page, and spun it round to face me. It was a list, about twenty names running down the left-hand column, and then a series of dates along the top of the double page. Various amounts had been crossed out: debt paid. Alexander's books. He didn't trust computers. Computers could be hacked. Every amount was stored in two key places: his head and Zane's. The basement held the third copy, the paper copy. The back up.

I gave the list one more glance. This was my job for today. I reached out and lifted the book, but Zane slammed his hand down, knocking it back to the tabletop. He shook his head. The list didn't leave the basement, apart from in my head.

I memorised all twenty names, and the amounts they owed. It was an odd register. They were all girls, the cash sums paltry in comparison with most of Alexander's deals. That didn't bother me, though. There was less chance of trouble that way. Once I could repeat it by rote for Zane three times without making mistakes, he took me back upstairs, handed me a jacket and a phone.

"What's the number?" I asked.

The mobiles I was given only ever had one telephone number logged into the directory, and that was the only one they could call.

"Mine," Zane said. I grimaced at the floor as I shrugged my way into a tight-fitting denim jacket. "You've got until four this afternoon," he said, shoving the rucksack into my hands. "Don't make me have to call you."

"Right," I muttered.

"Lizzie?" a voice behind me called my name. It was Samuel.

"She's going out," Zane said curtly, his harsh Northern Irish accent jarring again Samuel's soft Welsh one.

"Where to?"

"St Paul's."

I didn't say anything. I was used to being talked about as if I wasn't there. It was nice to see Samuel make a face when he heard my destination, though. We shared a dislike of the Central Zone.

"Come here," he said, reaching into his inside jacket pocket.

"She's leaving now," Zane protested, putting a hand on my arm when I moved.

Samuel stared at him, and Zane stared back, but only for a moment. Then he dropped his arm, and his head. Zane might be Alexander's right-hand man, his shadow, but Samuel was Alexander's brother. That meant he won the weigh in, just.

I trooped forward, scuffed and tatty Cat boots clumping loudly on the wooden floor. My eyes were on a small jar in his hands.

"You'll need this, if you're going to the Zone," he said, dunking two fingers into a beige cream and smearing it across my skin, over the interwoven lines running a never-ending circle around my cheek. "It's not a perfect match," he said, rubbing it in. "You're too pale. But it's better than nothing."

He finished his work, but left his hand against my cheek. His touch was warm against my skin, comforting. His eyes – Alexander's and yet absolutely not – stared down at me. I gazed back, saying nothing, doing my best to think nothing, waiting to be dismissed.

"Why is she still here?" Alexander's voice cut through the moment as he descended the stairs. I half turned my head to look at him, and Samuel dropped his hand at once. Not fast enough for Alexander's quick eyes to miss it, though. He paused on the bottom step, exuding a deathly calm, but for the snakelike narrowing of his eyes. No one spoke, we were waiting for Alexander.

"Elizabeth," he murmured. "Go."

I went, shouldering past Zane on my way out of the door.

"Four o'clock," he hissed in my ear as I passed.

CHAPTER THREE

The door slammed closed behind me before I'd made my way down the four steps onto the street. A man eyed me thoughtfully from the safety of a blue hatchback idling by the curb as I started walking, but I didn't pay him any attention. He was either undercover police, in which case I was definitely not important enough for him to follow, or, more likely, he was part of Alexander's security, watching who went past the building.

It was a warm day, muggy beneath a thick layer of cloud, so I was far too hot under the layers of my T-shirt, light hoodie and the denim jacket. The rucksack was heavy on my back, weighed down by the package, and sweat quickly began to collect between my shoulder blades. I really wanted to shrug off the denim jacket, but I didn't. I'd been handed the thing, which meant Alexander wanted me to wear it. Whether there were reasons behind the decision or not, it was smarter just to follow orders, spoken or otherwise, to the letter.

There was no question of my taking off the hoodie either.

Even with the thick make-up Samuel had coated on my face to hide the tattoo – the same stuff they give to burn victims – I felt like there was a spotlight on me as I walked. I wished I had thick, heavy curtains of hair, like I used to have, to hang forward and hide half my face, but Alexander liked my black hair chopped short, elfin-like, so that was how I wore it. Self-consciously I yanked the hood up, locking in the heat but covering up my deformity.

Alexander's headquarters was on Bancroft Road, in the midst of the Underground triangle of Bethnal Green, Mile End and Stepney Green, but I didn't head to any of those stations. The Underground was the government's favourite way of playing big brother. All tickets were issued, paid for and tracked using the government's ID card scheme. Sharp cameras kept watch for anyone whose face didn't match their card, and Alexander's claws hadn't quite dug deep enough to make a contact who could get him official ID cards. Not yet.

I wasn't walking either. It was three miles to St Paul's, and I had to make my drop-off then get myself to Kensington and back by Zane's deadline. I checked my watch. Just after eleven. I should have plenty of time, barring complications.

The Underground might have been tied up tight with security, but the trains were lagging sadly behind. They were much less popular, having been an early target of the various Celt terrorist groups, and without the ticket money coming in, the government couldn't justify the expense of updating the infrastructure. Only the underclass, the poor, used the overground trains. The ones who couldn't afford their own transport and had reasons to want to avoid the more heavily monitored Underground. People like me.

I made my way to the station at Whitechapel, bought my ticket to Blackfriars with cash I found in the denim jacket pocket, then stood unobtrusively beside a pillar to wait. The platform was fairly empty, a few youths loitering on benches, oblivious to the old woman with heavy shopping bags who really wanted to sit but was wary of opening her mouth. Down at the other end, as far from the ticketing booth as he could get, was an old man, homeless by the state of his clothes and the loaded shopping trolley that he'd somehow managed to get down the steps. There was one more person; the one I looked at the least, but was most acutely aware of. He was maybe mid-twenties and thuggish looking, and he was staring at me.

Alexander was having me tailed. That was both galling and reassuring. He wasn't doing a very good job; I'd clocked him when I was buying my ticket, and the more I watched the more obvious it was that he was following my every move. I sniffed, looked at him for long enough for our eyes to lock and let him know that I knew exactly what he was doing. I smirked to myself as I looked away. If I wanted to leave him chasing my shadow I could, I was positive of that, but I'd just get us both into trouble.

The train rattled in and groaned to a stop. The door

that halted in front of me was buckled and warped, the glass a spider's web of cracks. It refused to open when I hit the button, forcing me to jog along to the next one and throw myself in behind the old woman before the door closed at my back.

The inside of the carriage was dimly lit, the tightly meshed cages over the windows cutting out a lot of the light. They were more for show than anything else. If a bomb went off they would provide little protection. I sat on a plastic seat that had been warped and blackened by matches, and stared into nothing as I recited Alexander's list in my head.

At Blackfriars I got off, as did my shadow. We made our way up the hill along Queen Victoria Street, turning left onto New Change. The dome of the cathedral peeked at me at intervals, looming between the roofs of assorted buildings, guiding me in.

The closer I got, the more nervous I became. The streets were full of business people and policemen. GE patrols drove past me every few seconds. Of course the Central Zone would be on high alert after the events of last night. There was no more dangerous place for the guilty bomber to be. Was this Alexander's idea of a joke?

I stopped in the small square outside the cathedral, sitting down on one of the white stone steps, the rucksack between my legs. My minder hovered behind the columns of the building opposite. I had a feeling he'd disappear once I was no longer in possession of my – or more specifically Alexander's – valuable cargo. Trying to look like I was just bored, I surreptitiously checked my watch. I was here exactly when Zane told me I should be. That was good, because if I'd been late I was sure it would have been reported. Clockwork, I told myself.

"You can't sit here!"

I jumped at the harsh voice above me. Black boots came to a stop in front of my face. Above them, black uniform trousers and a black jacket. A red GE logo adorned the left breast of the jacket, as well as the hat. I gulped. Was this the man I was supposed to meet, or was this just another one of the hundreds of GE crawling over the Central Zone?

"I'm sorry," I gasped. "I was just waiting for my friend."

"Oh really, and who would that be?" He didn't stare at my face – didn't seem to notice my accent.

"Riley," I stuttered out the name Zane had given me, but there was no spark of recognition in the man's eye. He continued to glare down at me.

"What have you got in the bag?" he barked. "Come on, open it!"

I resisted the urge to look at the thug Alexander had sent to tail me. I was afraid of being caught exchanging wordless communication, and there was no guarantee he'd know who I was supposed to be meeting, either.

With trembling fingers I unzipped the bag, pulled the two seams apart to show him the inside. The little brown package nestled on top, impossible to miss. The GE officer hunkered down, stretched a finger out to stroke the top of the paper. He looked up at me, his expression unreadable, and I felt a cold hand squeeze my chest. He was only a foot or so away. Was Samuel's make-up good enough to hide my tattoo? Had I got the right man? If not, was I about to die?

He licked his lips. "Is it all there?"

Not trusting myself to speak, I nodded.

His fingers curled around the parcel. He lifted it, tested the weight, then in one swift movement, snatched it up and stuffed it down the front of his jacket. It was too big and bulky not to stand out, but it could just as easily have been a firearm. Few people were going to question a GE.

"Tell Alexander this will do him a month," he said. Then he straightened up and marched away.

My lungs unfroze as I watched his departing back and I hauled in gulps of humid, polluted air. My eyes searched the columns for my minder, but he was already gone. I wasn't valuable enough to watch.

I got up and made my way to a little fast-food shop across the street and bought myself a cheeseburger. It was limp, tasteless and difficult to swallow, but I persevered. Then I went into the bathroom and threw it straight back up. I was shaking, tension and adrenaline spiking in my veins like the drugs I'd just delivered. Flushing away the contents of my stomach, I sat down on the pan, my head in my hands, trying to get a hold of myself. I needed to get back in control; I still had another job to do.

Sighing, I reached for the bag, unzipped it and peered inside.

"You have to be joking!"

The change of clothing that Zane had packed in the bottom of my rucksack consisted of a short black skirt and cardigan, a white shirt, red striped tie and sensible black shoes. A school uniform. At the bottom of the bag my searching fingers wrapped around a sheet of paper. Alexander's spiky handwriting had scrawled across the surface.

KING'S COURT COLLEGE

Underneath was an address in Earl's Terrace, one of the most exclusive streets in Kensington. He wanted me to go and collect drug money in a school? No wonder he hadn't been able to send any of his usual lackeys; they'd stand out a mile down there. I was unlikely to fare much better. However, I wasn't going back to Stepney without every penny of his money.

I quickly stripped down to my underwear and dragged on the new outfit. It looked ridiculous. In the grubby mirror outside the stall I looked at myself critically. It was all wrong: the good little student who also had piercings covering her face? I'd never make it within a mile of the place without some overprotective parent or teacher calling the police. I drummed my fingers against the cold porcelain of the sink, thinking. Then I kicked off the flats and shoved my feet back in my Cats, leaving the laces untied. I yanked the short skirt up to obscene levels, opened the top four buttons of my shirt and stuffed the tie down inside it, like it was an arrow pointing the way to my non-existent cleavage. I already had the hair and the piercings for the look. When I was finished I studied myself. Much less posh, much more convincing. Every private school had misfits like this.

I stuffed my old clothes in the rucksack and zipped it up before I pushed my sleeves through the cardigan. It had a hood, a rare show of consideration from Alexander that caught me by surprise. I flipped it up. Now I definitely looked like a good girl trying too hard to be bad. Perfect.

Back at Blackfriars, I tripped on my way in, knocked into a girl dressed similarly to me, who was digging in her bag for her ID card. We both went sprawling, the contents of her satchel spilling across the ground.

"I'm sorry!" I said, helping her pick up pens and make-up. She didn't have an awful lot of books in there, I noticed. But then, if she went to classes she wouldn't be out in the middle of the school day. I left her growling just outside the entrance, still hunting in her bag, whilst I used her ID card to buy my access to the Circle line.

I got off at Kensington and headed for the High Street. It was another world; stately apartments over boutique shops, the roadside lined with expensive-looking cars. Housewives window-shopped, looking as if they didn't have a care in the world. It was like the last five years had never happened.

I fixed the look of contempt of a troubled youth on my face and started forward. My attire and my attitude afforded me plenty of stares, but they were disapproving and critical rather than suspicious.

It was half one, the very tail end of lunchtime, but the kind of girls I was looking for weren't likely to be rushing back for afternoon Latin. They'd be loitering somewhere, just out of sight of the school grounds, smoking, maybe drinking, congratulating themselves on putting two fingers up to the establishment and wasting the thousands their doting parents were spending on their education. They'd be easy to find.

In fact, I struck gold with the first cluster of girls I came across. They were huddled just off the High Street, on Edwardes Square in the shade of a wall overshadowed by huge oak trees, cover enough to hide the spirals of smoke issuing from their roll ups.

"I'm looking for Amy C," I said, walking right up to them.

One of them pouted, exhaling what was possibly supposed to be a ring of smoke from ruby red lips. It didn't work.

"You don't go to King's," she accused.

I smiled. "No, I don't."

I wondered if I'd found Amy C.

"Why are you wearing the uniform then? Why are you here? And what sort of accent is that?" she eyed me suspiciously.

I ignored the first question. "I'm here to collect." And ignored the last.

There was a moment of silence, strained on their part, triumphant on mine. Their expressions ranged from fearful to resigned to disgruntled. The girl who'd spoken was definitely in the latter group.

"How do we know who you are?" she demanded.

"Have you got any proof?"

I stared at her, my face immobile except for one eyebrow, which I arched incredulously.

"Just pay her, Amy," another girl sighed, her purse already opened.

"Name?" I held out my hand expectantly.

"Naomi."

"That's one hundred and twenty."

Naomi handed it to me without a word.

After her I went around the little group. Amy C was the last to hand over her cash. I wasn't surprised; hers was the biggest bill by a long way. Still peanuts, though, comparatively speaking. Alexander was just playing with these girls, waiting for them to grow up before he starting charging them the big bucks.

"Do you work for Zane then?" One of the girls, Marie, was eyeing me curiously.

I smiled thinly. "Sort of."

"Oh, you're so lucky! Isn't he fit?"

I said nothing, wondering if she'd fancy him quite so much if she'd seen him choke the life out of a man with his bare hands.

I counted the cash in my hands. I was at the bottom of my mental list.

"Where's Tanya?" I asked.

No answer. I looked up, but no one else was waiting to hand me over their unearned pocket money. They all looked a little shifty.

"Where is she?" I asked again.

"She's not here," Marie answered. I waited. "She's at home. She's not feeling very well."

I sighed. Here was my complication.

"Where does she live?"

They all avoided my gaze. I locked in on Marie.

"Marie?" I tried to make my voice soft, like we were confidantes. She squirmed. Time to turn the screw. "Marie, I'd hate to have to tell Zane you weren't helpful..."

I let that hang there, and three minutes later I was on my way, an address for a street on the edge of Chelsea scrawled across the back of my hand.

It was a long walk, but I didn't know the routes well enough in this part of the city to jump on any of the buses that were whizzing past. I could have taken any of the taxis meandering slowly by with their yellow lights on, but the cash I'd been given with the jacket was quickly dwindling and I wasn't foolish enough to spend any of Alexander's. At least the streets were safe, devoid of the junkies and thugs who roamed the less affluent areas.

Tanya's house was very posh. A town house, with fresh white paint, a glossy black door and flowerbeds hanging off each of the many windows. Her father was probably a politician, or a crooked businessman. They were the only type who had survived the recession.

I didn't hesitate on the street, but marched straight up to her front door. Anything else would have looked suspicious, and besides, the watch on my wrist was ticking on towards three. I was running out of time, and I really didn't want to have to phone Zane.

I rang the bell, listening to a series of chimes echo inside. Shortly after, a small, middle-aged woman opened the door. She was dressed neatly in slacks and a blouse nowhere near expensive enough to be the wife of the man who owned this place. She had to be the housekeeper. Good.

"Hi," I smiled warmly. "Is Tanya in?"

She looked at me, eyes raking over my distorted uniform, and her lips pursed.

"I'm afraid Tanya isn't feeling very well," she said, making no move to open the door.

"Yeah, I know," I grimaced my sympathy. "I'm a friend of hers from school. I brought round her homework."

I held up the rucksack, my excuse for being there.

"Oh, I see," she checked her watch. "Isn't it a little early to have finished school?"

"I had study last period," I lied smoothly.

That seemed to satisfy her. She swung the door open, gestured me in.

"Tanya's upstairs in her room," she said.

"Thanks," I hurried past, ran lightly up the stairs. The housekeeper watched me from the doorway. I hoped she wouldn't be able to see me once I hit the landing, because I had no idea which room was Tanya's. The first door I tried was a bathroom the next a large, grand room with a king-size bed, the sheets a sensible beige shade of satin: her parent's room, or a very sumptuous spare. I came up trumps on the third door. The television was on, and watching it from the large wrought-iron bed was a girl with heavy eyes, a red nose and a mountain of screwed-up tissues beside her.

"Hi Tanya," I smiled.

She stared at me. "Who the hell are you?"

"I'm collecting for Zane."

Straight to the point. I didn't have time to be nice.

"And you had to come here? To my house? When I'm sick?" Her voice rose in volume and pitch with each question.

Did she think the men peddling her their little white powder cocktails cared about the fact she had a cold?

"Yes."

"Well, I haven't got any money here."

I stared at her. We both knew that was a lie. There was cash in this house. Whether it belonged to her or not was a different thing, but she had access to it.

"You would be better to pay me," I said. Pay me, rather than the thug Alexander or Zane would send round if the debt went unsettled.

The implication of the threat was enough.

"Wait here," she huffed, traipsing past me out of the door in a pair of pink silk pyjamas. She was back in less than a minute, stuffing a wad of notes into my hand. I counted it carefully, twice, then handed her back a ten.

"Thank you so much," she muttered darkly.

I didn't see the housekeeper on my way out of the house, but I had the feeling she was watching me. It didn't matter. I was out of the place in seconds and I had no plans to come back.

I grabbed a bus headed for Victoria, knowing I didn't have enough time to run down King's Road. I had less than an hour to get all the way across London, and traffic was starting to build.

"C'mon, c'mon, c'mon!" I muttered, bouncing up and down in my seat as the bus snaked its way slowly back towards the centre, back into the Zone. I was the first one off, jumping from the open rear of the vehicle before it had even cruised to a stop; then I ran like hell towards the train station.

There were a lot more people on the platform this time, and when the train finally came I had to squeeze myself in beside a grandmother with a baby, and a man who looked too young for the office suit and tie he wore. I ignored all three of them, wrapping my hands around the rucksack which now held a good couple of thousand pounds of Alexander's money, and trying to mentally calculate if there was any way I could hope to make it back to Bancroft Road before Zane's deadline. I had the phone; I could ring him, but I'd rather avoid that outcome if at all possible.

"You still at school then?" The boy-man in the suit interrupted my thoughts.

I looked down at the school uniform, then back up to him. What did he think?

The grandmother caught the expression on my face and turned away; smiling to herself as she rearranged the swathes of blankets around the baby she was with.

"Right," he had the good grace to colour somewhat.

"Stupid question."

I smiled. It was.

"It's just, you look a little old, I mean... mature, to be at school still."

"Thanks," I told him coolly, wishing he'd stop talking to me. I had a quick glance around the carriage, but there weren't any alternative seats.

"Do you think you'll go to university when you're finished?"

University? That had seemed a far-off dream before, when I'd been a child. Now, I had more chance of flying to the moon.

"I doubt it," I said, not needing to fake the sadness in my voice. I did try to take the edge off my accent, though. Probably unsuccessfully. There were just too many people around, too many listening ears. I didn't need suspicion following me home.

"Right," he grinned. "Me, too. Had it all planned out, but that was before the world went to shit. Bit inconvenient really." He gave me a friendly, optimistic smile, and I returned the gesture half-heartedly. There was something not quite right about hearing him describe the end of the global economy and the destruction of my life as a 'bit inconvenient', but I knew he was trying to make a joke.

I didn't joke any more.

"Are..." he looked shyly at me, "Are you seeing anyone?"

What a question. Absolutely not, but I definitely wasn't available either.

"No. And yes."

He looked confused.

"It's complicated."

"Oh. I just wondered if maybe you wanted to go out sometime. We could talk about how the older generation have ruined the world."

He stared at me like a round-eyed puppy, like a little boy. And though I wasn't particularly interested, I wished with all my heart that I could say yes.

"I don't think that's a good idea," I hedged.

"Right. Well," he struggled to keep the embarrassment and disappointment from his face, and I felt both flattered and sorry for him, emotions I hadn't experienced for a long time. "Maybe I'll give you my number, just in case you change your mind?"

There it was again, that eager smile. Ordinary, normal, and something I so rarely saw.

"Sure, go on."

He almost fell over himself he was so keen. Ripping a page out of a diary, he wrote 'Mark' and then a mobile phone number. I took it with a smile.

"Hi, Mark," I said. "I'm Lizzie."

Then I bit my lip, because I knew shouldn't have given him my real name. But what harm could it do?

"Well, this is my stop." I stood up, slinging the rucksack over my shoulder as the train slowed at Whitechapel.

"Hope I hear from you," he said.

I smiled a goodbye, knowing he never would.

Outside the train station I paused, stared down at the little piece of paper, the line of digits written with blue ink in a loopy hand. Would I remember the number if I ever wanted to call it? Probably not. I sighed, then I scrunched it up and chucked it in the bin.

"What was that?"

I jumped, spun round. Zane filled my field of vision, my eyes level with his huge barrel chest.

"You're late."

I checked my watch. It was ten to four.

"No, I'm not. It's not four yet."

"And you're not back yet. What was that?" He gestured with his head down towards the bin.

I shrugged.

"Nothing."

"I'll decide if it's nothing."

I considered not telling him, but he'd make a meal out of it. Worse: he'd tell Alexander. Any excuse to drop me in it. And Alexander would have the truth out of me, one way or another.

"A boy on the train tried to give me his phone number."

"And you took it." It wasn't a question.

I met his stare, determined not to look guilty.

"I put it in the bin."

"After you took it." He smirked at me, and I knew he had me, because that was how Alexander would see it. Sensing victory, he dropped his gaze to my chest, my bare legs. Leered. "The outfit looks good on you."

"Shut up, Zane." I pushed past him, shoved my hands in the pockets of my cardigan and started walking towards Bancroft Road.

He caught me up before I'd turned the first corner. "Problems?"

I shrugged, knowing I'd have to explain every detail to Alexander anyway, and not really wanting to do it twice.

"Lizzie—" His tone was a warning. He wanted a heads up if there was anything Alexander wasn't going to like.

"The drop was fine. He said to tell Alexander the package would do him for a month." Zane sucked in a breath and I realised for the first time I might be the bearer of bad news. Oh well.

"And the money?"

"Easy-peasy. One of the girls was off school sick, so I had to go to her house and get it. That's why I'm so late."

"Huh."

No compliments. No slap on the back for a job well done. Zane wasn't like Samuel.

We walked the rest of the way in silence, arriving at five past four. I gritted my teeth, knowing Alexander would give a pointed look to his watch. Five minutes.

Zane took the rucksack from me at the door, then he headed to the basement to count it and then bank it in the safe, and I made my way up to the office. I knocked, waited, and heard the low lilt of Alexander call, "Come".

As predicted, he raised his arm to check his watch when I opened the door, but halfway through the gesture he caught sight of me, and my outfit, and he burst out laughing.

CHAPTER FOUR

"Well, look at you, Elizabeth," he grinned, looking me up and down.

Samuel, sitting on the other sofa, smiled wryly.

I resisted rolling my eyes with some difficulty.

"I'm going to change," I announced, heading for Alexander's dressing room.

"No, you're not." His words halted me before I'd taken three steps. "I like it. Keep it on."

I turned to face him, licking my suddenly dry lips. "If you want."

"I do. I'm thirsty, get me a drink. Samuel will take one, too."

I looked at Samuel for confirmation. He gave me the briefest of nods, then I marched in the direction of the kitchenette.

"And Elizabeth," Alexander called over his shoulder, raising his voice as loud as I had ever heard it. "Get one for yourself, just for making me laugh."

I raised my eyebrows at the cupboard full of glasses. He was in a really good mood, it seemed.

I grabbed three glasses, low, round tumblers, and added ice from the fancy machine on the outside of the giant, American-style fridge. Then I went straight for the whisky: Alexander's neat, Samuel's with a splash of water, mine with a generous serving of Coke. Real Coke, one of the advantages of working for Alexander. I loaded them on a tray, took a deep breath, and turned back to face the room. Zane was just sliding his way in the door. Thankful for the chance to linger a minute longer in the kitchen area, I turned back to the array of alcohol and reached for the Vodka. I added ice and nothing else. Zane was another one who liked his drink straight, and large.

I arrived at the sofa, depositing the tray on the stainless steel and glass coffee table, just as Alexander began cross-examining Zane about my success.

"Everything there and accounted for?"

"Every penny."

"Good."

Alexander nodded, satisfied. Then he looked at me as I went to sit down. Before the back of my legs could touch the soft, cool white leather he reached out, in one of his lightning quick moves, and grabbed hold of my chin. He tilted my face to the side, exposing my left cheek.

"Go wipe that muck off your face," he snarled. "I want to look at you, not a mask."

He dropped his hold and turned away from me. I stared at the side of his head, my skin stinging like he'd slapped me.

In the bathroom I gazed at myself. I looked normal. A little orange, perhaps. The make-up wasn't quite right, too dark as Samuel had said, but I looked just like anybody else. I could walk down the street and not have to hide my face. Sighing, I ran the water until it was warm, then scrubbed at my cheek with soap. I grabbed a towel to dry myself and held it over the lower half of my face as I straightened up to look back into the mirror. Straight, dark eyebrows, wide grey eyes, pale skin. Nothing unusual. Then slowly, hesitantly, I lowered the towel. Just an inch later the upper curve of the tattoo reared its ugly head, like a killer whale arcing out of the waves.

My face. It was never beautiful, never smooth and perfect and beautiful, but it had been *my* face. Mine. Now I barely recognised it. The tattoo that was like a barcode; the eyes that were too old, too cold. Only the lips, turned down in sadness, were still me. I sighed. I needed that whisky.

"Better," Alexander commented as I returned to the room. He patted the cushion beside him and I took my place. As soon as I sat down he threw an arm around my shoulders, playing distractedly with the school tie still knotted around my neck. I waited for the third degree to begin. Step by step: what had I done; who did I see; who did I talk to; what, exactly, did I say? Every detail of my trip into the outside world to be mused over, analysed. Just to let me know he was watching. He was always watching.

But he wasn't interested in me. Not right then. His eyes were fixed on Samuel.

"I hear what you're saying," he said, picking up again on a conversation I'd missed. "But you need to see the bigger picture. We have to focus on our business ventures. The money needs to keep coming in, Samuel. That's what keeps us moving forward; that's what keeps us alive. Elizabeth's little adventure today is proof of that. The police, the GE, the politicians, they keep demanding more, and we have to make sure we can pay, or none of us have a future, and some of us stand to lose our lives."

So Zane had given him my message from the GE officer. Yet he didn't seem angry. Instead his voice was... persuasive. Not a tone I often heard him take. What had I missed? What were he and Samuel arguing about? Zane was no help, his hostile face impassive and calm. I stared down at my drink, at the ice cube slowly rotating as it melted, but my ears were pricked, listening keenly.

"It's not about lining our pockets, Alex. This is about more than that, about more than the two of us. We're supposed to be fighting for something."

"And what, exactly, is that?"

The sudden change, the sudden iciness in Alexander's voice made me look up. But it was Samuel's eyes that caught my gaze, and they were fire. Mesmerising fire.

"For freedom. For the chance to bring our families out of the wilderness. For the resolution of the United Kingdom. Dammit, Alex, you are allowing yourself to be distracted by the money, by the power."

I held my breath. Nobody talked to Alexander like that. Nobody.

"It is my money that keeps you alive, Samuel." Alexander spat each word at his brother. His fingers were clutched so hard around his glass I feared the delicate crystal would shatter under the pressure.

Samuel stared at his brother, took two deep breaths.

"Yes. It is," he conceded; then he stared hard at Alexander. "But I want more. We need to do more."

"We will," Alexander's voice was a purr, placating, reassuring. "I promise you we will. But these things take time. You have to be patient. Elizabeth," he said my name in the same soft tone, but my head jerked round at once. His lips twitched in a mockery of a smile. Caught. I was obviously listening in. Though I was allowed to stay in his presence, I wasn't supposed to pay attention; not unless he told me to. Still, he let it slide, holding out his glass to me. "I need another drink."

I thought about what they'd both said as I made my way slowly back over to the kitchenette, Alexander's empty glass in hand. Samuel and Alexander called themselves 'freedom fighters': the government called them terrorists. They planted bombs, like the one I'd set up at the Home Office Information building, to further their cause, to tell the English National Party, or the ENP, the current ruling power, that the Celt countries would not disappear quietly into the abyss of poverty and disorder, but would keep fighting until the United Kingdom was reformed.

Instances like those, though, were few and far between. The majority of the brothers' work revolved around drug deals and violence. It brought in wads of cash, but did nothing to further the 'cause', as Samuel called it. From the sound of it, recent activities were not enough for the youngest of the pair.

He needed to be careful, though. Alexander could only be pushed so far.

They'd moved on by the time I returned with Alexander's second drink.

"They're getting greedy," Zane was saying. "Six months ago the package Lizzie delivered today would have been enough for a season; now it's a month. In few months more, it may be a week. If they keep upping the price on us, it's going to become a problem."

"We can afford it," Samuel argued. "And we need their protection."

"We do," Alexander agreed. "And we can. But some of our government friends are starting to take advantage. I don't like to be taken advantage of."

"What do you suggest we do?" Zane was leaning forward, his face eager. This conversation was going in a direction he liked. Sending messages, getting payback, involved blood, pain and violence. His favourite things.

"Alex, let's not get too ambitious," Samuel warned. "We don't want to start a war with government officials."

"I thought that was exactly what you wanted!" Alexander shot back.

"You know what I mean. These are business deals."

Alexander considered his brother for a long moment.

"I'll think about it," he said. "But I won't have these people thinking they can get one up on me. I—" he broke off, looking angrily at the door. "What is it?"

One of Alexander's thugs had opened the door, forgetting to knock. His head was peeking round into the room, the nervous expression on his face at odds with the scars and lines and piercings covering almost every inch of his skin.

"There's been an incident, Mr Alexander, sir. Someone's been brought in – Murphy." The name meant nothing to me, but Zane stiffened in his chair. "He's been caught passing information to a GE officer, sir."

"Where is he?" Samuel stood up, an ugly look on his face. Traitors were the one thing likely to provoke his temper. Alexander was riled, too. Although his expression didn't change, he had tightened his grip on the tie still around my neck, half choking me. .

"In a room in the basement, Mr Samuel, sir."

The basement was a jumbled maze of rooms, and I had only been in two or three at the very front: the stores, where drugs and guns and money and everything else Alexander peddled, were kept. Further back were small rooms, windowless rooms, rooms like this one, where the walls were lined with breeze blocks and the floor was poured cement, with a drain set into a shallow dip in the middle. The lighting was low, a single bulb hanging naked from a wire. The only furnishings were a small metal table and two uncomfortable-looking chairs. Only one of those was filled.

The man was forty, maybe, his body was tall and thin, his skin jaundiced yellow. His hair was short, a buzz cut, and the jagged ends glittered silver grey. His outfit was nondescript: a scruffy grey T-shirt and combat trousers, torn and muddy at the knees. I'd never seen the man before, but I'd never forget his face after today. I couldn't stop staring. It was mutilated: swollen and bruised and bloody. He looked as if someone had set about him with an iron bar; as if his hands had been held behind him – like they were now – tied with rope, leaving him vulnerable, defenceless. His left eye was glued shut and he peered around the room with his right, little more than a slit, the pupil gleaming underneath as it danced from side to side, watching, waiting.

Alexander stopped just inside the door, his hand on my neck guiding me to a halt beside him. Zane entered a step behind and moved to take up a position against the wall, visible and yet invisible. It was Samuel who strolled forward, who grasped the back of the empty chair and dragged it across the concrete, metal legs squealing, until he was able to sit himself down directly facing the beaten stranger.

Samuel reached behind him, dug into the waistband of his trousers and pulled out a gun. I stiffened, my eyes widening as I watched him slowly draw it out and place it carefully on the table. The man in the chair saw it, too. He was supposed to.

"Tell me," Samuel said softly, sounding much more like his older brother. "Tell me why one of my men saw you meeting with a GE officer in Camden."

"I... didn't." The words came out a mush, barely recognisable, and it was clear that speaking was painful. I wondered if they'd broken his jaw.

"Don't lie to me."

Samuel leaned forward, his hands clasped together and resting on his knees. His face was intent, eyes staring keenly at the man in front of him.

"It's the truth," came the garbled reply.

"No, it isn't. Perhaps you need something to jog your memory... Zane?"

At the sound of his name, Zane stepped away from the wall, cracking his knuckles in anticipation. The man in the chair attempted to twist away as he approached, but he was tied in place. There was nowhere to go. I tried to turn my head to the side, unwilling to witness the violence that was about to follow, but Alexander threaded his fingers into the tie around my neck and forced me to look straight ahead.

There was little noise as Zane's massive fist connected with the man's stomach, then his upper arm.

"So, Zane tells me some boy made a pass at you today on the train," Alexander's voice was a whisper in my ear, making me jump and distracting me from Zane's assault. His thumb began to rub circles into my neck and his touch both thrilled and terrified in equal measure. I couldn't have moved even if I'd wanted to.

"I... never..." I managed to splutter, keeping my voice low enough not to travel in the crowded room.

"Shhh," Alexander crooned.

The word did not calm me, however. My stomach convulsed, an involuntary response, and I had to swallow back the vomit that rose in my throat.

He let go of my tie and let his hand slide up into my hair, fingers pulling gently at the short strands, making my scalp tingle.

"Can I trust you, Elizabeth?"

I turned my head to stare at him, my eyes black as coals in the muted light, and he gazed back. He wasn't looking for an answer, but I nodded anyway. Just a tiny dip of my head, almost imperceptible.

"I hope so," he said, emotionless eyes boring down into mine. "The next time you accept so much as a smile from another man, I will make you truly sorry."

I believed him.

"Yes, Alexander," I murmured, dropping my gaze. He used his grip on my hair to pull my head back up.

"Good," he said.

Not a single other person in the room heard our exchange. Zane was still circling his prey, looking for new areas to inflict damage. Samuel, however, held up his hand.

"Enough," he said. "I'll ask you again. Why were you meeting a GE officer?"

This time the man didn't hesitate; the words tumbled out of his mouth, along with a thin stream of blood that dribbled down towards his chin.

"I was trying... to get information. Trying to find out what they knew about us. I didn't tell him anything, I swear."

"On whose orders?"

"What?" The man looked confused. His eye rolled in its socket before swivelling round to fix on Samuel again.

"On whose orders did you meet with him?"

"I was..." he stalled, "trying to use my own initiative."

"I don't believe you."

Samuel picked the gun up off the table top. The man's breathing started coming in great gasps. I felt my own pulse begin to quicken in sympathy and fear. More pain was surely coming. Slowly, calmly, Samuel cocked the gun and held the end of the barrel against the man's thigh.

"Time to go," Alexander murmured to me, pulling me backwards out of the room.

We made it as far as the base of the stairs before the sharp crack of a gun exploded in the air.

CHAPTER FIVE

Life went on as normal for a few weeks. Alexander sent me out on various errands, making deliveries, collecting information, spying, but most of the time I remained in his office, permanently at his beck and call. There were no more arguments, and no more bombs. Then one day I woke to an empty bed. Surprised, I lifted my head to see Alexander already up, dressed in a tight vest T-shirt that showed off his impressive muscles and a light pair of jogging trousers. He had a towel slung over his shoulder, and he was deep in conversation with Samuel.

I yanked the sheets up higher to cover my naked skin and the small movement made both men turn their heads.

"She's awake," Alexander said. "About time."

I turned, squinted at the clock on the wall. It was barely after seven.

"I'm going to hit the weights. She's all yours."

He clapped his brother on the shoulder as he passed, and headed out of the door without another glance at me. I stared at Samuel a little apprehensively, my heart punching out a sudden staccato rhythm. What did Alexander mean by that?

He took a few steps towards me, then stopped as he registered my bare shoulders. His eyes dropped to the rest of my body, shrouded by the sheet, but just as unclothed, and then he turned his back, giving me some privacy.

"Get dressed," he said over his shoulder. "We're going out."

"Where are we going?" I asked fifteen minutes later as I belted myself into the passenger seat of a faded red Astra. It was several years old, but it gleamed outside and in. The upholstery smelled of jasmine and lavender and the scents of other popular cleaning products. Somebody had gone over the thing with a fine-tooth comb.

"Scouting," Samuel answered, twisting the key so that the engine roared to life.

I didn't ask anything else as we wove our way out of Stepney. If he'd wanted me to know precisely where we were headed, he would have told me.

"Are you hungry?" Samuel asked as he twiddled the radio on. He stopped on a station pumping out harsh guitars, the drumbeat heavy in the background.

I was, but I didn't know whether to admit to it or not. Alexander would have been irritated by the inconvenience. I gnawed on my lip.

Samuel looked over to me when I didn't respond, and smiled.

"I'll take that as a yes."

He pulled over at a corner, handed me a note.

"Go grab us a couple of bacon rolls," he said, nodding in the direction of a little white hut. "And some tea."

I stared at him blankly.

"But—"

"Don't worry about your face, not with Clive."

He gave me a reassuring smile, so I took the money and rolled out of the car. It felt strange to walk along the street in the daylight without my hood and without any of the make-up. I looked around warily, but there were few pedestrians about this early.

I walked quickly to the street vendor Samuel had pointed out and gave my order. The man in the hut looked at me keenly, then gazed at the car. He half raised his hand in greeting. He must have recognised the model, because it was impossible to see through the tinted windows.

He said nothing to me, but hurried to put together my order. I paid, then turned to head back to the car, two steaming cups and two paper bags balanced precariously in my arms.

"Hey," he called. "Samuel will want ketchup."

So he did know who it was for. He stuffed a couple of sachets in my fingers, then watched carefully as I headed back to the car. When Samuel drove off I saw him staring after us.

"Is he a Celt?" I asked softly as Samuel accelerated away, holding his tea and simultaneously smearing ketchup on his roll. Only a lifted knee steered the car.

"No," Samuel shook his head. "But his wife was, and they shot her, so he's sympathetic to the cause. Throws information our way every now and then. He hears a lot of things he shouldn't, working where he does."

We drove on in silence for fifteen minutes. I stared out of the window, watching the houses get bigger and more impressive, more imposing, with each turning Samuel made. Finally he stopped outside a wide set of wrought-iron gates. From where he parked, on the other side of the road, I could easily make out CCTV cameras and a fingerprint entry pad. On either side of the gate was a tall, red brick wall. The top of the wall glittered slightly: spikes of glass.

"Who lives there?" I asked, craning my head to try to see the building behind the fortifications.

"Edwin Bowles."

"The defence minister?"

"That's him."

I stared in wonder, and hatred. It had been Edwin Bowles who had pushed through the dissolution of the United Kingdom, had erected the walls, had championed the twisted laws that allowed the Scots, Welsh and Irish to be branded, and to be shot without trial. Edwin Bowles was an all-round bastard. If he'd walked out of his house right now, I would have begged Samuel to put his foot down and put the rest of the country out of its misery.

"Why are we here?" I asked, leaning over Samuel,

trying to get a better look at the place.

"This is your next job." His voice was husky in my ear, his breath tickling my neck.

I pulled back, stared at him.

"What?"

"This is your next job."

I looked back at the house. Now, rather than grand and magnificent, it looked like Fort Knox.

"In there?"

"In there. See the alleyway?" Samuel rolled the car forward, revealing a narrow cobble-stoned alley lined with giant bins and side gates.

I nodded.

"That's where you'll go over. We've had a section of the wall tarred. You'll have to go over that exact spot or the security glass will cut you to ribbons. The garage is just on the other side. The door isn't alarmed, but there are CCTV cameras pointing at every angle. You'll have to keep out of their sight. There are two cars in the garage. One is a Jaguar, that's the one you're after..."

Samuel's voice was low and hypnotic. The gentle cadence made the impossibilities he was suggesting seem plausible.

Three days later I found myself parked back in the same spot, only it was dark. We were in a different car and Samuel was going over the exact plan once again. The explosives I had to plant were laid out in my lap, more complex than anything I had ever constructed before.

"Do you know what you have to do?" he asked me.

I nodded, trying to breathe around a hard knot in my chest.

"When you come out, I'll be right here."

"Okay," I whispered, my voice barely audible over the gentle hum of the engine.

"Lizzie, you can do this."

"I know," I lied.

He smiled at me, raised a hand to my cheek. His thumb gently traced a slow circle around my tattoo. That staccato beat started up in my chest again as I gazed at him, saw his confidence in me, his belief in the job we were about to do. Felt his faith in me slither its way across the darkness to warm the ice in my belly. Then he dropped his hand and I knew the time had come to ghost out into the darkness.

I walked down the alley like I had every right to be there. Then, at the precise spot, marked out by a discreet chalk 'X' on the floor, I scrambled up the wall, agile as a cat, the apparatus for my bomb evenly distributed around my body. The top of the wall was smooth and cool, the tar that one of Samuel's contacts had laid protecting me from the sharp edges of the glass spikes. I dropped down inside the wall, astonished that it seemed as easy as Samuel had said it would be.

Low lights lit up different areas of the garden; the garage I was heading for stood just twenty paces to my left. It was tempting to head straight for it, taking the shortest route, but I knew if I did that, the Bowles's personal security would be onto me in a heartbeat. Floodlights would pool down, alarms would sound, and I'd be face down in the grass. Instead I took a winding path, counting my paces, twisting and changing direction, following the route Samuel and his detailed planning had laid out for me. When, at last, I stood before the garage door, all was quiet, all was still.

Thank you Samuel.

Bending down, I twisted the garage handle and slid the door upwards. I stopped dead at six inches, knowing a motion detector kicked in at eight. Then I dropped to the ground and wriggled on my belly until I was inside. At last I relaxed. Now it was time to work.

Putting the bomb together was easy. I used a short knife to split the grey putty explosive into three sections. I secured each block to different areas of the car: the front and rear axles, and the petrol tank. Then I ran wires between each section of the bomb, so that if any segment was detonated, all three would blow. The hardest thing was the trigger. From underneath the car, I had to reach up through the mechanics of the engine, something I was not familiar with, and hunt out the ignition system. Even with all of Samuel's diagrams and coaching, the inner workings of the car were still just a gigantic puzzle of wires and pipes. The pinpoint glare of my tiny flashlight illuminated only a few inches at a time, making my task almost impossible. For a while I panicked, eyes raking across alien mechanics, but I forced myself to breathe, calm down; to concentrate. Eventually I saw the segment

I was searching for; I stripped it down, slicing the rubber tubing from the wire. My trigger clipped on to the exposed copper threads. Any electricity passing down the wire would generate a chain reaction that could not be stopped.

I tried not to think about the person sitting in the driver's seat when that happened. Edwin Bowles was a bad man.

Job done, I flicked off the light and spent a moment breathing deeply in the darkness. Time to get out. Incredibly carefully, I eased back out from under the car. Without the pinprick light of the torch, the dark was absolute, cloaking me like a thick blanket. Only a thin grey streak of light whispered under the garage door, still open several inches at the bottom and my only escape route. Feeling my way, I braced myself against the brick wall of the garage, my sleeves over my hands as always. I still had the short blade clutched firmly in my other one. Leaving it would have ruined the whole operation, because surely Bowles's security detail would sweep under the vehicles.

I'd taken one single step towards the garage door when a low sound stopped me in my tracks. I listened, but there was silence. Then a tiny tinkle, like a bell, close to the ground. A moment later the low buzzing again. What was that?

I took another step and the buzzing intensified, building until it broke off in a sharp yap.

A dog.

"Shit," I hissed.

The dog barked again.

It didn't sound very big, maybe a terrier or a chihuahua, but it was going to be loud enough to call attention to me. I needed to shut the damn thing up, but in the dark I had no idea where it was.

"Where are you?" I murmured to the dark. "Come on, where are you?"

I took another step and there was a snarl, followed by an extended tinkle, like whatever was attached to the bell was running, coming closer. Good, that was what I wanted.

"Ow!" I yelled before I could stop myself. Something razor sharp attached itself to my ankle and chomped down. Instinctively I yanked my leg back, but the thing held on, twisting left and right, worrying at me, digging deeper into my flesh. It was growling and snarling as it bit, making one hell of a racket.

"Shhh! Shut up!" I hissed. I reached down, thinking I could maybe pull it off me, but the knife was still in my hand and as I threw my arms towards the ground, the blade sank into something – something that resisted, then yelped. "Oh hell. Oh hell, no!"

I flicked my torch back on, shining it downwards and hoping vehemently that the brightness wouldn't be visible under the door. The dog – it was a chihuahua – was still attached to my ankle, but it wasn't moving and its neck and shoulder were covered in thick, wet blood.

"Christ." I wriggled my foot and this time it let go. It flopped, lifeless, to the floor. I looked down at it, thinking fast. I couldn't leave it here, it was obvious evidence, but what was I going to do about the blood pooling onto the cement floor? And what about the blood coating the animal's teeth – *my* blood?

I was going to have to take it with me.

I looked around, flashing the penlight, and caught sight of a carrier bag against one wall. My sleeves over my hands again – now I really needed the gloves – I emptied the bag of car oil and anti-freeze, then stuffed the dog's body inside. There wasn't much I could do about the bloodstain, though. Using the knife, I trimmed off a section of my shirt and used that to wipe it up, then I smeared some of the car oil over the top, hoping the black stain would disguise it. It was messy, and it was glaringly obvious, but there wasn't an awful lot else I could do.

I was so panicked and harassed I almost forgot to turn the torch off before I dragged myself back under the door, the carrier bag in my hand scraping noisily against the gravel of the driveway. I looked out towards the house as I got up into a low crouch. Lights were on, but no one was staring out of any of the windows and there were no doors open. Where the hell had the little bugger come from?

I recited Samuel's pathway to myself as I ghosted across the garden, ducking and weaving out of sight of the CCTV cameras. Getting over the wall was tricky; the roses planted along the base scratched at my clothes and the weight of the little dog threw me off balance. My ankle was throbbing, too. I hoped I wasn't leaving a little trail of blood across the garden. When I sank down to give myself a good push upwards, my leg twinged savagely and my one scrabbling hand almost missed the top of the wall. I got there, though, heaving and straining the muscles of one arm, pulling the bloodied bundle along with the other. The next second I was over, dropping down into the narrow back lane. I limped along at an awkward jog until the car came into view. The door was open.

"What's that?" Samuel asked sharply as I collapsed inside, tossing the carrier bag onto the backseat.

He didn't wait for my answer, but engaged the central locking and hit the gas, taking us away from the scene of my botched crime.

"The dog," I gasped, wincing and reaching down for my ankle. Now that I was a little more comfortable, in the warmth of the car, it was really starting to hurt.

"You killed the dog? Why the hell did you do that? What went wrong, Lizzie?"

"I didn't mean to," I stammered, alarmed by the tone of his voice and the fierce set of his brow. "It bit me!"

"Jesus!" Samuel rubbed at his forehead. "Tell me what happened. Exactly."

So I did. I went over how I got into the garden, laid the bomb, and how I'd met the dog on my way out.

"You left the garage open?" he asked, raising an eyebrow and shooting me a look.

"Inches," I said defensively.

"Inches were enough," he barked back. "Then what?"

"It came at me and the damned thing wouldn't let go. I reached down to try to pull it off, but the putty knife was in my hand and it must have stabbed it in the neck. It killed the thing instantly. I would have left it, but, well, it would have been pretty obvious that I was there, and my blood was all over its teeth! I'm sorry, Samuel."

I lifted my foot up to rest it on the edge of the seat and tentatively felt around my ankle. One touch was enough to send sharp stabs of agony shooting up my shin. I whimpered, hissing through my teeth.

"Are you all right?" he asked, looking down at my leg. It was impossible to see if his eyes were sympathetic in the dark.

"I think so. It's sore."

"Did you bleed in the garage or the garden?"

With trembling fingers I felt around my jeans. The thick denim felt ripped, but dry. Reaching underneath, my skin and sock were slick and wet.

"I don't think so. I think my clothes soaked it up."

"You'd better hope so," Samuel said under his breath.

"Is... is Alexander going to be mad at me?"

"That depends," Samuel gave me a rueful grimace.

"On what?" I whispered, frightened now.

"On whether the bomb goes off tomorrow."

"What about tonight?"

"Tonight maybe you should stay out of his way."

I didn't answer. My mouth was suddenly dry. How was I supposed to avoid Alexander when he dictated exactly what I did?

"Samuel—"

He held up a hand to silence me. His phone was

ringing, the caller ID screen lighting up lurid green in the dark. I didn't need to look at him to know who it was.

"Hello? Yeah... we're on our way back. Clockwork? Well, the bomb got planted okay. There was a... complication." He looked at me. "Lizzie had to kill the dog." He listened to Alexander's response. "No, she brought it with her. It bit her on the ankle. Yeah," he laughed at whatever had been said, but it was a mechanical laugh – no real humour there. I dropped my throbbing ankle to the floor of the car and hugged my arms around my middle. "No, I'll drive out further east then do the dumping in the river. Shouldn't take much to weight it down." Dumping in the river? Weight it down? Fear curled in my gut – were they talking about me? I wanted to butt in, to ask what Alexander was saying, but I knew I'd just be adding further trouble to the pile. The suspense was painful. I clamped my teeth together to stop myself from snivelling and one of my molars stabbed viciously. "Right. I'll see you when I get in." He hung up.

I, not we. I started to hyperventilate.

"What are you dumping at the river, Samuel?" I managed to whisper.

Samuel took a quick second to glance at me as he rounded a corner, alarmed by the tremor in my voice.

"The dog," he said. Then understanding dawned on his face. "You didn't think...?"

I didn't answer. I was too relieved to speak.

"Christ, Lizzie. I'm not going to kill you for getting bitten on the ankle," Samuel said, sounding exasperated.

I nodded an acceptance, but his words didn't make me feel an awful lot better. Because I'd still messed up, and he might not blame me, but his brother would.

We drove out to North Woolwich, to an area of the river beside the abandoned London City Airport. It was very dark and totally deserted. Samuel parked as close to the river as he could get, killing the lights so that the residential streets in Woolwich town, across the water, wouldn't expose us. Then he grabbed a couple of bricks from the boot – smiling wryly when he caught my expression: why the hell were they in there? – and added them to the carrier bag. He tied the handles in a knot, squeezed any air out, then lobbed the bundle as far out into the river as possible. There was a distant splash as the carrier bag connected with the calmly bobbing surface of the Thames.

"Now what?" I asked, still feeling anxious about whatever Alexander had said on the phone.

"Now we go home," Samuel told me.

One of the bricks from the boot seemed to drop its way into the depths of my stomach.

It took a surprisingly short time to wind our way back to Stepney, probably because I was dreading facing Alexander so much. I vacillated between worrying about that and trying to ignore the pain in my ankle, which was getting worse and worse. My foot burned and throbbed in my shoe, and the skin around the joint felt puffy and swollen. I hoped I wouldn't need hospital treatment, because I knew I wouldn't get it.

When we arrived Samuel handed the car over to another nobody – pausing to tell him to take special care because there would probably be blood residue in the upholstery and the carpets – then led me inside. Rather than heading upstairs, Samuel made for the basement rooms, laughing at the look on my face when I realised which way he was going.

"I need to look at your ankle," he assured me. "The medical stuff's down here."

I wasn't altogether reassured, although I was happy enough to delay seeing Alexander.

We passed by the stores, then the small windowless rooms used for holding and torturing and other nasty business, until we came to a large open space at the back. Samuel flicked a switch and two long fluorescent lights buzzed into life. I stared. The place was like a mini surgery with an operating table, a tray balanced on a stand with all sorts of instruments lurking under plastic sheeting, and cabinets against the wall.

"What's this?" I asked, astonished.

Samuel smiled at my flabbergasted face, then started pulling gauze and wadding out of a drawer.

"People get hurt quite a lot in our line of work, and you and I can't just step into the nearest hospital. We've learned to patch ourselves up pretty well. Now," he looked over at me, "You'll need to strip off your jeans, then jump up on the table."

I hesitated, not entirely comfortable with the idea of standing there in just my underwear. Being Alexander's plaything, my modesty in front of him had died a long time ago, but it was different with Samuel somehow.

"What?" he asked.

"Nothing," I muttered. My fingers went to the button of my trousers as I kicked off my boots. Closing my eyes so that I wouldn't have to look, I shimmied my jeans down my thighs, wincing as I eased them around my ankles. Samuel deliberately looked away so that I could slide onto the table, then he turned round with surgical gloves on when I was seated, my arms draped over my naked legs.

"Right, let's see," he said, bending over and examining my ankle. I peered around my knees to assess the damage.

My skin was a mess. The dog had grabbed me just where my sock met my shin and the cut was a tangle of ripped skin and wisps of nylon. Blood had congealed around it, sticking the fabric to my shin like glue.

Very gently, Samuel wiped at the outer edges of the wound with a damp tissue, clearing off most of the blood. Then he grabbed the edge of my sock and tried to prise it down. The nylon resisted, holding resolutely on to my skin. I sucked in a breath as I felt the cuts break open afresh. Little droplets of blood oozed through.

"Sorry," Samuel muttered. "Nearly there."

I closed my eyes and chomped down on my tongue, letting my teeth dig into the spongy muscle until the pain was enough to distract me from Samuel's treatment of my leg.

"Right," he said. "I can't stitch it. It's deep enough, you've got some really nasty lacerations, but the edges are a mess. I'll clean it up and bandage it, but we'll just have to keep an eye on it and make sure it doesn't get infected. When did you last have a tetanus?"

I stared at him. I'd no idea.

He made a face, then wrapped my lower leg in a bandage, knotting it tightly so that the whole area immediately began to pulse.

"Okay," he sighed when he was done. "Lift up your sleeve."

But I couldn't do that either, because my sleeve was too long, and too tight. After a moment's deliberation I shrugged out of my top, too.

"Is this going to hurt," I asked, as he approached me with the needle.

"Not as much as that probably did," he pointed to my ankle.

I grimaced. Fair enough.

He grabbed the big muscle in my upper arm, squeezed it, then stabbed the needle straight into the flesh, slowly forcing down the plunger.

"Ow," I complained as he massaged my arm.

He smiled at me apologetically, then looked up, towards the hallway. I followed his gaze and saw Zane standing there. He raised his eyebrows and half-smirked, eyes raking in my semi-naked state. I bristled, but didn't bother covering up; it was nothing he hadn't seen before.

"Alexander's waiting," he said.

"We'll be up in a minute," Samuel replied, staring hard at Zane until he went away.

I exhaled as his white-blond hair disappeared back into the darkness. Alexander.

"Don't worry about it," Samuel murmured, reading my mind. "You got the job done, that's all that matters."

I wished I believed that.

Samuel waited until I'd winced my way back into my jeans and yanked my top back over my head, then he walked along slowly beside me as I limped my way up the two floors to Alexander's office. Zane must have heard my thumping shuffle because he opened the door just as I reached the top step. The smirk was gone. He glowered at us as we passed, his expression sour for a reason I couldn't fathom. Surely he'd be delighting in my failure, my imminent punishment?

"Elizabeth," Alexander said, appraising me from the sofa. "Are you all right?"

My eyebrows drew together in confusion before I could smooth my expression. I hadn't expected concern.

"I'm fine," I stammered. I looked down at my ankle. "It hurts a little."

"Well, you shouldn't have made a mistake."

I waited for the rest to follow, but he astonished me by smiling with almost genuine warmth.

"You're lucky," he said.

"What do you mean?"

"Haven't you heard?"

I shook my head. I'd no idea where he was leading me.

His smiled widened into a grin and he waved Zane and Samuel out of the room, waiting until the door was closed before reaching for the remote.

"Our little present went off early," he said, turning on the enormous flat screen. "We didn't get Bowles. But we went one better. Well, two actually."

"What do you mean?" I whispered.

Alexander flicked through the channels until he came to the news. A face filled the screen. A child's face.

"Seems the dog went missing, and little Annabel was so upset she convinced her mother to take the car out so they could search for her. Tragically, the pair didn't make it out of the garage. Some awful person had laid a surprise for them." He stopped then, soaking in the moment so he could revel in my agony. His eyes drank in my horrified face, but he couldn't help himself from having one more dig. "Well done, Elizabeth. Well done."

I gaped at the screen. It wasn't real. No, surely not. It wasn't. It wasn't.

But the truth was staring me in the face, staring out at me from the screen.

What had I done?

"No! No, no, no!" I was almost yelling, forgetting, for once, Alexander's dislike of raised voices. "I killed a little girl? I killed a little girl!"

The child's face smiled out at me from the television screen, her big, beseeching blue eyes magnified, as was her carefree, innocent smile. In my mind's eye I saw her expression change in the split-second before she died.

Had there been time for realisation, shock, fear? Had there been time for pain?

"No, no, no, no, no!"

I fell forward onto my knees, my hands clutching my throat. Tears and sobs welled in my chest, choking me as they forced their way out. My stomach heaved, and I thought I might vomit.

"Oh God. What have I done? Oh God!" I couldn't take it in, couldn't stop seeing her face, even now the television report had moved on to interviewing a severe-looking man in a dark suit.

Alexander didn't even look at me.

"Stop crying."

I clapped my hand over my mouth, holding in the noise, but I couldn't stop the tears that streamed down my cheeks or the shudders racking my shoulders, my ribs. It was torture, knowing I'd murdered that little girl and her mother just as sure as if I'd held a gun to their heads and pulled the trigger. Only my method had been so much more cowardly; I hadn't had to look in their faces as they'd died.

I stayed there, silently grieving, for the rest of the night. Eventually Alexander tired of the news and he turned off the television, turned off the lights. Then he went to bed and left me huddled on the floor, drowning in a puddle of my own tears.

CHAPTER SIX

Just days later Alexander sent me out on a routine drop off: a small payment of cocaine to a man who specialised in smuggling Celts across the wall. It was in Brixton, awkward to get to, and dangerous, but he let me take a car and driver, Cameron. Cameron usually watched the door, or the street, or patrolled the various business premises and warehouses that Alexander owned. He didn't talk much, but he was big and mean, and he drove fast, so we had no problems and were back by mid-afternoon. Cameron dropped me off at the front door then sped off round the corner, where Alexander had his garages.

I headed inside, pleased that I'd have another clockwork mission to report. I rushed past the man on the door with a nod and a smile, then headed for the staircase to the upper floors. I'd just put my foot on the first step when a hand clamped down on my shoulder.

"Not today," the doorman said, shaking his head at me. I frowned. He wasn't one I recognised and I wondered if he realised who I was: nobody, but a nobody with access to just about everywhere.

"But I've got to report to Alexander," I protested.

Alexander always wanted to know exactly when I got back. He wasn't just interested in how it went; he liked keeping tabs on me, on my every movement.

"Not today," he repeated. "Orders from Mr Alexander. Nobody, but nobody, goes up there this afternoon. Not me, not you, not God."

I made a face and looked away, caught sight of Zane in a room down the hallway, doing the inventory by the looks of it and none too happy about that fact. That brought me up short. What sort of meeting would Zane be excluded from? Who was up there?

Slowly I took my foot back off the step.

"Well," I said, thinking. Now what? I'd nowhere else to go and I didn't fancy hanging about with Zane, whose face was like a black cloud and who despised my company at the best of times. "I guess... I guess I'll just take a walk, come back later. When they're done."

The doorman said nothing, but held open the door for me to go back out. My heart in my mouth, I flipped my hood back up, stuffed my hands in my jeans pockets, and marched back out of the door.

What was I doing? Alexander was going to be furious when he found out I'd just disappeared without permission. And where was I going? Stepney had never been particularly affluent, but now it definitely wasn't the sort of area you just wandered around. I was somewhat protected because most people who knew my face knew that I belonged to Alexander. But what about all the thugs and thieves and scumbags who didn't know me?

Strangely, none of these thoughts slowed my feet. If anything, they quickened them. Because there was a strange feeling bubbling in my chest, a feeling that made me want to break into a sprint and run as fast as my legs could carry me. Freedom.

But I didn't run. I just walked, a quick, clipped pace, and I let the streets fade by me without really thinking about where I was going. So I was surprised when I found myself at a standstill outside an old-fashioned red phone box, and even more surprised when I swung the door open and walked inside. I lifted the handle, stared at the display. Most of the coin-operated machines in the country were still set up to accept the Euro, and as the government didn't have the money to change all of them back to the pound we were operating in a weird half-and-half system. The pound was the currency, there was no doubt about that, but when it came to coins, Euros were the handiest to carry around. I dug around in my pocket, pulled out a €2 coin. It was far too much, and I knew I wouldn't get change, but I stuck it in the slot without hesitating.

Then I paused, took a deep breath, shut my eyes and tried to dredge up the image I was searching for: a scrap of paper with untidy, loopy writing in blue ink. I didn't have a photographic memory, not quite, but I'd tried to memorise the number like I'd memorised Zane's list, like I memorised the addresses of the various locations where Alexander wanted me to make drop-offs and pick-ups. I tapped out the digits like I saw them in my head, then waited. The phone began to ring in my ear, but that meant nothing. I could be calling anyone.

"Hello?" It was a male, a Londoner, but it was impossible to decide if it was the right voice over the white noise of the line.

"Mark?"

There was a brief pause.

"Yes." He sounded unsure, suspicious. I realised I hadn't identified myself.

"Mark, it's Lizzie. You probably don't remember me. We met a couple... a few weeks ago. On the train."

"Oh. Right." He sounded surprised, then he laughed. "Hi! I guess you changed your mind."

"Yeah," I breathed. "Sorry it took me so long. I lost your number."

What the hell was I doing? I knew this was insanity, but my brain seemed strangely disconnected from my mouth.

"You don't have to apologise. So... how are you doing? Does this mean you want to meet up sometime?"

"Sure. In fact," I crossed my fingers. "What are you doing right now?"

"Now?" he squeaked. I waited. "Well, nothing I guess. Yeah, I can do now. Sure."

"Where are you?" I asked. I couldn't travel far.

"At home. I live on the south side of Hackney."

Perfect.

"Well, I'm not far away. Could we meet in Bethnal Green? There's a nice little coffee shop I know."

I described it to him and he said he knew the place.

It was a safe location for me to go to; I knew the owner was sympathetic to Celts. He'd given me a cup of tea a few times when I was on the streets, before I met Alexander. We agreed to meet there in twenty minutes, but walking quickly, I was there in fifteen.

It was a nice place, cosy, with small windows that made it hard to see in from the pavement outside. The tables were small and round, with little stools instead of chairs so they could squeeze a few extra customers in when it was busy. It wasn't today, though, and I grabbed myself a seat over by the wall. I kept my hood up, knowing that if I sat right, and kept my face at a certain angle, most of my left cheek would be hidden. I didn't have any of Samuel's make-up on me today.

Mark arrived just a couple of minutes late. He gave me a wave before heading to the counter, bringing over a tray with two steaming cups of coffee and a monster-sized muffin.

"I couldn't resist," he said, indicating the cake. "I thought we could share."

"Thanks," I smiled, trying not to look too eager as I reached for a large chunk. I hadn't eaten since breakfast and I was starving.

"So," he said, staring back at me. "I didn't think you were going to call me. I kind of got the impression on the train that you weren't interested."

I shrugged. "I changed my mind."

"Ladies' prerogative, I guess," he smirked, rolling his eyes.

"Right," I laughed. This was so bizarre, sitting here, having a normal conversation with a normal person.

"Aren't you going to take your hood off?" he asked me, wiping the smile off my face.

I sat back a little.

"I have hood hair."

"C'mon, it's hiding half your face."

He leaned forward as if he was going to knock it off, but I jerked backwards. The movement shifted the fabric to the side for just a second or so, but it was enough. His face dropped.

"Oh, shit," he hissed, staring at me. I stared back. He'd seen it. Now what? Was he going to run, start screaming, call the police, the GE? This had been such a stupid idea. What was I thinking?

He broke eye contact, gazing frantically around the place, then back to me.

"You're... you're a *Celt*," he mouthed the last word, then glanced around the room again. I wished he wouldn't; his jerking, wide-eyed movements were attracting far more notice than my face. "Have, have they only just caught you? Is that why you didn't call? I thought they took you back across the border once you'd been tattooed?"

Well at least he wasn't running and screaming. I wasn't in any danger, but he was gawping at me like I was a live grenade, and I hated it. My experiment in being normal was over.

"I haven't just been caught," I said quietly.

But," he blinked, confused. "But you didn't have that

tattoo," – more mouthing – "on the train. I would have noticed. I definitely would have noticed."

"It was there," I said. "Just hidden."

I was disappointed. I'd wanted... well I'd wanted him not to find out, but that had been idiotic. I'd wanted him not to care, to see that it was just a tattoo, nothing more, but he was acting like I was an alien from outer space. What did I expect? He didn't know me from Adam. I sighed.

"I'll leave," I said, scraping my stool back to stand.

"No... wait!" He reached out and grabbed my hand where it leaned on the table. "Don't go just yet. I'm sorry. It... it was just a shock, y'know? I wasn't expecting it. I've never even seen one of those up close before, only on the news." His eyes were pinned on my cheek, one hand lifting, seemingly of its own accord. "Can I touch it?"

I wet my lips with my tongue nervously, didn't answer. Mark took my silence for assent, which I guess it was, because I made no move to stop him as his fingers continued to reach for my face. He ran the tip of his index finger twice round the circle, eyes following the movement while I stared at him, counting the seconds, waiting for him to look at me. *Me*. It took a while, but then he did, and when he caught my eye, he smiled. "So I guess you're not really a school pupil, huh?"

"No."

"Right. I guess I should have picked up on your accent too," I was hopeless at disguising it. "Anyway, why were you wearing the outfit? You're not..." he leaned in closer dropped his voice. "You're not a prostitute are you?"

"No, of course not!" I snapped back, outraged.

"Sorry."

I glared at him, not quite sure if he was forgiven.

"It was a disguise," I said coldly. "People don't ask so many questions when you're dressed like something they recognise."

"I see." He quite clearly didn't, but he sensed it was time to change the subject. "Well, I'm afraid I wasn't wearing a disguise. I'm just a plain old, boring office worker. I work in HR and Payroll for the Defence Department. It's the least exciting job in the entire defence unit, but it's a start," he grinned.

I could see that he was making an effort to make up for his reaction, to force the conversation back into the realms of normality. I appreciated it. What would be a normal response?

"So, you live in Hackney?" I asked hesitantly.

"Yeah," he brightened. "It's not much, a little one-bed flat, but it's mine. Well, rented. No parents, though. Finally! You could," he dropped his voice, then his head, and blushed. "You could come and see it sometime, if you wanted?"

I raised my eyebrows, and his blush doubled.

"Nothing like that! Just, I don't know. I could cook you dinner or something."

"That sounds nice," I said, but I didn't smile. Because it did sound nice, and I knew I'd never get to experience it.

I took a gulp of my coffee to cover the awkward moment, then looked off to the right, over his shoulder. Someone, an old man, was staring at me, frowning. Automatically I yanked at my hood, pulling it further forward. The old man's frown deepened.

"I should probably go," I said, flicking my gaze back to Mark. I was pushing my luck staying here so long. If the old man was the type to call the GE they could come crashing in the door any second.

Mark looked over his shoulder, caught the gaze of the old man, who finally looked away.

"You reckon?" he said.

I nodded. Definitely.

"Will I get to see you again?" he asked.

"I don't know."

"I guess it's still pointless to ask for your number?" He looked up at me hopefully as I stood, reaching into my pocket for change to cover my half of the bill. "Don't worry," he held his hand out. "I'll get this."

"Thanks." I looked down at him, grimaced. "I don't have a phone. Not one I could use to call on anyway."

I saw that my cryptic answer made little sense to him, but he didn't push me on it.

"But I've got your number," I tapped my forehead, where I had it stored. "If I can, I'll call you."

"I hope so," he said softly. I repressed a shiver, remembering when Alexander had said those exact words to me, right after he asked if he could trust me. If he found out about this, I was in serious trouble.

"Bye, Mark," I smiled at him, at his young, innocent face, knowing I'd probably never see him again. On a whim, I reached out. He matched the motion and our hands clasped, his engulfing mine. I let myself revel in the uncomplicated, unfettered warmth of his touch for the briefest of moments. Then I walked out of the coffee shop, marching right past the old man, who kept his eyes firmly fixed on his cup of tea until I was gone.

On the way back I was torn between the desire to run, knowing I'd been gone longer than I should, and the desire to slow to a funereal march, aware of the sort of reception that was likely to await me. I was annoyed at myself now. A five-minute date, a hot drink and a bit of cake were not worth the trouble I was likely to get into if anyone – i.e. Alexander – ever found out about it. I still couldn't even work out why I'd done it.

I'd no idea how long I'd been gone: maybe an hour, maybe more. If the meeting was still happening, there was a chance no one would have missed me. If not, well I'd make some excuse. If I got really desperate I'd tell Alexander I had to go out and buy some tampons. I ducked into a shop as I neared Bancroft Road to grab some, just in case, firming up my alibi. They weren't the make I liked, but it was hard to get anything now that was made in the States. Not unless you went through Alexander or one of his competitors.

When I got back the same man was watching the front door. I noticed Zane was no longer in the room through the back. Did that mean they'd finished upstairs?

"Can I go up now?" I asked, trying not to seem petulant, although nerves made my voice sound defensive.

"Knock yourself out," he said, gesturing to the staircase.

I made a face as I turned my back on him. What a strange thing to say.

At the top of the stairs I noticed the door to Alexander's office was wide open, which was unusual. I walked slowly towards it, the nerves from downstairs magnifying with each step. Before I could reach the doorway, Zane appeared in it, looking out to see who the quiet footsteps belonged to. He looked me up and down, then disappeared.

"It's Lizzie, sir," I heard him say.

"Elizabeth?" Perversely, I stopped, still in the darkness of the hallway. I didn't like the way he sounded. Soft and low, as always, but there was something else. Swallowing against my tightening throat, I started forward. It wasn't wise to keep him waiting.

Did he know? My eyes darted around the room as I entered, searching for signs. Zane stood just behind the door, against the wall. That was a weird position. He only stood there when... when Alexander was meeting with people and there was a chance it could get ugly. An obvious show of muscle, an in-your-face physical threat. Alexander was in the office area, his back to me, reading over something.

I waited, wondering if I should clear my throat or something to let him know I was there, but some inner sense told me to keep quiet. He knew I was waiting, he was just making me sweat it out.

He knew.

"Where have you been?"

He spoke before he turned, but then he did face me, fixing me with his eyes like a cobra, and I was held, hypnotised.

"What? I... nowhere."

"Nowhere," he echoed.

Then he looked to the left, to his bodyguard.

Zane pushed off from his position by the kitchenette and approached me. He was smiling, blue eyes for once alight when they looked at me. A foot away, he stopped, and his fist shot out. My legs buckled.

It was a move I had seen a dozen times: a short jab to the stomach and grown men fell to their knees.

I had never felt it before.

My stomach exploded with pain, shock waves ricocheting out to my intestines, my kidneys, the muscles of my abdomen. My lungs went into spasm and I couldn't breathe, my legs just folded under me.

I couldn't hold myself up and gravity toppled my upper body forward, arms stretched out to cushion my fall, but Zane had a hold of my hair and he wrenched my head back, kept me upright. I stared forward, into the muzzle of a gun. Alexander rested it gently on my forehead, right between my eyes.

"Where have you been Elizabeth?"

Refuse to tell him and die? Tell him and die?

Which one would be the quickest, the least painful? My head throbbed as I went cross-eyed, trying to keep the barrel of the gun in sight as I deliberated.

"I... I went out."

"Yes, I know that. Where did you go?"

He looked down at me, not a trace of anger or hate in his face, just calm composure.

I licked my lips, trying to eek some life back into them. "I went to Bethnal Green, to a coffee shop."

I was willing to bet he knew that, too. He also knew I'd met a twenty-year-old boy, and that I'd drunk a coffee and eaten half a muffin. He didn't know who the boy was. Once he had that information there would be nothing left to stop him pulling the trigger and blowing my brains out. He'd have to get a new carpet – a minor irritation, but I knew how attached he was to the luxurious, thick white shag – but that was a price he seemed willing to pay for the chance to deal with my misbehaviour personally. Having Zane take me downstairs to the basement wouldn't give him the same satisfaction.

"And who did you meet there?"

I hesitated, hanging on to my last few seconds of life. Zane adjusted his grip on my hair, pulling me up a few inches, taking the weight off my knees. Reminding me he was there. I swallowed, shifting my gaze from Alexander to the gun, to Alexander. He smiled at me, pushed the muzzle harder against my skin. He was waiting.

"Who. Did. You. Meet. There?"

"I... it was..."

I should have known. I *had* known. What the hell had I been thinking? Was my five minutes of ordinary life worth dying for?

Oh God. Make it quick. Please make it quick.

But he wouldn't. Alexander wasn't into doing merciful things like that.

"What's going on?"

I swivelled my eyes to the left, caught sight of a figure lingering in the doorway. It was Samuel; it had to be. No one else would have walked in without permission.

"What's Lizzie done?" Samuel stepped into the room, approaching the three of us: me kneeling on the carpet; Zane behind, holding me up; Alexander in front, holding a gun to my head.

"Elizabeth," Alexander said, taking care to roll my name around his mouth like a caress, "has been secretly meeting up with somebody in Bethnal Green. Behind my back."

"Oh, that."

I tried to look at Samuel, to see the expression on his face, but Zane held me too tightly. What did he mean by that? His tone was flat, unsurprised. How could he possibly have known? How had Alexander known?

"You knew?" Alexander whispered, anger for the first time creeping into his voice.

"Yeah. She was on a job for me."

My eyes widened. What was Samuel doing?

"A job for you?"

"Yes. I told her to keep it quiet. I didn't mean from you, but obviously she misunderstood."

Alexander stared down at me, his eyes thoughtful. I stared back, knowing my life depended on whether or not he believed his brother. I was too frightened to construct a look of innocence, or even hide my shock at Samuel's lies. Why was he covering for me?

"Is that true, Elizabeth?" he asked.

I tried to nod, but my head was jammed between Zane's hand and the end of the gun, still pressed hard enough into my forehead to leave a dent.

"Yes," I whispered, my throat choked with fear.

"Who is he?" Alexander was still looking down at me, but he wasn't talking to me.

Out of the corner of my eye I saw Samuel shrug.

"Just someone I thought might be a useful informer; his dad has connections. But it didn't work out. The boy hasn't got the balls for it."

"Is that so?" Alexander murmured. He still held the gun to my head – still hadn't decided.

"Look, Alex, kill her if you want. But that job's next week, so you'll have to get me a replacement sharpish, and a good one. We don't want to let the Davis mob down."

Samuel's voice was casual, unconcerned. If he was trying to save my life, he was doing a very good job of making it look otherwise.

"Hmm." Alexander twisted his mouth to the side, then slowly lowered the gun. I gasped with relief, closing my eyes to try to hold back the tears that shimmered, threatening to overspill. "On your feet," he said.

My legs didn't feel like they were working yet, but Zane was lifting me, my full weight supported by a fistful of my hair, so I scrambled to get my feet beneath me. I swayed slightly, but managed to stay standing when Zane released me. My eyes were locked on Alexander's. He took both hands and placed them on either side of my head, then he leaned forward and softly kissed the spot where his gun had dug into my head. The skin throbbed slightly; I was going to have a bruise.

"I don't like people plotting and scheming behind my back," he said, addressing me, but making sure his words reached Samuel as well. "It makes me think they're doing things they shouldn't be. Understand?"

I nodded, one traitorous tear sliding down my cheek.

Alexander smiled, then his hand whipped up and smashed me across the face. He was still holding the gun.

My eyes rolled backwards in my head as I hit the ground for the second time. I was still conscious, but only just. The room spun, and when I clapped my hand to my face I could feel that the skin had split. Blood oozed over my fingers. I pulled my hood around to absorb the hot, sticky liquid, my eyes on the pristine carpeting. I didn't look up, but I felt the light vibrations of the floorboards as Alexander walked away.

On my hands and knees, I crawled my way into a corner. And I stayed there.

CHAPTER SEVEN

Alexander kept me around because I had two skills he considered valuable. The first was my ability to get into – and out of – awkward places. I was small enough and agile enough to wriggle through windows or shimmy up walls, but more than that; I was invisible. Even with my tattoo, my piercings and my alternative haircut, I was inconspicuous. The eye tended to rove right over my head whenever anyone scanned a crowd. I could never work out if that was self-preservation, if they sensed I might be one of those contemptuous, easily aggravated teenagers who looked to cause trouble; or if it was because I was so defeated, such a nobody, that they couldn't bear to look at me. Either way, my presence more often than not went unnoticed, and time after time I came back from errands for Alexander that I shouldn't have.

The second skill was exponentially more valuable: I knew how to make bombs.

It wasn't an innate skill, I wasn't born with the ability to create chaos and destruction; but the inner workings, delicate connections and wirings, just made sense to me.

I'd always been fascinated by puzzles: from connect the dots and mazes to Rubik's cubes and sudoku. They were logical, rational. The answer was there, somewhere, if you just looked hard enough. In the turmoil of my life as a child – passed from parent to parent, foster home to care home – they were a comfort; they were something I could control, something I could fix. The complex, interlinking circuitry of a bomb was just another puzzle, another brainteaser to solve, only this time a deadly one.

Alexander had uncovered my talent quite by accident. At that time all of his terrorist bombings were planned, organised and executed by two men: Kieran and Patrick. They were Irish, and they'd done their apprenticeships trying to instigate a resurgence of violence in Northern Ireland. It was ironic that the first bombs they'd made were to separate Northern Ireland from the rest of the UK and now they were working to repair that fracture, but no one ever mentioned that fact. They were dangerous men.

They didn't often visit Bancroft Road, preferring to keep a distance, receiving orders through intermediaries for whatever job Alexander planned for them next, and although that meant Alexander couldn't control their every movement as he would have liked, he consented to let them work their own way, so long as everything ran like clockwork. It did, for a while, but then things began to go wrong. I don't know if they started to get lazy, if they were skimming more off their fee by getting in cheaper components and explosives, or whether they didn't realise quite who they were working for, but a job

– one Alexander had gone to great expense to set up access to, buying blueprints and paying off security – went disastrously wrong. The bomb didn't detonate and it was discovered. The neutralised vestiges found their way to the police and then, mysteriously but not surprisingly, to Alexander, and he was not pleased. The Irishmen were summoned.

I was in Alexander's office – curled up on a sofa, quiet and discreet, there but not there – when they arrived. It was the middle of winter and it must have been snowing hard outside, because both men had unmelted flakes clinging to their hair and shoulders when they entered Alexander's lair.

Zane let them in. Alexander remained sitting on another of the oversized sofas, twiddling something in his fingers. He refused to look at either of the bombers, but stared down at the thing in his hands like it was the most fascinating object in the world. Kieran and Patrick stood waiting, arms behind their backs, legs slightly apart like soldiers, or like pupils brought before the headmaster. They looked more annoyed than fearful, as if they thought this treatment was beneath them. One of them, Kieran, cleared his throat to let Alexander know he was there. I suppressed a grin. Alexander already knew.

"Mr Alexander, you wanted to see us?" he prompted, after his more subtle hint had evoked no response.

Alexander smiled down at his hands.

"Do you know what this is?" he asked, voice like velvet.

Kieran held his hand out for the object, but Alexander's

fingers tightened around it. He had no intention of giving it up, and after a few awkward moments Kieran's arm dropped back to his side.

It was Patrick who spoke.

"It would appear to be the remains of a bomb," he remarked, his tone sarcastic, his eyebrows knitted together in a scowl. Clearly he was unimpressed at the less than warm reception he and his partner were receiving.

"Yes, it is," Alexander said, twiddling at the wires, making a little black box spin. "And do you know why I'm holding it?"

Silence.

The correct answer was because it hadn't gone off, but neither man wanted to admit to that, because that would be tantamount to accepting responsibility, accepting failure.

Alexander drew the moment out several seconds longer, enjoying the way both men shifted uncomfortably.

"I'm holding it, because the police recovered the whole device, intact, at the scene. Now," he paused, looked up at them for the first time. Kieran looked away, but Patrick held his stare. "Can you understand how that might present something of a problem for me?"

"There was nothing to link the bomb to us, or you," Patrick shot back. I had to admire his bravery, but he was dicing with death answering back to Alexander. "We didn't leave fingerprints, and the parts are untraceable."

"I should hope not," Alexander murmured, smiling coolly. "But it takes time and resources and contacts to set up access to a job like that. So when you mess up, I lose money, and I lose face."

That was the real issue. Alexander was very careful about his reputation. He was known as a cold-hearted bastard, a good businessman, and someone who got things done. A botched job looked bad, it sowed seeds of doubt in the minds of his associates, made him look unprofessional.

"It won't happen again," Kieran assured him, glancing up briefly from the hole he was trying to burn into the carpet with his embarrassed and angry glare.

Alexander stood up. He was at least two inches shorter than either man, but they seemed to have shrunk during the length of the conversation.

"I want to know why it happened this time!" He raised his voice, just a little, just to the volume of any normal conversation, but it was enough to make Kieran flinch and Patrick drop his gaze. He waved the device in the air. "Why did this not go off?"

Kieran shrugged. "I don't know. Everything was set up perfectly. There was no reason for it not to detonate. Maybe there was a fault in the wire, maybe the C4 was bad, maybe—"

"Maybe, maybe, maybe," Alexander hissed.

Kieran took the hint and shut up, his teeth coming together with an audible snap.

"Useless," Alexander tossed the device over his shoulder. It landed lightly on the cushion beside me on the sofa.

Now that I could see it clearly, it was more obviously the inner workings of a bomb. There were several wires, all lines in different colours of rubber tubing, all leading to a little black box. Their other ends were exposed and frayed, with the residue of some pale blue substance the consistency of play dough sticking to the copper threading. I glanced up at Alexander, but he was still talking, the broad shoulders of his back to me. In one quick, decisive movement, I reached out and snatched up the black box. Still nobody turned to me.

With nimble fingers I eased the cap off and peered inside. It was a fairly simple system; a switch to connect the circuit and set off the charge. I didn't see a trigger, like a timing mechanism, but that was probably remote controlled so that whoever set it up would have time to get far enough away to escape the fallout of the blast – a few metres or a block, depending how much explosive was attached to the end. I *did* see what was wrong with it, though, straight away. It was fairly obvious.

"It's been wired wrong," I murmured.

"What?" A harsh Irish accent whipped out the word and I jerked my head up. I hadn't meant anyone to hear me.

Patrick was staring at me, his upper lip curling in a sneer.

"It's been wired wrong," I repeated, a little louder. My cheeks coloured and I felt my pulse pounding in my throat. I was very aware that my presence in the room was supposed to be silent.

"Don't be stupid," Patrick snapped.

"How would you know?" His partner, too, was eyeing me with distain and dislike.

Alexander turned to me, raised one eyebrow questioningly. I knew that look. It meant I'd better be right, or I'd be sorry for opening my mouth. I was already sorry; but I was right, too.

"No, really. Look." I held the little black box out for Alexander's inspection, my fingers pointing to the mistake I'd spotted. "The wires come into these inputs, but the switch is linked to the wrong connectors. The circuit couldn't complete, that's why it wouldn't detonate."

"Let me see that," Patrick snatched the device out of my hands, making sure to give Alexander a wide berth as he moved back to stand beside his partner. The two of them bent over it, examining their handiwork. After several seconds Patrick raised his head and stared hard at Kieran. "You idiot," he whispered.

Alexander grinned wolfishly. He didn't need to see the inside of the device for himself, the truth was written all over their faces.

"Well, that's not a mistake I expect we'll be needing to repeat," he said. "You got an advance for the job, but as there was no boom, you won't be getting the rest of your fee."

Neither man looked happy with that, but they weren't about to argue.

"See Zane, he's in the basement. He'll give you your next assignment." Alexander lingered ominously over the final word, but Kieran and Patrick didn't notice, they were too eager to get out of the room with nothing less than a hit in the pocket and an unhappy boss.

Alexander's office wasn't soundproofed, and a couple of minutes later I heard two muffled pops. Patrick and Kieran would not be doing any more jobs for Alexander.

I didn't waste any time feeling sorry for them. I was under the spotlight now, uncomfortably so.

"Tell me how you knew there was something wrong with this." Alexander had returned to the sofa, the device back in his hands, and he tapped me on the knee with it, punctuating each word. I watched the little plastic box bounce off my jeans as I wondered what the right answer was.

"I don't know," I mumbled. "It's just... logic. Circuits are circles and switches are open or closed, and you can follow the connections round. It's like a map or something."

"Has anyone ever shown you how to build something like this?"

I shook my head, my innocence and my fear clear on my face.

"Hmmm." Alexander narrowed his eyes as he looked at me, but his expression was thoughtful and calculating rather than angry.

Patrick and Kieran were the last two explosives agents Alexander brought in from outside. They had proved untrustworthy, and he wanted his finger more firmly on the pulse, wanted to oversee every part of the operation, from set up to implementation. He took to organising these forays into terrorism in-house, using as his operative someone he had total and utter control over: me. I was given a crash course in rudimentary bomb construction – which mostly consisted of someone taking me to an Internet cafe and keeping watch whilst I plugged searches into Google that would almost certainly flag up on the big brother communications monitoring the government claimed it didn't do.

There was no time to practise. The first time I laid my hands on C4 explosive was my first job. It was a small target: nothing political, nothing to do with the 'cause'. A small-time drug dealer had failed to pay his debt to Alexander. He'd had warnings, but the money had still to come in, so now it was time to send a stronger message. The man – I didn't know his name – had a garage he used for 'storage': cannabis cultivation in reality. I was going to go and blow it up. Usually Alexander would have sent a lackey in to torch the place, but he thought it was an ideal opportunity for me to prove my worth.

I didn't go alone. Though it wasn't a difficult task – the garage was in a run-down industrial area and would be all but abandoned at the time of night we planned to visit – Alexander didn't like the idea of me being out of his sight with a jacket full of explosives. It was also awkward to get to, and I couldn't drive. It would have been easy enough to learn, Alexander owned countless cars and anyone could have taken a few hours to teach me the basics, enough to get me from A to B. But then I would be independent. Then I might be able to get away.

Alexander's reasoning stopped there, never considering that I had nowhere else to go.

Samuel took me. He was keen to become more involved with Alexander's terrorist activities, and though this wasn't anything to do with that, he knew where Alexander's schemes for me were leading, even if I didn't. I didn't really know Samuel at that point. He had been in Cardiff for years, since before the wall was built and the Welsh Assembly fell apart, running his brother's business deals in their hometown, some above board... some less so. But now that he was living in London, he was eager to carve out his own niche in Alexander's world.

We drove there in total silence. Samuel didn't speak, and I knew that with his brother it would be best to keep my mouth shut. I still didn't know how alike they were, and how they differed.

"This is it," Samuel said, coasting to a stop and motioning to a large metal gate. "Thomson's garage is in there, number thirty. I'll stay here with the car."

"Okay," I whispered.

I sounded like a frightened little girl, because that's what I was. My eyes were huge in the dark, drinking in the sight before me. Thomson's garage was curled away inside a rickety wall of corrugated iron. Floodlights glared down at odd intervals, creating bright pools of light and deep corners of shadow. There was no one in sight, but that didn't mean there weren't people – or dogs – lurking in the gloom.

Funnily enough I wasn't worried about the bomb.

There was no chance of me blowing myself up. I knew I had wired everything correctly. All that was left to do was attach the explosive in situ and set the timer. Simple.

Getting in and getting out was what terrified me.

Samuel heard the nerves in my voice.

"Do you know what you're doing with that?" he asked, indicating the small bag that I carried the bomb in.

"Yes," I nodded, my voice a little stronger.

"It's time," he said.

I took one deep breath and then got out of the car. Samuel had killed the lights of the Ford Focus, but I felt the force of his eyes following me as I stepped round the front of the vehicle. The road was empty, but I still jogged lightly across it, eager to be in the shadow of the pavement. The padlocked gate looked the easiest access, but the telltale winking green light of a CCTV camera was mounted on one of the floodlight poles. Rather than risk being seen, if there was any security watching from inside, I walked along the fence a little way until I found a patch of darkness between two streetlights. I took a moment to stare left and right, making sure I wasn't being watched by anyone other than Samuel, then vaulted the fence in one smooth movement. I landed on the other side, bending my legs against the impact and crouching down low to the ground to look around. Empty and silent.

Cautiously I made my way around the back of a long line of garages, pausing to peer down the narrow slit alleyways to read the numbers along the row opposite. Number thirty was right at the far end, tucked neatly into a corner. It had its own camera, hanging off the top left-hand corner and marking it out as different to the rest of the rundown storage boxes, but it was still the same construction, it still had the tiny window at the back; and that's where I was heading.

The glass was black, reflecting the inky darkness inside. I picked up a rock from the ground and, holding my breath, smashed it hard against the pane. The glass shattered, and immediately a burning light began to glare out of the hole, streaming across the darkened wasteland behind.

"Oh Christ!" I hissed. Anyone looking out would be able to see that for miles around! Why the hell were there lights on?

Panicking, I jumped up and shuffled my way into the tiny hole I'd made. It was six inches by twelve inches maximum, and if I'd been ten pounds heavier I'd never have made it through.

I hit the floor, totally blind. The whole space seemed to shimmer at me, like staring at the sun through binoculars. There was a funny smell to the place and it was stifling hot. Walking forward, I reached out with my hands, trying to feel my way as I couldn't see. My foot connected with something, sending it tumbling to the ground with a dull *thunk* before my scrambling fingers could grab hold. There was a low tinkle of breaking glass, then at once the light was halved.

I sighed with relief. I could see. And I'd never seen anything like this.

The cannabis plants grew higher than my head, sprouting up in rows under a system of silver vents pouring out hot air. The air was thrumming with the low grumble of a generator and a lamp – the partner of which I'd knocked over and shattered – shone artificial sunlight, while tinfoil on the walls multiplied the effect. Gathering my senses, I flipped off the working lamp, aware of the tiny broken window, which must have been filled with blacked-out glass to hide the brightness. I replaced the brilliant lamp with a tiny flashlight, clamping it between my teeth as I set to work constructing my little device in the middle of the room. There wasn't much to it. I'd already linked all the connections and stripped the ends of the wires. All that was left to do was attach the bomb to the stuff that went boom. I shook my head as I eased the copper ends into the C4. I didn't understand how putty could explode like it did. It looked completely harmless, like something from a children's art class, only much, much more valuable. And dangerous.

I set the timer to fifteen minutes – Samuel wanted it short enough so that we'd have time to get out of the area but still be close enough to know if it worked – if I really did know what I was doing – or so we could come back and hide the evidence if I messed up. Then I took a quick second to check it over. I didn't want to have to face Alexander like Kieran and Patrick had. Everything seemed fine.

Standing up, I shuffled my way to the rear of the building and struggled out of the minuscule opening, then

I crept back the way I'd come, over the fence and into the road. It wasn't until I saw Samuel's car waiting for me, engine running, lights dimmed inconspicuously, that my pulse started racing and a sheen of sweat broke out on my forehead. I'd done it. I'd just planted a bomb. All it had to do now was go off.

"Problems?" Samuel asked as I got in the car.

I shook my head, not wanting to mention the lights. After all, I'd got away with it.

"Good," he smiled. "Alex likes clockwork."

We drove for two blocks, then pulled in at the side of the road to wait. I don't know what I expected – maybe a huge fireball to erupt into the sky? – but it was nothing so spectacular. There was a flash, the tiniest vibration, and then the low cloud around the building in front of us glowed a dull orange. I stared forward. Was that it? Did it work?

"Let's go home," Samuel murmured, smiling to himself as he drove away.

From then on Samuel was always my driver. As the jobs got more complicated, more risky, he brought in others to smooth the way, like the hired thugs at the Home Office Intelligence building whose timely vandalism set up my escape route. I wasn't afraid of Samuel like I was of Alexander, but I knew without a shadow of a doubt that we weren't friends. To him, I was something of Alexander's that he could borrow when he needed it, like a car.

I was useful, I was reliable, and I stayed alive.

CHAPTER EIGHT

There was no fallout from my excursion to Bethnal Green. Alexander had accepted Samuel's word, I'd been punished for keeping secrets, and as far as Alexander was concerned that was the matter dealt with. He would be watching me, of course. Very closely. But then, he was always watching me.

I found out two days later what the big job was involving the Davis mob – whoever they were. Alexander took me down to a tight, windowless room on the ground floor, where Samuel and Zane were pouring over a large sheet of paper pinned to a table. A moment later I realised it was a map. Either Zane or Samuel had inserted little coloured pins going from north to south in a jagged line and as we entered they were discussing each of the dots, pointing and running their fingers over tiny lines of red and blue.

Samuel looked up, his hand still hovering over the map.

"Rhys Davis has been in touch," he said. "They're looking at the section between Abergavenny and Knighton. It's a big stretch of nothing bordering on the

Brecon Beacons National Park. It's a good move. That area should be much quieter. They'll expect more trouble on the busier routes."

"We're looking at two main points," Zane chipped in. "Here," he pointed to a large red pin, "at Monmouth where the A40 used to cut the border, or here," he raised his fingers north a few inches, "at the A465. Rhys prefers Monmouth, but we're pushing for the more northern point. If there's any trouble, any complications, it would be easier to disappear from there."

Alexander nodded. "Take the northern. And tell Davis to set up a dummy attack at Monmouth, twenty minutes before. That might draw some of their security away from where we'll be."

"Good idea," Zane agreed sycophantically.

Alexander just smiled. He knew that.

"It'll put them on the alert, though," Samuel disagreed, his forehead furrowed in concentration. "They'll bring in reinforcements, maybe a helicopter."

"Yes, but by the time they arrive at Monmouth, our main assault will have happened. When they realise their mistake and turn round, we'll be long gone."

Samuel nodded. "Okay," he relented. "But an issue we're going to have is that when we head back, there's only one road. We'll have to go a long way down the A465 before we can pull off onto another route. We'll be easy to trace."

"Then we'd better make it a fast car," Alexander smirked, a gleam in his eye.

Samuel made a face.

"A fast car isn't going to outrun a helicopter," he complained. "We're leaving ourselves too open."

"It's a risk," Alexander conceded, "but an acceptable one."

I stood silently through their exchange, keeping my face impassive, though I had to stifle a wry smile at Alexander's final comment. That was easy for him to say; it would not be him in the line of fire, taking the risk.

So they were planning an attack on the Wall, then. Now that I'd heard some of the place names they were considering, I realised it was the Welsh border that was their target. That made sense: both brothers were Welsh and their families and friends were still back in Cardiff, struggling to scratch a survival out of the civil chaos gripping the little country. It was less of a stretch to head east than to make the long trek to the northern wall and risk being cut off on the road back to London. But it was a dangerous job. I'd never seen the Welsh wall, but its Scottish counterpart was an astonishing structure to behold. Cutting a swathe across the landscape as far as the eye could see in either direction, it was over ten metres in height, topped with electrified wire and guarded at regular intervals by huge towers with state of the art cameras and armed soldiers. For hundreds of metres on either side the land had been stripped clear and booby-trapped with wire and mines. The thing made the Berlin Wall look like a garden fence.

The brothers were getting ambitious; although I couldn't

help thinking, as I watched them plan and scheme, heads bent low over the map, that this new direction showed Samuel's influence. Alexander only ever acted if there was something in it for him, and I failed to see how he would profit from this venture.

"Who's going to do the construct and drop?" Zane asked, eyes on Alexander.

Samuel snapped his head up instantly, stared hard at his brother. "I want Lizzie," he said. "She knows what she's doing and I trust her. I don't want to walk into the lion's den with a stranger."

A little bubble of warmth bloomed in my stomach and I smiled at him tentatively. It went unnoticed, though. Samuel only had eyes for his brother. Alexander rubbed his jaw, scratching at the designer stubble dappling his lower face. He looked thoughtful.

"You're going to do a scout?" he asked.

"Today. I've got a fresh plated car ready. Even if anyone from the GE clocks us, they'll have no idea who we are."

Alexander nodded his approval. Then he turned to me, and both Zane and Samuel swivelled their gaze to my face as if they'd been waiting for his permission to acknowledge that I was in the room.

"Get your things," he murmured.

I was back inside two minutes, my jacket in hand. I owned almost nothing else. In that short time Samuel had rolled up the map and was sliding a rubber band in place to hold the tube.

"Let's go," he said, motioning to the front door with his head.

"Samuel?" Alexander's brother paused at the door, his hand on my shoulder. "Take someone with you. Take Cameron."

With Cameron's company I was relegated to the backseat of the car. A Fiesta this time, much smaller than most of the cars in Alexander's ever-changing fleet and a three door, so I had to scramble awkwardly into the tight space at the back. It was a long journey, taking the M4 east, then cutting up north at Swindon and following the A417 through Cirencester all the way to Gloucester. All the way Samuel and Cameron chatted quietly, the low drone of the radio drowning out their words. They didn't turn to include me, so I contented myself with staring out of the window at the countryside. It reminded me of home, the real home from my early childhood on the outskirts of Glasgow. Only now the fields were not wild with grass and grazing sheep. They were farmed, the soil intensely filled and stripped and filled and stripped. Electric fences lined the largest, and CCTV cameras rested on poles, far more of a deterrent that the scarecrows of old. Food was scarcer now, and nothing was imported so the government took great pains to protect what it grew.

At Gloucester we changed direction again, moving further east. The roads deteriorated and Samuel cursed as the car dipped and jolted over potholes and cracks. The Welsh border lingered just over the horizon, and its close proximity added a thrill to the air, cloaking the car in a tension that killed off conversation. There were more GE patrols here, hoping to catch rogue Celts who had somehow managed to penetrate the Wall's defences, and it was rumoured that the residents in the villages close to the border were paid for every successful capture, and for collecting information.

"Lizzie," Samuel said softly.

I jerked upright, leaning forward to rest my face between the two seats.

"That's the Wall. That's our target."

"Oh my God," I breathed.

Either this wall was much more impressive than the one cutting Scotland off from England, or I had forgotten the true enormity of the structure. Ten metres had never looked so tall, poured concrete so thick, so completely impenetrable. Even from this distance, several miles away, staring down at the way the wall curved through a shallow valley, I could make out the complex web of security: interwoven lines of cameras; lights; surveillance towers; rolls of wire, crackling with electric charge. Just to get to the base meant crossing a minefield of barriers, traps and explosives. I doubted a field mouse could cross the space without being spotted and blown to smithereens.

"That's impossible," I murmured.

I was so awestruck I hadn't even realised that Samuel had stopped the car, pulling discreetly in to the side. A pair of binoculars was nestled loosely in his huge hands.

"It's not impossible," Cameron sniped. "People cross the border every day."

And how many of the ones who try, die? I thought. But I didn't voice my concerns. If Cameron knew the answer, I didn't think I wanted to hear it.

"Lizzie, you need to pay attention. The next time you're here it'll be dark," Samuel told me, his voice quiet and serious, the binoculars glued to his eyes. "It won't look the same. You need to memorise the place, set points of reference in your head so you know exactly where you are. That central tower for instance."

I looked at the watchtower he was pointing to. It was circular with a panorama of windows at the top, almost like a lighthouse. Bizarre and out of place in the bleak, desolate dystopia before me.

Trying to do as he said, I stared ahead, letting my eyes dart from building to building, logging windows, cameras, wires, hillocks, exactly where the old road ran into nowhere; but his words had unsettled me and it was like trying to hold water in my cupped hands. The details trickled away as soon as I moved on.

"You'll be here, though, won't you?" I asked tremulously.

Samuel didn't even bother to respond, he just gave me a look. Of course he would be there. He always took me, and this was such a big job, one so central to his all-important cause, he would never miss it. Never.

Still, the squirming in my stomach refused to go away.

Cameron and Samuel sat there a long time, discussing the plan. Samuel pointed out the exact spot where I was to plant the bomb, the only detail I was able to cram into my head. It was easy: they wanted to blast a hole in the wall right where the A465 used to sweep into Wales. They wanted to reopen the border.

"Samuel," I whispered, hoarse after keeping my mouth shut and listening for so long, "how big will the bomb be?"

I was trying – and failing – to imagine the amount of C4 needed to cut through such a solid object.

"About the size of a briefcase," he said.

I bit my lip. More explosive by about half than I'd ever had my hands on before, but still...

"Is that going to be enough?"

"No," Samuel smiled at my puzzled expression. "That thing's six feet thick and the centre's reinforced steel. But our package is only half of it."

"What do you mean?"

"That's why Alex has been communicating with Rhys Davis. He's organising a second bomb at the exact same spot, on the other side of the wall. So Lizzie," he paused, made sure he had my complete attention. "You have to be in place at precisely the right time. We're coordinating it so both bombs go off at once. There can't be any mistakes.

"Clockwork," I murmured.

He nodded. "Clockwork."

We left not long after that. The same red Micra had driven past us three times and Samuel was beginning to get restless, checking his mirrors so often he looked like he had a twitch. Samuel swapped over and let Cameron drive for the return leg. Cameron pushed the Fiesta too hard, too fast, but even so he couldn't get close to the speed limit displayed on the signs dotted along the road. They were an unattainable goal, a mockery, reminding drivers of a time when the roads had been smooth and flat. Now, in just a few short years, potholes rutted the surface, deceptively deep, and the edges of many routes had begun to crumble, narrowing the lanes until it was impossible for two cars to pass side by side on all but major carriageways. Even driving along at forty Cameron struggled to keep the car under control, to prevent tyres exploding and axles snapping, and I bounced about in the back seat until the sharp edge of the seat belt rubbed a raw weal on the soft skin where my shoulder met my neck.

Even with Cameron's overenthusiastic driving, it was pitch black by the time we wound our way back into Stepney, and I was dog tired. My head ached; Samuel had made me describe the scene and the plan to him over and over again until my brain felt like it was going to haemorrhage, and sitting still had drained me.

Cameron dropped Samuel and me off to report back to Alexander. Or rather: for Samuel to report back and me to return to my keeper. My pulse began to thud as we ascended to the first floor the way it always did whenever I'd been away from him – what sort of mood would he be in? – and at first I didn't notice that a musical beat was pounding through the house. As we reached the door, however, the whine of guitars and high-pitched singing cut through my jangled nerves, along with the rumble of male laughter. Slinking into the room in Samuel's wake, I peered around his broad shoulders, intrigued and uncertain.

Alexander's office was a haze of smoke, both cigarette and something stronger. The lights had been dimmed and men crowded the pool table, the television and the sofas. No one turned round as we entered; all eyes were fixed on the centre of the room, where I knew Alexander would be. Impatiently, Samuel pushed his way through, and I shuffled along behind, eyeing the strange faces warily. I recognised almost nobody, but it was clear from the hardened faces, expensive suits and gleaming gold that these men were some of Alexander's underworld partners. The air was heady with the damp of smell sweat and alcohol, cloying under the cloud of smoke.

We found Alexander lounging lazily in a huge stuffed armchair. On his knee was a blonde; legs bare and ample bosom on display. She was crowing with pleasure at having the attention of the most dangerous man in a room full of dangerous men. She stroked Alexander's face and whispered and giggled in his ear. He responded by letting his hands rove over her indecently.

I stared, not quite sure how I felt. That was my place; though at times – most of the time – I loathed it and loathed him. Seeing myself superseded was both a relief and a concern. If Alexander was done with me, would he dispose of me? Unconsciously I edged closer to Samuel, seeking protection. To him, at least, I was still useful.

"Alex!" Samuel had to call his brother's name three times before he had his attention.

When he saw we were back, Alexander lifted a remote

and, at the touch of a button, the pounding music died instantly.

"All right, everybody out," he said.

Just moments earlier the quietly spoken phrase would have been impossible to hear, but on his command everyone began to filter from the room, immediately and without complaint. The blonde wriggled forward on Alexander's knee, trying to extricate herself so that she, too, could leave, but Alexander's arm tightened around her like a vice.

"Not you," he murmured. "You stay."

She beamed, and nestled further into his lap, fingers kneading his chest. I tried to keep the revulsion off my face as I studied her. How could she flaunt herself so flagrantly? How could she enjoy being so close to one who'd committed and commissioned so many wicked deeds that he was, in fact, more a monster than a man?

And, though I refused to admit it to myself, perversely, deep down, I knew I was jealous.

Staring into her unfocused eyes, I realised she wasn't really there. She was on a pleasure trip, some of Alexander's white powder burning in her veins. What was startling was that his eyes, too, were wild and bright as he looked to Samuel. But rather than make him warmer, less cold, now he seemed even more terrifying. Alexander, with his rigid control, was lethal and ruthless. Out of control, what was he capable of?

"Well?" he asked, smirking blearily, his head dipping down to analyse the blonde's plentiful assets.

I felt my cheeks burn. Was this display designed to humiliate me, or did he really not care that I was there? Knowing Alexander, the truth would lie somewhere between the two.

"We checked the place out. It'll be complicated, and dangerous, but it's doable. We just need to construct the package, then make sure Davis holds up on his end."

"Good. This should make you happy, little brother. Fighting for the cause."

I saw Samuel shoot an apprehensive look at the blonde, uncomfortable discussing the subject in front of her. Alexander seemed unconcerned. His hand was now running up and down her thigh.

"We'll talk more about it tomorrow," he said, directing his words at her neck as he leaned in to nuzzle it.

Samuel left without comment and after hovering uncertainly for a microsecond, I rushed to follow him. On the staircase, however, he abandoned me, disappearing up to the second floor where he had his own flat, opposite Zane's. I stood alone in the darkness of the hallway, indecisive. Since I'd been rescued by Alexander, if that was what you could call it, I had always slept in his bed. Though the building was full of rooms, none of them belonged to me, and I was frightened to go too far in case Alexander decided he needed me. He would be annoyed if I was not there to answer his call, and the gash on my cheek from the last time I'd displeased him had only just healed. I was in no hurry to earn myself a new one.

Miserable, I dropped down onto the floor outside his office, curling up like a discarded dog, my arms wrapped around my legs, chin resting on my knees. I would just have to wait it out.

I was still there an hour later when Samuel came jogging down the stairs, but I drew my legs in and kept quiet, and he ran past towards the front door, seeming not to have noticed me. I was ashamed to have him see me there, waiting whilst his brother screwed the drugged-up blonde. My luck didn't last, however. Just minutes later he came back up, walking slowly this time, and with company. I recognised the simpering voice of Natalie, an English girl who was his sometimes-girlfriend. She ignored me, sticking her nose up in the air, but Samuel caught my eye, his expression pitying. I grimaced into my knees. His sympathy was painful, stoking the ashen embers of my embarrassment. I was relieved when they moved on, their low conversation fading away as they entered his flat.

A high-pitched laugh bubbled through the office door and I clapped my hands over my ears. I didn't want to have to listen to this.

"Lizzie?" My name came from above.

I looked up to see Samuel standing on the upper landing.

"Come on, up you come."

Desperate to get away from the sound of Alexander and the blonde, I scrambled to my feet and rushed to his side, not pausing to think through his invitation.

"Thanks," I muttered, grateful.

Samuel's flat was small but clean – though it was obvious a man lived there. There were few personal effects on display and the place had an unloved feel about it, as if the owner used it as somewhere to sleep and nothing more. Adding to the atmosphere was Natalie, who glared at me when I entered. Samuel headed straight for the bedroom, leaving us eyeing each other across the room: her furious, me awkward.

"What's she doing here?" Natalie asked as soon as Samuel reappeared. He had a heavy blanket clasped in his arms, which he deposited on one of a pair of two-seater black leather sofas.

"*She* is sleeping on my couch," he replied, sounding a little belligerent. Natalie folded her arms across her chest but said nothing more, though she still looked far from happy. "Goodnight, Lizzie," he said, grabbing Natalie by the arm and marching her into the bedroom, where he shut the door.

Glad to be alone, I spread the blanket out and got under it without undressing. I didn't think I'd sleep, but the cool leather was soothing against my red cheeks, the plump cushions surprisingly comfortable, and I quickly drifted off.

In the middle of the night I woke to the sound of love-making. It was both easier to listen to and more painful than the squeals and raucous laughter that I'd heard coming from Alexander's office. An uncomfortable tightness gripped my chest and I squirmed into the sofa, suddenly restless. If I'd had anywhere else to go, I'd have fled the room. But I didn't. I buried my head under the blanket, pressing a wad of material hard against my ears until I drowned them out.

CHAPTER NINE

I left Samuel's room at the first rays of dawn, folding the blanket neatly and leaving it balanced on the arm of the sofa before easing silently out of the door. One floor down, there was no sign of stirring, though I knew it must be close to Alexander's waking hour. I pressed my hand to the door, even went so far as to twist the handle, but I wasn't sure what I would find inside, and so, gently and noiselessly, I let it go.

I was feeling petulant, and – annoyed as I was with myself for it – Alexander had hurt my feelings. I wanted to do something to annoy him, to get back at him in some small way. I knew I'd only be hurting myself into the bargain, but I pushed that thought to the back of my mind.

The trouble was there wasn't much I *could* do. I didn't have transport, I didn't have money, and, though I hated to admit it, it wasn't safe to stray too far. I chewed on the inside of my lip as I pondered my paltry options, but nothing came to mind.

Then I heard a thud and a low groan, as if someone

was stretching. Alexander was up. With nothing more firmly decided than that I was getting out of the way for a little while, I threw up my ever-present hood, ran lightly down the stairs and headed out of the door.

I needed a haircut. The tendrils of my fringe were reaching down to tickle my eyebrows and at the back it had grown to ruffle over the collar of my clothes. It was getting to a length where I'd have to spend time styling and coaxing it into shape, and time to myself was a luxury I rarely had. Alexander's pixie cut might leave my cheeks naked to the eye, but it was convenient and I had grown accustomed to it. It was also something I could do without needing any money. My face was my payment; the hairdresser was one of many businesses operating under Alexander's protection.

The place wasn't open by the time I arrived at the tiny line of shops, but I could see a light burning deep inside and so I banged hard on the glass door. An agitated face appeared at the window, puckered lips tight around a cigarette, hair held up in an untidy platinum blonde knot on top of her head. Her eyes screamed 'go away', but when she saw it was me she unlocked the three bolts and stepped aside to let me in.

"Take a seat," she said flatly, then she turned her back on me and stormed towards the rear, where I knew there was a towel room and, beyond that, a snug little space where baggies of white powder could be exchanged for bundles of notes.

I settled myself into the worn leather chair, scrutinising

my face in the mirror. I looked tired, and irritated. It irked me further to think that Alexander would be pleased I was hacking my hair back to his favourite style.

"The usual?" She was back, appearing out of nowhere, sharp scissors in one hand, a comb in the other.

"Yes. No, wait." I stared at myself, and she stared at me. One pencil-thin eyebrow rose impatiently. "Blue," I said.

"What?"

"I want some blue. Not all, just a bit. Then you can do the 'Alexander'." That was my name for the pixie chop.

"That'll take longer," she moaned. I said nothing. We both knew she'd do it, no matter how many bookings she had that day. Favours for Alexander always came first.

It took two hours. Customers came, and waited. No one complained about the hold up and she didn't apologise, rushing around trying to wash and dry and cut and dye all at the same time. I watched her, and I watched the clock, feeling a perverse pleasure as I realised Alexander would definitely be getting annoyed. Maybe he'd shout, throw something. I imagined the way his eyes would narrow, daydreamed about him taking his anger out on Zane. I avoided thinking about what was actually going to happen when I turned up again. At no point did I consider disappearing for good.

"Well, what do you think?" The tone in the hairdresser's voice told me she didn't give a damn what I thought, she just wanted me out of her shop so she could try to get her schedule back on track. I ignored her, staring critically at myself. My fringe was vivid blue, slanting forward over my eyes in a shock of colour. The rest of my hair was my natural glossy black. Combined with the piercings and the black tattoo against my chalky white skin, the look was almost punk. I grinned. I loved it; and I was pretty sure Alexander would hate it.

"Thanks," I said, hopping off the chair.

"I'll just put it on your tab, shall I?" she asked dryly, but I was already halfway to the door.

Feeling brazen, I left my hood down. I stopped outside the shop to grin up at the ugly grey sky.

"Lizzie."

I jumped.

My silent observer emerged from the shadow of the building.

"You shouldn't wander off. Alex was looking for you."

I tried to shrug, like I didn't care, but it was a poor pretence. Samuel shook his head, amused and exasperated.

"Blue?" he commented.

"Blue," I agreed.

"Okay." He grimaced in a way that plainly said 'your funeral'. "Come on, you're going home."

There was no point arguing.

"Did Alexander send you to find me?"

Now that we were heading back I was starting to feel the first stirrings of unease. Blue hair flapped in and out of my vision as I walked, waving a warning. I was beginning to regret acting so rashly.

Samuel sniffed and shifted his jaw, but didn't answer. His silence spoke volumes. I pressed my lips together.

Would it be better to invoke Alexander's rage with my childish statement of independence or run back to the hairdresser, have her change me back, and keep Alexander waiting that much longer? There was little difference between the two, except if I chopped off the fringe I'd lose face in front of Samuel. Alexander cared a lot about losing face. Did I?

"Lizzie! Hey, Lizzie!"

I turned, then my eyes widened as I saw Mark running across the road towards me. Samuel had stopped dead at my side. I risked a glance at his face and saw it was stone.

"Hey," he huffed to a stop, breathless. "I thought it was you. Wow, look at your hair. I love it; it looks great!" he grinned at me.

I grimaced back tightly, aware of Samuel's scrutiny.

"Hi Mark. What are you doing here?"

My words were meant to be a friendly greeting, but they came out like an accusation.

"My friend lives round the block," he said, his face the picture of innocence. He looked from me to Samuel to me again, raising his eyebrows slightly and half-smiling, waiting for an introduction.

Shit.

"Mark this is my," – how the hell to introduce him? – "boss, Samuel."

Mark held out his hand at once, but Samuel hesitated before reaching to shake it. Mark's eyes tightened slightly as they shook and I wondered if Samuel was trying to break his fingers with his grip. The hostility was rolling off him in waves, though I was the intended target, not Mark.

"Nice to meet you," Mark said.

I gnawed on my lip.

"Samuel, Mark is a friend of mine."

I tried to smile through the lie. Samuel and I both knew I didn't have any friends.

"So..." Mark looked at me, hoping for a conversation opener, but I couldn't think of a single safe thing to say. I dropped my gaze to the floor, wishing he would just evaporate. Or maybe I would.

Samuel rescued me.

"We're late, Lizzie. We need to get going."

I nodded at the ground.

"But—" Mark looked disappointed.

Samuel had already turned to go. I hesitated, torn.

"Sorry," I blurted to Mark as Samuel's feet took him five, six steps away from me. "I have to go."

I moved to follow Samuel but a hand around my upper arm stopped me.

"Lizzie, are you okay?" Mark kept his voice purposefully low so that Samuel, who had paused and was eyeing me with a look of quickly escalating impatience, couldn't hear.

"I'm fine, Mark," I said automatically, throwing him a smile that felt plastic on my face. "Really, it's fine. It's..." I tailed off.

"Complicated?" He was looking at Samuel so he didn't see the brief flash of confusion that crossed my face before I realised what he meant. Complicated. That's what I'd told him on the train.

That wasn't the half of it.

"Yeah," I said softly. Then I glanced over my shoulder. "Look Mark, I really have to go."

"You're sure you're all right?"

No, I wasn't. But there was no point admitting that to Mark. As often as possible, I avoided admitting it to myself.

"It's fine, Mark," I repeated hollowly.

"Call me," he said suddenly, stepping closer, his expression growing more intense.

"What?"

I wanted to step back, put that space between us again, but Mark kept a firm hold on my arm.

"Just... call me. So I know you're okay." His eyes flicked to Samuel. "Promise me."

My heart was beating fast, panic oozing into my veins. I could all but feel Samuel's glare stabbing into my back; I was trapped between that and Mark's earnest determination.

"Okay," I whispered, not sure what else to say, just wanting out of the conversation.

"Promise?" he pushed.

I wet my lips, tried to drag air into my lungs.

"Lizzie!" Samuel barked my name and I flinched. He was angry. Angry enough to tell his brother? If Alexander found out about any of this conversation...

Mark's hand shifted from my arm, running down to grip my fingers. Squeeze them. He was comforting me.

As soon as the gesture registered, my mouth short-circuited my brain.

"I promise," I breathed, then said, louder, for Samuel, "I'll see you around Mark." I spun on my heel, saw Samuel was back to striding off again. With an apologetic wave to Mark, I hurried after him. I didn't look back.

We walked out of earshot, down the street and around the corner, in total silence. I had to jog to keep up with Samuel's loping strides but I didn't complain. The rusting sign of Bancroft Road was in sight before he spoke.

"So, is that why I lied to Alex?"

His tone was clipped, curt. I fiddled with my zip, gazing down at it as if it were made of solid gold.

"Who is he?"

I stuck my tongue between my teeth, held it there. Why did I feel bad about this? Why did I feel like a traitor? It was Alexander I had betrayed, not Samuel.

"Lizzie?"

"No one," I finally mumbled. "Just someone I met for coffee. I hardly know him."

I sneaked a peek at Samuel. His face was drawn, a frown blackening his features.

"You're playing a dangerous game, Lizzie," he told me.

That much I knew. I just didn't quite know why I was playing it.

I kept my eyes on the floor as I trudged up the stairs to Alexander's Bancroft Road headquarters, the bounce well and truly sucked from my steps, so I didn't notice the door open. I would have walked right into Alexander if Samuel hadn't grabbed the back of my top and jerked me to a standstill. I looked up, startled, to see a pair of green eyes boring down into me.

"You found her," he said softly.

Then he tilted his head to the side, reached out a hand to stroke the wave of electric blue hair. I suppressed the urge to flinch away.

"Interesting," he said. Then he stepped past me, shrugging his way into a tailored charcoal grey jacket. "See Zane," he addressed Samuel. "Have him deal with the issue in my office."

He took one more step then slid deftly into a waiting car that I hadn't even noticed was idling by the curb.

I stood motionless as he drove away, not quite sure if I was in trouble or not. His quiet calm was unreadable. Alexander's anger burned slowly, and he never acted rashly. I would just have to wait. My stomach twisted queasily, unsettled by the thought.

Samuel went straight to the basement to find Zane whilst I dragged my heavy feet up to Alexander's office, wondering idly what the issue might be. Knowing Alexander, it could be anything; and knowing Zane, I might find out, and I might not.

I did find out, and quickly. The buxom blonde was still in Alexander's bed, her body draped like art amongst the smooth creamy silk sheets. I avoided looking at her at first, but I was like a moth to a flame. Despite myself, I found my steps leading me closer, and a cold, forbidding dread enveloped me. Something was wrong. She was too quiet, too still. Her head didn't move with heady dreams as she rocketed down from the high, her chest didn't rise and fall with each breath. Another step and I saw that her eyes were open, gazing right at me, completely unseeing.

My hand crept over my mouth as I stared at her dead body.

I had seen death. It surrounded Alexander. But it was always shocking, always violent and bloody. This was peaceful and cold, and it was all the more horrific for that. A trembling step at a time, I made myself walk right up to the body, forced myself to gaze upon her face. She hadn't overdosed. Instead bruises encircled her neck, blue and green and black against marble white skin. She'd been murdered.

The vomit rose in my throat without warning. I only had time to bend over before bile and acid spurted from between my lips, coating my shoes, the hardwood floor and the edge of the bedding, where it pooled like liquid pearls on the floor. I groaned, reaching out to grip the mattress as my whole body retched again.

"I'm not cleaning *that* up," Zane snapped, appearing from thin air behind me. In his arms he carried a large black bag, a zip running the length of it. Without pausing to look at the girl in the bed, he laid it out on the mattress and unsheathed it with a single sweep of his arm. Then, with no trace of empathy or pity on his face, he began to fold her limbs into the bag until she disappeared. I watched him, still bent over, waiting for more waves of nausea. He didn't look at her face once, not even when he stopped to tuck in the tresses of her hair so they wouldn't catch in the jagged teeth of the zipper. Sliding both hands underneath her enclosed body, he swung her up and over his shoulder in a practised movement, then padded from the room.

When I was sure I was alone, I stood up and began methodically to strip the sheets from the bed. I was glad I'd ruined them. I would never have been able to sleep on them again. Rolling them up into a ball, I waddled over to the kitchenette and stuffed them into a black bin bag. When Zane came back I'd have him incinerate them. After that, I remade the bed, deliberately choosing something vivid – this time ice-blue satin – to try to wipe the memory from my brain. It didn't make a difference. I could still see her there every time I caught sight of the bed in the periphery of my vision. A reminder of what happened to those who overheard things they shouldn't. I wanted to get out of the room, but I knew I had to be there, waiting, when Alexander came back.

He made me wait for hours. Lunch came and went, and I marked the time by eating a disgusting Pot Noodle I'd found gathering dust in one of the kitchenette cupboards. The afternoon dragged by. The evening light was dimming through the large sash windows at either side of the building and the light-sensitive spotlights had flickered on to illuminate the room in a muted glow when he finally strolled through the door. I was positioned for penance, curled up in a ball on the sofa, silent and in silence, the television blank.

I looked at him and he ignored me, walking quietly to his desk and slinging his jacket over the computer chair. I had to clamp down on my lower lip, bruising the soft skin to stop myself from speaking. Alexander fiddled with a few things on the desk, then walked to the very back of the room, where the pool table lay, glistening coloured balls already laid out in a perfect triangle. He strode past the rectangle of bright green felt to where the cues and assorted aids were held against the wall. My eyes widened as I watched him curl his fingers around the glossy shaft of a cue.

He headed in my direction.

Before, I'd had to hold in my words, now I couldn't have spoken if I'd wanted to. My voice had died, choked into silence by fear as my eyes followed the cue's progress across the room. Was he going to attack me, beat me to a bloody pulp? I tried to retreat further back into the sofa, but the soft leather refused to yield.

He stopped dead in front of me. His fingers caressed the length of the highly polished maple, a ring on his little finger glinting menacingly, hypnotising me.

"I want to play," he said, and then he tilted the cue out towards me.

It took a few seconds before I could move. Tentatively I reached out and he surrendered the pool cue into my hands. He half smiled at me, then returned to the pool table, selecting another cue before I'd reached the area.

"I'll break. You get us both a drink," he suggested.

I did what he said without a word. I was completely bemused. Where was the anger, the punishment I'd expected?

The sound of crashing balls collided with the clink of ice as I dropped two cubes into each of our glasses.

"You're spots," he said as I returned to him. I placed the glasses down on a side table before I picked up my cue.

"I'm not very good," I said dubiously.

He smiled at me. "I know."

I was nervous of taking my eyes off him to focus on the white ball, still not convinced this wasn't a trick to lull me into a false sense of security, but he was waiting for me, leaning in a relaxed stance against the wall, green eyes warm, amused. Swallowing against my better judgement, I dropped into a low crouch, aimed, and sent the white skittling past the ball I was aiming for, instead knocking one of his conveniently over the pocket.

"That's a foul," he commented. "Two shots to me."

He took his two shots and made them six, easily knocking in four balls. I took a single shot, this time managing to hit my own ball, but sending it in completely the wrong direction. He potted another four, moving confidently and smoothly around the table, each time leaving the white perfectly placed to strike another ball. Only the cluster of spotted balls – mine – eventually held him at bay, crowding his single remaining stripe into the edge. On my third attempt I at last potted a ball: the black.

"Does that mean you win?" I asked, as he laughed.

"It does. Try again. Do you know how to rack?"

I nodded. I'd watched him play with Zane or Samuel often enough. He'd never asked me to join in, though. I couldn't help but wonder why he was being so... nice to me.

I pulled his balls from the pockets and gathered mine from where they lay scattered across the felt, forcing them to coexist inside the plastic triangle. He broke again and the balls went spinning off in all directions. This time none found their way into the pockets, although one teetered on the brink. Alexander glared at it, like he could force it to drop with the power of his mind.

I eyed the ball, determined this was going to be my first mini-victory. I leaned low, lined the white up, drew my hand back, and thrust forward. The white ball shot towards the corner, connected exactly where I wanted it to. Then I blinked, and there was a second sharp crack. The two balls kissed together, then both tried to slide into the pocket but each choked the other in the narrow alley. My teeth snapped together in annoyance. How had that happened?

A bark to my side made me jump. Alexander was laughing, his eyes on my infuriated face. I scowled at him, but that only made him laugh harder. Eventually I was forced to smile ruefully back, though inside I was reeling. We were interacting like normal people, like friends.

I froze as his fingers wrapped themselves around my cue. He took it from me, then moved to stand behind me, curving his body round mine.

"You're lining up all wrong," he said.

His weight pushed my upper body down until we were both leaning over the table.

"See the white? You need to hit just below the middle. There," he slid the pool cue through my slack fingers until the chalked end lightly tapped the white. "And don't hit it too hard, or it'll bounce back. We'll aim for that stripe." His fingers pointed to a ball mid-table, then closed over mine, guiding my hand back and forth until he stroked forward. The white cruised across the felt, pushing the ball into the middle pocket where it fell with a satisfying thunk.

"See?" His body shifted away from mine and I immediately straightened up. My heart was pounding, from fear... and something else.

I twisted round to find myself face to face with him, his eyes inches from mine and burning into my soul. He reached up a hand and tugged my fringe.

"I really do like the blue," he said softly.

Then he grabbed me by the waist, lifted me up onto the table. A hand cupping my chin, he kissed me, tenderly as a lover. I kissed him back, my eyes open, watching him warily, but as the movement of his lips intensified I found them closing. My legs wrapped themselves around his middle and he carried me awkwardly to his bed, his mouth never leaving mine. Slowly he undressed me, then he took me, and he was the gentlest he'd ever been.

Soon afterwards his quiet snores filled my ears, and I cried myself to sleep.

CHAPTER TEN

The morning dawned chilly and grey, and with it Alexander's strange warmth faded, replaced by cold indifference. He barely spoke to me, except to snap orders. I was bewildered, but oddly relieved, by this return to normality. At least I knew where I stood, and I had perfected the obedient, mousey persona that I withdrew into.

I didn't leave Alexander's office for the whole day, spending prolonged bouts on my own with nothing but the quiet rasp of my breathing for company. The next three days followed the same pattern. I left only to spend frustrating hours in the basement with Samuel, where I recited road names and camera positions and checked, rechecked and triple-checked the wiring on the biggest bomb I'd ever seen. I knew everything about the job – the journey, the bomb, the complicated route to the base of the wall. The only thing I didn't know was when I was going. That was kept a secret from me, until the moment Samuel turned to me from the desk around which he, Zane and Alexander were crowded, and fixed me with a sombre look.

"It's time."

'Time' was late afternoon on a Friday. There was no warning, no preparation, no chance to gather myself. I collected my jacket and, without so much as a goodbye from Alexander, the two of us left his office. We headed to the ground floor, out of the front door, down the steps, then Samuel walked me to the passenger side of the waiting car. I stared at him, suspicion beginning to tingle at the base of my spine.

I sensed rather than saw a figure already sitting in the driver's seat.

"You're not coming," I accused.

I finally understood why he'd insisted that I know the plan inside out, from every angle; why he'd made me go over, again and again and again, every minute detail.

"I'm not coming." Samuel's eyes were hooded by the encroaching night, his expression unreadable.

"But... but you always come with me," I said.

I'd never done a job without him before. At least, not this type of job.

"Not this one," he replied. "Alex needs me to stay here."

"Oh."

I felt a sudden anxiety swirl in my gut. It left me unbalanced, disorientated, like I was drunk. He must have heard the uncertainty in my voice, because his lips twisted up into a smile.

"You'll be fine, Lizzie," he promised me. "You will be."

Then he did something really odd. He hugged me.

Just quickly, for a second or two at most, letting his chin rest briefly on the top of my head before he pulled back. I caught the scent of his aftershave, the heat of his body under his clothes. My fear vanished, replaced with a feeling of complete and utter security, but it was all too brief. As he let me go, I felt the weight shift in my left jacket pocket. I frowned and opened my mouth, but he put a finger to my lips, shook his head infinitesimally. He dropped the finger to my shoulder, and pushed me down into the car.

"You've got the phone?" he asked Cameron.

My driver nodded back curtly, then twisted the key hard in the ignition. The engine roared to life as Samuel shut my door. I gazed at him through the window in the short second before we pulled away, searching for reassurance, for an answer to the puzzle in my pocket, but his face was carefully blank.

I waited until we'd driven out of Stepney, heading north on the Westway, taking the long route to the M4 that avoided the Central Zone, before I let my fingers slide into my pocket. They closed around two things: a small rectangle with a criss-crossed surface that I was almost certain was a phone keypad, and a crumpled bit of paper. A note? Why was Samuel passing me a note? Why not just tell me? I looked to my right, at Cameron. He stared straight ahead, ignoring me completely. Slowly, cautiously, I eased the paper out of my pocket. Then I stopped. There was no way to read it without Cameron noticing. It was too dark in the car, I'd have to hold it right up for the passing streetlights to flash in and reveal whatever was written there. Grimacing, I returned it to the depths, took my hand out and stuck it firmly between my thighs.

Forty-five minutes later I decided enough time had passed.

"Cameron, can you pull over? I really need to go."

He looked at me in total disbelief.

"Please Cameron."

"I'm not stopping," he said flatly.

"Please," I beseeched. "Even if you just pull over at the side of the road. It's an emergency." I bounced up and down on the seat a little to emphasise the seriousness of my words.

"We left less than an hour ago. How can it be an emergency?" He shook his head, his foot firmly down on the accelerator.

I bit my lip. "It's a girl thing," I said. "I've got... y'know."

I hoped he was too ignorant of the biological workings of females to argue. He looked at me, clearly irritated, but uncertain.

"And you have to stop, right now?"

"Yes!"

He drummed his fingers on the steering wheel, then slammed his foot on the brake and skidded into a lay-by.

"You have three minutes," he warned.

I jumped out of the car and slipped and slid my way down a short grass embankment. Just in case he checked, I yanked my jeans open, then hunkered down in the grass. Thankfully there were no houses on the short stretch of road, and little passing traffic at this time. That also meant that there was very little light, but I'd brought my tiny flashlight with me and I twirled the top to turn it on. Risking a quick glance behind me to make sure Cameron was still safely behind the wheel, I drew out Samuel's note. I recognised the handwriting at once. The scrap of paper was filled with his angular block capitals.

DON'T TELL CAMERON YOU HAVE A PHONE.
IT CALLS ME. ONLY IN AN EMERGENCY.
S.

I gawped at it, perplexed, for a long moment, then stuffed it and the torch quickly back into my pocket. I'd heard the soft click of Cameron's door opening.

"Hurry up!" he growled, sounding far too close. Craning my neck I saw that he stood feet away, at the top of the embankment. Had he spotted me stowing away the note?

"Right!" I snapped. I half turned, my hands gripping the top of my jeans. "Turn around!"

He looked at me suspiciously, but did as I asked. Thirty seconds later we were back in the car, speeding off towards the motorway.

"I'm not stopping again," he said, slamming the car into fifth gear and pushing as close to the speed limit as he could go, sending us rocketing over potholes and sections of riveted tarmac.

I ignored him, folding my arms and staring out of

the side window. My head was spinning, and an ominous nausea was creeping into my stomach. I didn't understand why Samuel would not want Cameron to know that I had a phone. Unless there was an extra part to the plan that Cameron knew, but I didn't. And Cameron would only do explicitly what he'd been told by his boss. So what did Alexander have in store for me?

I felt the shape of the phone through the fabric of my jacket. I wasn't sure that I was altogether reassured by its presence, because now I knew there was something to be scared of.

I was so wrapped up in my thoughts that I didn't realise we had reached the end of our journey until Cameron yanked up the handbrake and killed the engine. The sudden stillness shocked me awake.

"We're here," he announced unnecessarily.

I nodded, staring out of the windscreen. Night had fallen as we'd driven across the English countryside and the scene before me looked nothing like it had when Samuel had taken Cameron and me on the scouting mission. It was nothing like the map I'd constructed in my head.

The ground directly in front of us was submerged in inky blackness, but beyond that the world was brilliant white, blinding. Floodlights sent pools of yellow light into the searching dark, whilst sweeping searchlights illuminated the remaining shadows in arcing semicircles.

"It's almost nine," Cameron said, checking his watch. "You have half an hour."

I nodded again, refusing to turn my head to look at him. I couldn't drag my gaze away from the brightness.

"Lizzie..."

"I know!" I snapped. Adrenaline and panic were beginning to thrum their way through my system, and Cameron's pugnacious tone shredded the last of my nerves. He raised his eyebrows at me, annoyed, but I stared him down. I was the one about to try to outsmart one of the most heavily guarded structures in the country, not him.

I shut my eyes and tucked my chin into my chest, gulping in several deep breaths. Then, without looking at the wall, I got out of the car. Reaching into the rear, I pulled out a rucksack and slung it on my back. It was my delivery package.

"Here?" I asked, ducking to look at Cameron's silhouette.

"Here," he agreed, then he turned away. No good luck or goodbye. If I didn't return in an hour or so he'd give me up as dead and drive home, and he'd probably enjoy the journey a whole lot more.

I shut the door, wishing for the thousandth time that night that Samuel was in the driver's seat, and turned to face the dark and light before me. Then the strangest thing happened. A calm spread throughout my body, stilling my pounding heart and clearing my befuddled brain. Every nerve tingled with energy. I felt alert; I felt ready. Tightening the straps on my backpack, I jogged slowly forward.

For the first half mile I met nothing. This road went no further, the nearest town was miles back the way we'd come. Only the wall lay ahead, imposing and impenetrable. The first indication that I was reaching the government's border defences was a sign stating 'ROAD END'. I ignored it, and the one that followed twenty metres later. Fifty metres after that I met a barrier. On either side, tight curls of barbed wire wound across land that had been left to grow wild. I paused several feet before the horizontal wooden bar, its red and white warning stripes hidden by the night. I knew that it was fitted with motion detectors. Another pace forward and I'd be surrounded by bright light, and moments after that by armed men. Instead I stepped off the road, feeling my feet sink into the softness of long, wet grass. I counted seventy-six paces, stretching them to match the stride of a man, then stopped and faced the wire. If Samuel's informants were right, I was in a foot and a half of no-man's-land where the motion detectors couldn't see me. Time to find out.

I shuffled forward one pace, then another. My knees were slightly bent, ready to throw myself to the ground at the tiniest noise or flare of light. Nothing happened. I took one more half pace, then reached out with steady fingers. The cold smoothness of wire connected with my skin. I wrapped my hand around its thin, twisting length, then ran it through my fingers. Within inches I came to a sudden end, slicing my thumb on sheared metal. Holding tightly to that edge, I waved my hand to the left. Empty air. I allowed myself the briefest of smiles, then walked forward through the gap that had been cut for me.

Abruptly everything around me was flooded with blinding white light. Startled, I reacted instinctively, throwing myself to the ground.

"Jesus Christ!" I hissed.

What had gone wrong? Samuel had told me I should be able to sneak through here undetected, so long as I kept to the narrow path, and I had. My heart hammered in my chest, my confident calm shattered. I knew in seconds I would be surrounded, guns pointed at my head. Turning my head to the side, I squinted against the glare, trying to see if there was anything coming for me. I locked eyes with something just ten feet away; something huge and terrified, motionless as a statue. The stag's antlers streaked black lightning against the white.

I relaxed and froze in the same instant. I hadn't been detected, but was my friend about to get us both shot? I held my breath and waited.

The sound of a screaming engine cut through the quiet thud of my pulse. Brakes screeched as the car rollicked to a stop less than a hundred metres away, at the road's end. I heard car doors open and close, three, maybe four of them. Enough men to kill me several times over.

"What do you see?" The call was loud and deep.

"Another bloody deer. This one's huge."

"Shoot the bugger. I'll radio and tell them to kill the floods."

I waited for the shot to ring out, still staring at the stag – who hadn't moved an inch – but it never came. Instead I listened to the car doors open and close again, and the rumble of an engine starting up. Moments later I was doused in darkness. Not wanting to give the wildlife another opportunity to expose me, I crawled quickly forward on my hands and knees. Once I knew I'd cleared the wire, I stood and scanned the wall in front of me, trying to get my bearings. The curved tower that I had likened to a lighthouse was dead ahead. Instead of heading straight for it, I cut across the grass at a forty-five degree angle. Samuel had told me that the tufted grass was peppered with mines, and my path, slicing diagonally like a bishop on a chessboard, was the only safe route to the base of the border wall. I had to pick up my pace, breaking out into an all-out sprint to avoid the beam of light sweeping towards me, chasing the shadows that kept me hidden. At last, however, I crashed into the solid concrete that was my target.

Now for the most frightening part: I risked exposure by flicking to life my little torch, shining it left and right, hunting for the tiny 'X' that would tell me where to drop the bomb. It had to be exactly right, exactly opposite the Davis mob's package, or the mighty wall would withstand our assault. I found it, then killed the light and listened intently. Had anyone seen that? I couldn't hear anything over the thrum of the electric wire high above my head. There was nothing to do but carry on, and hope.

I dropped to my knees, wondering if there was another person just feet away on the other side, doing exactly the same as me. Caught in a mad moment of fancy, I lifted a hand and pressed it to the wall, imagining my counterpart mimicking my movements, but the grey concrete was cold and rough, and it jerked me out of my fantasy. Shaking my head to regain my focus, I wrenched off my backpack and nestled it firmly against the base of the wall, digging a little way into the mud and grass that had accumulated over the foundations, to ensure it didn't budge an inch. Then I unzipped it, reached in and exposed the device. I'd done all my preparation beforehand. All I had to do was set the timer.

The faded green light of my cheap digital watch told me it was 9.17 p.m. I was cutting it close. Trying not to rush and make my fingers clumsy, I set the timer to thirteen minutes. Was that time enough to get back to Cameron, back to the car and start speeding away? It would have to be.

However, there was no time to check my work for the umpteenth time, though I'd planned to. I just had to trust in my earlier handiwork. I'd done it right; I knew I had. Without wasting another second, I clicked a button to activate the device, reassured when it started flashing and the timer began to wind its way down.

Then I turned and ran.

All the way across the grass I expected to hear a crack of gunfire, or to feel the burning agony of a bullet tearing through my flesh, but nothing came. I could only assume that Samuel's decoy, miles away at Monmouth, had been successful. Or perhaps I was just lucky.

How long would I remain so?

Not willing to leave my life to chance, I pushed myself harder. I was running blind, just hoping my feet would find the safe route, that God or fate or fortune would lead me to the gap in the wire. It didn't. I missed the wire, but I hit the light, triggering the motion detectors and dazzling myself. I threw one hand to my forehead, narrowed eyes desperately searching, but all I saw were the curls of barbed wire.

Where the hell was the gap?

I knew I had only seconds before the men in the car came hurtling back, guns drawn. Left or right? Left or right? I could only guess.

Left. Please God let it be left. I skirted the wire, my presence blindingly obvious to anyone looking from the height of the wall. How far did their guns reach? It was impossible to know. I heard a puttering sound, like gravel on the underside of a car, and the ground around me exploded in little puffs of grass and mud. That was my answer.

Where the hell was the gap?

There! There, right in front of me! I headed for it, running at full tilt, hoping the lights and my speed would make me a blur to the snipers trying to fix me in their sights.

Through the coils, I kicked left, skirting along the line of wire. I was still within reach of the guns, still in sight, but getting less so every second. Then I was at the road, the glare of headlights nowhere in view. Only the black of the tarmac.

My feet pounding onto solid concrete, I stepped up a gear, flying away from the border, heading to Cameron. And safety. Please, please still be there, I thought desperately.

The route back seemed to take much longer. It felt like I was running uphill, though I hadn't noticed a decline on my way there. But there was only one road, so this had to be it; I had to be almost there.

How far now? How many leg-burning, lung-bursting paces before I saw the car? With every step I felt safer, with every pump of my arms I inflated the hope in my chest that was beginning to believe I'd got away with it. Impossible, but I was still moving, still breathing.

At last I saw the car, a faded gleam of metal in the moonlight, just metres away.

"Cameron!" I gasped, hauling open the passenger door. "Let's go."

Then two things happened at once. Behind me, the world exploded in a cacophony of noise and light. In front of me, the windscreen shattered and the silhouette of Cameron was blasted backwards, slamming into the headrest.

I hit the ground, though from the force of the explosion or my own survival instinct I couldn't be sure.

"Cameron," I hissed in the open door. "Cameron!"

But I knew he was dead.

And if I stayed there, in a few seconds I would be too.

That thought got me back on my feet, got me moving. Foolishly ignoring the car – a much faster mode of transport than my exhausted legs – I ran, not knowing if I was headed for the wall, or safety, or straight into trouble. I didn't know who was here, but I knew it wasn't shrapnel from the bomb that had torn through the windshield and murdered Cameron. We'd been found.

I was more obvious on the road, so I darted right, vaulting a drystone wall and cutting across a field. My feet sank into the softness of recently ploughed mud, the undulating surface testing the strength of my ankles. Behind me, in front of me, echoing all around, I heard the sound of dogs. The noise sent a shiver through me, and though my ankle had healed, I felt the ghost of a twinge shoot through my leg as I sprinted. This time it wasn't the shrill yaps of a chihuahua. These were gruff barks, rumbling in deep chests. Alsatians, or Dobermanns. The GE were going to hunt me out.

Crying in between gasps, I tried to push myself faster through the heavy dirt, but it was like one of those dreams where you know you need to get somewhere, can see it, are reaching for it, but find you're running through treacle. No matter how hard you try, your limbs just won't move fast enough. How long before the dogs caught my scent? How long before a sniper's dot found its mark on my back?

I was running so hard I hit the barbed wire fence before I saw it. The force of impact sent the tiny barbs straight through my clothing, into my flesh. I yelped, the sound dragged out of my mouth as my torso wrapped around the top wire.

"Here!" I heard someone yell to my left.

Hissing in pain, I wrenched backwards, tearing my clothes from the snarling knots, and used a fencepost to hurdle the obstacle. A flash of white light lit me from behind for an instant, silhouetting me against the dark. Shots rang out, one of them whizzing past so close to my shoulder that it shredded the sleeve of my jacket. My arm immediately began to burn, but I was too panicked to stop and realise I'd been hit.

On the other side of the fence, my feet found purchase on solid ground. A road! Sobbing in relief I took off, not thinking about direction, just trying to lose the beacon shining on me, telling the GE, the shooters, the dogs, where to find me.

"Where did she go? Can you see her?"

"No. Spread out. She can't be far."

Shouts ricocheted in the darkness, though at least they were behind me this time. I was losing them. But I couldn't hope to hide, not from dogs. I needed some way to move faster. I needed a vehicle.

Hoping desperately that the road I was on ended in a house or a farm, I kept running, trying to ignore the burning, stabbing pains in my chest, my legs, my arm. I was getting tired. I knew I couldn't keep going much longer.

Then a miracle appeared. Behind a line of trees I hadn't been able to see in the dark, glowed the square rectangles of life. A building.

"Please, please let there be a car!"

I rounded the invisible trees, feeling the hard dirt road beneath my feet change into the loose gravel of a driveway. A thin filter of light dribbled from a porch, bouncing off the curved roof of a car.

"Oh thank God!"

I headed straight for it, tried the handles. The doors refused to budge.

I didn't have time to be restrained. The GE were only moments behind. Bending my elbow into a point, I slammed it as hard as I could against the driver's side window. Nothing happened, but agony shot up my arm, doubling where it hit the ragged cloth ripped to shreds by the shot.

"Christ, open!" I mouthed, pulling frantically on the door and kicking at the front wheel. Spinning, I searched the ground. Most of it was hidden by darkness, but edging the gravelled driveway were little stone statues, including one about twice the size of a brick: a lion. Lumbering over, I snatched it up and threw it at the window. This time it splintered, bending inwards, the glass just about holding together. One more solid jab and it disintegrated onto the seat. I didn't spend time trying to unlock the door, I just grabbed the roof and undulated my way through the hole I had made.

There were no keys inside, but I scrabbled around at the ignition, ripping out the wires. My Internet research, and Samuel's coaching on the Bowles's bombing, had taught me the rudiments, and seconds later the car started.

"Yes!" I squealed.

I'd never been taught how to drive, but I'd watched, and watched carefully. The car, by some mercy, was an automatic. I shoved at the stick until it went to D – which I hoped stood for 'Drive' – then I slammed on the pedal. Nothing happened. I shifted my foot over, searched for the other pedal. This time when I pressed down, the car rocketed forward, straight into the darkness. Fingers fluttering at the dash, I hit buttons until the lights exploded into life.

I looked out. There was no time to gasp with horror; I was about to smash into an agent and his snarling beast. They hit the bonnet and the agent bounced over it, his startled face flashing by me before he disappeared over the roof. The dog was less fortunate, rolling beneath my tyres. Squeezing my eyes closed in sympathy, I pushed down harder on the accelerator.

My steering was erratic, causing the car to leap from one side of the road to the other.

Soon enough, the road straightened out – it was little more than a lane I now realised – and I killed the lights. I needed them – it was pitch black – but they made me far too obvious. Fighting against my flight instinct, I slowed down, too, hoping quiet stealth would serve me better than engine-roaring speed. I kept watching the rear view, searching for headlights chasing me down, but there was nothing but darkness. To the side I saw flashlights sweeping across the fields and behind that the smouldering yellow of a fire out of control. I didn't allow myself to smile, but I felt a slight twitch of relief.

At least one thing had gone right tonight.

The narrow road ended with a junction onto a proper highway. I followed the sign for the M5, accelerating up to fifty miles an hour – as fast as I dared – and flicking the lights back on, knowing, now, that I drew more attention to myself without them. I couldn't relax though, cringing in terror each time another car came my way. Mercifully, none of them were topped with the blue lights of the police, or the altogether more terrifying red flashes of the GE. But rather than calming as the miles passed, I just got more and more tense. That couldn't be it; I couldn't be safe. After ten miles I was a nervous wreck, tears shimmering in my eyes and blinding me, my hands shaking so hard they could barely hold on to the wheel. The cold air blasting in through the smashed window didn't help. I had to pull over. Unable to wait until I came to a lay-by or a side road, I steered the car over onto the grass verge, jolting forward as the wheels sank into a hidden dip, the underside scraping loudly against the ground. As soon as I stopped, I extinguished the lights. The dark was a relief.

What was I going to do? What the *hell* was I going to do? I dropped my head to rest on the steering wheel, panic paralysing my brain. I felt lost, frightened.

Then a thought occurred to me. Samuel.

With trembling fingers, I pulled the phone out of my pocket and hit dial. A pre-set number jumped up on the screen and I pressed it to my ear, listening to it ring one, two, three times.

"Hello?"

"Samuel?" My voice came out as a frightened squeak. I tried to swallow, but there was something sharp lodged in my throat.

"What's happened?"

"I... everything! It's all gone wrong!"

"The job?"

The job? I'd almost forgotten about it in all the panic. I thought about the wave of noise, the riot of colour. So much more spectacular than anything I'd ever constructed before, and I hadn't even had a second, a moment to look. I'd felt the fiery heat of success, though.

"No, that was fine. It went off. Both sides, I think. But then... Samuel, I don't know what happened."

"Tell me."

I took a deep breath, trying to control the juddering sobs that were shaking my shoulders.

"Cameron's dead. They shot him through the windscreen. I don't know who it was, but I think it was the GE. They were everywhere. They had dogs and men with flashlights. They were just... everywhere."

I squeezed my eyes shut against the memory.

"Christ! Are you all right?"

Yes. No.

"Kind of. I got shot in the arm, but I think it just grazed me. It's bleeding, but not really badly."

"Where are you now?"

"In a car. I stole it. I had to, the dogs were chasing me."

"Don't worry about the car, Lizzie."

Just hearing my name made me bubble. I gripped the steering wheel, trying to get a hold of myself. His voice was soothing; I already felt more in control. Reason was returning. With it came a strong desire to see his face.

"I'll come back. I can drive, I think. The car has plenty of petrol."

"No," I could hear the cogs of Samuel's brain whirring. "It's better if you don't arrive on your own. Not right now. I'll come and get you. Tell me precisely where you are."

Samuel's words didn't make sense, but I couldn't think straight. In faltering tones I told him exactly where to find me.

CHAPTER ELEVEN

After I'd hung up I had nothing to do but wait. I was okay at first, concentrating on trying to stem my tears, calm my ragged breathing. But then, as minutes passed and I became subdued, the atmosphere in the car started to turn. The silence was smothering. I felt like I was in a glass bubble, unable to see or hear anything beyond my protective walls, but naked to anyone approaching. The dirt verge I'd pulled into had no cover. Two of my wheels were still angled up onto the rutted tarmac and the passenger window was smashed open. I needed to move, but my hands were shaking so much I knew I'd never be able to start the car, and I wasn't getting out. Instead I stared out into nothing, recoiling from every imagined shadow or sound. Surely it was only a matter of time before the GE found me?

But no one came.

An hour passed, then another. My senses remained on high alert: ears pricked, eyes wide. This late, this far out into nowhere, there was no other traffic. It was just me and the dark. So when I saw the pinpricks of light appear far off in the distance, my first reaction was terror. It was the GE. I was sure of it. They'd found me. Even if they didn't know I was here, they'd soon be on top of me, and I was impossible to miss. I had to go, had to hide. I maybe had five minutes, and if I was on foot I needed as much of a head start as possible.

Yet as the lights drew painfully closer, I didn't move. Because it might be Samuel.

I stayed there, pinned, like the proverbial rabbit, watching the glare, staring right into the source of light, deliberately blinding myself. The car pulled up in front of me and the light instantly died. Not for me, though; spots of colour danced in front of my eyes, and though I heard the door open and the measured footsteps tapping on the road, I couldn't see who was coming for me.

I started to hyperventilate, torn between panic and terror, knowing it was too late to move but desperate to flee. I was still trapped in indecision when the door wrenched open.

"Lizzie!"

Samuel.

I looked towards the sound of his voice, still blind, and relief welled up in me like vomit. My mouth opened and closed, but no sound came out.

"Lizzie, come on, let's go. We need to go." Samuel's voice was impatient and clipped, but even its harshness couldn't rouse me from my traumatised paralysis. All I could do was reach for him, the coloured spots dissolving from my eyes just in time for tears to blur my vision.

He sighed, but I felt strong arms wrap around me and pull me from the car. That feeling he gave me, the feeling of complete and utter safety, wrapped around me like a warm blanket. Strangely, though, it only made me cry harder and little sobs hiccupped out.

He carried me across the short stretch of road to his car, somehow managing to get the passenger door open and depositing me awkwardly on the seat. I didn't want to let go, my arms clinging round his neck, face pressed into the warmth of his shoulder, but he was too strong for me, breaking my grip easily and shutting the door. I curled into myself, drawing up my legs and crying into my knees. Seconds later he slid into the driver's seat, flicked the lights back on and turned the car in a tight circle, accelerating away from my stolen vehicle.

Samuel didn't speak until we'd put twenty miles between ourselves and the scene. He didn't touch me, smile or even look at me. The only concession he made was to turn the heater on full, trying to warm away the shakes wracking my body. Finally, once my sobs had quietened to sporadic sniffles, he opened his mouth.

"Are you all right?"

I nodded jerkily, but he wasn't looking at me, he was staring straight ahead at the emptiness of the road, so I tried to clear my throat.

"Yes." My voice sounded hoarse and strangled, the muscles in my throat stretched tight and raw.

I wasn't, not really. I ached all over, I was exhausted, and the whole ordeal had left me feeling fragile, like glass; but I was alive, and I wasn't badly hurt. Cameron was back there somewhere with a bullet in his head, so I supposed compared to him...

"Thank you for coming to get me." I addressed my gratitude to my knees, but it was heartfelt. Tears threatened to gush again, but I swallowed them back.

"You're welcome." Samuel's answering nod was curt.

I bit my lip, uncomfortable in the awkward silence, but not sure what else to say.

Since I'd started making bombs for Alexander, Samuel and I had spent a lot of time together, but I couldn't say that I knew him. There was a clear chain of command: he told me what to do, and I did it. But then he'd changed the dynamic – he'd lied to cover up for me, and he hadn't told Alexander about Mark. He'd given me a phone tonight, a phone that called only him, and then he'd come and rescued me. But now, now he was treating me with... if not cold indifference then certainly not warmth. We were back to being soldier and commander, but I couldn't play my role. I needed... I needed him to hug me. Needed that feeling of safety back, that sense that everything was okay.

Because I was pretty sure it wasn't.

Confused and spent, I leaned my head back against the headrest and closed my eyes. The heat and the gentle vibration as the car rumbled along slowly lulled me into a dreamless sleep.

I woke up briefly when cold air slapped my face. The door was open and Samuel was fumbling at my hip, trying to unlatch the seatbelt, but it was like trying to resurface from the depths of the ocean, and my eyes closed themselves without command. I was vaguely aware of being lifted, but I couldn't concentrate on where I was being taken, and I passed out again as soon as Samuel laid me down. All I cared about was that it was somewhere warm, and soft, and quiet.

When I came to, properly this time, light was streaming in through a large window, tickling my eyelids. I opened them, squinting through the brightness, trying to make sense of where I was. Not in Alexander's bed, though it was a place I dimly recognised. A living room, clean and sparse and empty. The two-seater leather sofa I was lying on was the biggest piece of furniture in the room, along with its twin.

I was in Samuel's flat.

Fully dressed, I was sweltering under the thick blankets someone – probably Samuel – had draped over me. I threw them off, then peered at the digital watch I still wore. It was almost lunchtime. With some effort I pulled myself into a sitting position, then groaned. My back and my legs were aching, and my head pounded and spun like I was hungover. The worst pain, though, came from my arm, stabbing the large muscle just below my shoulder. Where I'd been shot, I suddenly remembered.

Gingerly I twisted myself to stare at it, expecting to see a bloody mess of skin and torn fabric, but the sleeve was missing, snipped cleanly away. A huge plaster dressed the wound. Hesitantly, the fingers of my other arm reached round and prodded experimentally.

"Ow!" I sucked my breath in through my teeth as the muscle twitched and a bolt of pain cut right to the core of my arm. I was glad I hadn't been conscious for the cleaning.

Now what? I sat and stared straight ahead, thinking. I was tempted to stay where I was, hiding in Samuel's flat, waiting until someone came looking for me, but there were questions in my head that wouldn't go away. Had the bombing been a success last night? What were the news channels saying about our attack? More importantly, were the GE and the police looking for me? Had they found any of my DNA at the scene? I'd been swabbed when I'd been tattooed, so I knew they had me on file, my fingerprints too. More importantly still, what was Alexander going to say about the bombing, Cameron's death, my survival, Samuel coming to get me?

Staying here wasn't going to get me any answers.

I stood carefully, swaying as the blood rushed to my head. I'd been off my feet for too long. How long had I been asleep? I'd no idea what time Samuel and I had arrived the night before. After midnight was the best guess I could make. Grimacing, I limped across the room, making my way to the cool darkness of the stairwell. I paused at the top of the stairs, searching for my courage. Light spilled out from Alexander's office on the floor below. I frowned at that: it was unusual for him to leave the door open.

If he was in, though, it might give me a chance to sound out how the land lay before I had to face him...

As quietly as possible, I descended the stairs, using the wall and the banister to ease my weight slowly down onto each tread, wincing with every minute creak of the wood as it shifted under me. It was painful, my stiff muscles protested at the slow, careful movements, but it was worth it. I reached the landing without Zane's white-blond hair poking out. Holding my breath, I inched forward until the sound of voices wafted out of the open door.

Alexander was speaking, his voice low and intense.

"It's about time we ramped up our actions. After last night, this is the next logical step forward."

"But why Lizzie?" My eyes widened and I leaned forward. They were talking about me, and Samuel sounded angry.

"Why not?" Alexander purred, unperturbed by the heat of his brother's response. "It's what she does."

"She can make the thing, but why does she have to wear it? You have a hundred other idiots you can use for that. It's a waste, Alex, pure and simple."

What the hell were they talking about? What could I wear?

"A waste?" Alexander's voice had changed. It had a dangerous edge and I dropped the puzzle, for now, to listen. "Is that the only reason?"

"What do you mean?" Samuel sounded defensive.

There was a prolonged moment of silence, interrupted only by the fierce pounding of my pulse.

"I need her," Samuel snarled – there was no other way to describe it. "She knows what she's doing and she gets the job done. That's it."

"Is it?"

"Say what you have to say, Alex."

Samuel's voice was getting louder and louder, echoing out of the door, but I had to strain my ears to hear Alexander's quiet response.

"You have a girlfriend."

I frowned to myself, totally confused by the change of direction.

"You would know," Samuel had lowered his voice, but not by much. "It's at your insistence that I'm sleeping with her."

"Her father's a man it's useful to know. But that's not my point."

"What is, then?" Samuel's voice was ice. Someone – Zane? – cleared their throat: a warning.

"What does Natalie say about Elizabeth sharing your bed? Or doesn't she know? That's twice now, Samuel."

What?

"Lizzie isn't sharing my bed!" Samuel spat the words. "She slept on my sofa. I had to put her somewhere – your bed was full," he accused.

"Good." Alexander's voice had dropped again, and I took another step forward, trying to catch the murmured reply. "Because I'll kill her before another man touches her. She is mine."

My diaphragm convulsed, pushing the air out of my lungs. I'd been claimed. But there was no warmth in hearing the words. Does a watch feel warmth for its owner? That's what I was – a possession. Alexander wouldn't kill me out of jealousy: just out of spite.

But there was no sense in the threat. Was Alexander trying to say that Samuel... wanted me? Surely that wasn't right. There were six years between us, and he had a girlfriend. Natalie was beautiful and rich and well connected, none of which I could claim. But then, what had Samuel said? Something about being with her at Alexander's request?

My head was spinning. The only thing I was sure of was that being caught listening in could only end badly for me. Quietly, I shuffled backwards. I'd go back to Samuel's sofa, stay there. I turned, my foot reaching for the first step, and caught my toe on the overhanging lip. Losing my balance, I toppled, clattering noisily into the banister.

"Dammit," I hissed.

I just had time to right myself and turn to face the open doorway when Zane appeared. His eyes narrowed with suspicion, but I tried to make it look like I had just descended. Attempting to gloss over the awkward moment, I smiled at him, realising just a second too late how out of character that was, considering our relationship. His lip curled in distaste, then he turned his back on me.

"It's just Lizzie," I heard him say to the room.

That was it, then. I had to enter now. I took one calming breath and tried to assemble a look on my face like I hadn't heard their conversation for the last five minutes. I couldn't manage neutral, but nervous was a good enough substitute. It's how I'd been feeling anyway, before I'd heard whatever it was that I'd heard.

The three of them were sitting on the sofas, and they were all looking at me. I didn't have to work at the nervous expression now. It formed itself as my empty stomach twisted and flipped. I ignored Samuel and Zane, keeping my eyes firmly fixed on Alexander, looking for a signal as to where he wanted me to go, what he wanted me to do. He just stared straight back, leaving me in a quandary. I wanted to sit, because, hovering in the middle of the floor, I felt like a duck in a fairground shooting gallery, but the only space was beside Samuel. Did I want to sit there, given what they'd just been talking about? What message would that send to Alexander? Then again, if I hadn't been listening in, if I was none the wiser, would I just have sat there without thinking? Or would I have sat at Alexander's feet, retreated to the bed, taken one of the hard chairs around the desk in the office area? I was tying myself in knots, spinning round in circles.

Aggravated, I decided the safest thing was just to ask. "Can I sit?"

Alexander nodded, once.

I realised I hadn't been specific enough.

"Where?"

With the slightest tip of his head, he gestured to the space beside Samuel. I tried not to grimace, then sat pressed against the sofa arm, as far from the splayed length of Samuel's thigh as I could get.

I looked up to see Alexander watching me quietly, a strange smile on his face, eyes cold as ice. Samuel, I saw out of the corner of my eye, was staring resolutely ahead, his eyes on Alexander's bed.

"So you survived again," Alexander commented. "My little cat-bomber. When will you run out of lives, I wonder?"

The threat was veiled, but it was there. I tried to smile.

"I have a few more, I think."

"Do you?" He spoke so quietly I might have imagined it.

"What happened to Cameron?" Zane cut across the tense silence.

I shrugged, not sure what Samuel had already said. "He was shot."

"And why weren't you?"

I paused to send him a filthy look before I answered. "I dropped to the ground, then I ran."

"Did you even stop to see if he was dead before you abandoned him?"

"He was dead." I glowered at Zane.

"Really?" Zane smiled into my furious face. "And how did you manage to phone Samuel?"

"What?" I stuttered, a second too late, trying to stop the shock from showing on my face and only succeeding in flushing bright red. Beside me, Samuel stiffened.

"How did you call Samuel?" Zane repeated.

I stared at Zane, not sure if this set up was designed to trap me, or Samuel.

"Elizabeth?" Alexander prompted.

A gleam came into Zane's eye as he waited.

My brain frantically whirled, trying to come up with a lie that would protect the pair of us. I couldn't tell the truth, couldn't say that Samuel had slipped me the phone. I owed him that, after the way he had covered for me when I'd gone to meet Mark.

"There... was a phone in the car," I said.

"Yes. And it was programmed to call me." Zane leered a smile, a cat about to pounce on a mouse. "But I didn't receive any phone calls last night, not after the one from Cameron telling me you were there, and that you were headed for the target."

I decided to brazen it out, while Samuel continued staring into the distance.

"I don't know Zane. I hit dial, and it went through to Samuel. It must have had the two numbers stored, or maybe you programmed it wrong." I left that hanging and Zane scowled.

"Where is it?"

"Where's what?" I knew perfectly well what he meant.

"The phone, Lizzie. Where is it?"

"I dropped it."

More importantly, where was my jacket? Because the phone Samuel had given me was still in the pocket, and if Zane found it he'd know at once that it wasn't the one he'd given to Cameron. Surreptitiously I tried to let my gaze wander around Alexander's spotlessly clean office. My jacket was nowhere in sight. Did Samuel have it? I hoped so.

"You dropped it?" I started at the change in tone of

Zane's voice. He smelled fresh blood.

"Yes."

"Dropped it with your fingerprints all over it?"

I didn't hesitate.

"I was wearing gloves."

All three men looked at me: Zane sceptically, Alexander curiously, Samuel unreadable. I understood the scepticism: I never wore gloves. They made me clumsy, sausage-fingered. But there was no way Zane could catch me in the lie.

He turned to Samuel.

"Was she wearing gloves when you found her?"

I looked to Samuel. This was a much smaller lie than the one he'd told before. Surely he'd back me up. He didn't.

"No."

"Did you see any gloves?"

"No."

Zane looked back to me, smiling cruelly.

"I did," I whispered. "I swear I did."

My word against doubt. With Zane, at least, I knew my word counted for nothing.

"Well," Alexander cut off whatever snide remark lingered on Zane's lips. "The police are not looking for you. Yet. We will see if that changes."

I nodded, grateful for the temporary reprieve. Zane looked sour. I knew he'd be watching me even closer now, searching for some slip up, something he could make stick. Something to get me out of his way for good.

Alexander sent Zane out for food and the atmosphere in the room was even worse with just the three of us sitting there. Alexander and Samuel kept up a conversation, talking about supplies of US imports – which were getting more expensive and harder to sneak in – and I stared off into nothing, trying to be inconspicuous. They ignored me for the most part, both focussed on the business, but I couldn't help thinking Samuel looked uncomfortable. Just something about the way he held his body, the tightness in his jaw. Maybe there was truth in what Alexander had said. Or maybe I was just imagining things. I didn't really know him well enough to tell.

After we ate – fish and chips, the grease soaking into the paper and my stomach lining, making me nauseous – the three of them disappeared, heading to Romford to 'reassure' an unhappy supplier, leaving me alone with my curiosity and my conscience. I still had no idea what had happened last night, other than that the bomb had gone off. What were the GE saying? Had I succeeded in blowing a hole in the wall? How had EBC News spun the story? Who was being blamed for the attack? Was there any mention of Cameron's body and the car? I'd only the empty room to ask.

Frustrated, I uncurled myself from the sofa and strolled around Alexander's office, swinging my arms, clicking my fingers and looking for something to do. The bed was made, every surface spotless and dust free. I needed to shower, but just as that thought formed in my head, my eyes fell on Alexander's laptop. It was open, the back of the screen gleaming red, the shiny Dell logo winking at me.

My fingers suddenly felt tingly, singing with a strange urge that wouldn't go away even when I curled my hands into fists. Trying to fool myself that I was acting nonchalantly, I idled over to the desk, running my fingers over the smooth satiny surface of the wood. I let my hand pause beside the mouse, drumming a rhythmic pattern with my nails on the desktop. The computer chair was pulled slightly out from the curve of the desk and turned a fraction to the side, towards me, like it was an invitation to sit down. It was too tempting.

Taking one more glance at the closed office door, I slid neatly into the seat and flicked the mouse. Instantly the screen flickered to life.

"Dammit," I muttered.

It was locked. I pursed my lips as I thought about what Alexander might have set as his password. I doubted it would be anything too difficult – so few people had access to his computer, just him, Zane and Samuel. Never me, never anyone who didn't make it up the stairs. I was actually surprised that he'd left it here at all. But not enough to be suspicious, not enough to stop. Letting my fingers rest on the keys, I thought for a moment more, then decided to start with the obvious. I tried 'Alexander', 'Cardiff ', 'Samuel', even 'Zane'. Nothing. I didn't know why, but I was sure it would be a name. I even tried 'Bancroft'. Thankfully there was no limit to the number of times I could try. If I locked the thing permanently it would be rather obvious that I'd been prying where I shouldn't.

I was almost ready to give up, when I typed in 'Elizabeth'. Password incorrect. I smiled wryly. There was no way Alexander would have that as his password. Just for the hell of it, I plugged in 'Lizzie'. To my astonishment, the log-in screen disappeared and Windows began booting up. Alexander's wallpaper flashed onto the screen – a silver Celtic cross against a blood-red background – then a host of icons popped up on the left-hand side. I stared at the folders, all titled innocuous things like Accounts or Documents. Intrigued, I rolled the mouse over one entitled simply GE, but that wasn't what I'd logged on for, and I let it be, firing up Internet Explorer instead. The programme loaded quickly, and I typed in the EBC News address. It took a while to load – even Alexander couldn't get around the strategic government throttling – but eventually the headlines and images appeared across the page. It wasn't hard to find what I was looking for: it was the lead story.

TERRORISTS TARGET WELSH BORDER.

Underneath the huge bold headline was a picture of the wall. It was hard to tell if the image was taken from the English side looking out, or the Welsh side looking in. I supposed it didn't really matter. The main focus of the picture was a huge 'U', gouged out of the concrete maybe ten feet across as its widest point. The photographer had a good eye for layout. He'd captured the way the road ran off into the distance, nothing now obstructing its path except for a wide crater at the base of the wall.

Well, I had at least one of my answers. The proof before me was indisputable. We'd succeeded in biting a huge chunk out of the GE and their border. Eagerly I turned to the article, keen to read the EBC report, biased as I knew it would be.

My hand guided the mouse across the beautiful walnut finish of Alexander's desk as I scrolled down, shifting an old, but mint condition, copy of a luxury car magazine out of my way as I read the bitter, twisted words of the reporter. Is this what he'd say if he weren't censored? Was it what he really believed? Probably. I snorted, skimming the rest of the article, not wanting to read his delusional drivel. I nudged the mouse again, easing the magazine out of my way, thinking maybe I'd have more luck with a different news site – unlikely – when there was a loud clatter as something dropped down off the desk.

I jumped, hissed out a swear word as I dived under the desk, searching for whatever had made that nasty crunching, clattering sound.

"Don't be broken," I beseeched it. "Oh, hell."

My hand curled round the remains of a phone. Alexander's mobile. It must have slid under the magazine because he'd never have purposely left me with this, not in a million years. Scrambling the bits together, I emerged to survey the damage. The screen was still in one piece but the SIM card, battery and back cover had sprung loose. With fumbling fingers – I really didn't want another reason to be in Alexander's bad books right now – I slotted everything back together and switched it on.

"Come on, come on," I begged it. It took several painful seconds, but eventually the provider's symbol flared onto the screen. Seconds later the phone fired up properly. Running my fingers across the touch screen, I sighed in relief. It was fine.

Then I sat back in Alexander's plush black leather computer chair and surveyed the room from this, his throne. Empty. Completely empty. I was utterly alone.

My eyes went back to the phone, one finger running the smooth length of glass, inadvertently causing the electronic keypad to spring up. I gazed down at the numbers, trying not to do what I knew I was about to do.

In Alexander's office.

On Alexander's personal phone.

Stupid. Beyond stupid. But a promise was a promise, and I had promised. Not thinking any further than that, I let my fingers drift over the keypad, tapping out the number I'd somehow memorised despite myself.

He answered after just one ring.

"Hello?"

"Mark?"

"Lizzie." My name came out on a breath. He didn't say it like Samuel, who made it almost musical, but I liked it nonetheless.

"Yeah," I breathed back. "Hi."

"You called. I didn't think you would."

"I promised," I reminded him.

"You did," he agreed. There was a pause that I wasn't sure how to fill, then he went on, "I thought about you this morning."

"You did?" My stomach did a strange flip-flop. I shifted

in the chair.

"Well, yeah. Haven't you seen the news? Someone blew up the Welsh border last night."

"And you thought of me?" My voice was high-pitched, tight, while my mind raced. Had they somehow got DNA from the bomb? The car? Had the police released my name, my face? Automatically I looked to the door, waiting for Alexander to burst through it and tell me it was over. I was over.

The door remained closed.

"Well, you're the only Celt I know," Mark laughed down the phone.

"Oh. Right." Relief crashed through me. It must have bled down the line because the silence was instantly deafening.

"You... you weren't involved, were you? Lizzie?"

It took a moment to make my lips work.

"What?" I whispered woodenly. That was the best I could do. If I said one more word I'd give myself away.

Apparently I had anyway.

"Jesus Christ, Lizzie!" Mark's voice was suddenly so loud I had to jerk the phone away from my ear.

"Mark—"

"They talked about it, on the news. The men they suspect might be involved in this. They're dangerous." That was the understatement of the year. Mark gave me a moment to consider this, then continued, much more quietly. "What are you into, Lizzie?"

Tears gathered in my eyes. To stop them falling down

my cheeks, I closed them. I couldn't answer him; didn't want to confess – to me or him – exactly what I'd got myself into. Or how deep.

Distant yelling on Mark's side of the line made me blink my eyes back open.

"Bollocks," Mark muttered. The word sounded funny in his clipped English accent.

"What's going on?" I asked.

"I'm at work," he explained.

"Oh." I thought about that. "On a Saturday?"

"Overtime," he explained. "Look, Lizzie," he started.

"If you have to go—" I mumbled at the same time.

We both paused, then Mark sighed.

"I do," he said. "I have to go. But—"

"But what?" I asked when he didn't continue.

Another sigh.

"These people they're talking about in the media, Lizzie, they're not the sort of people you want to be involved with." That I knew. Irrefutably. "You need to get away from them."

"Mmm." I made a non-committal sound, knowing that was impossible. Mark seemed to hear what I couldn't say.

"I'm serious. No matter what promises they make to you, you aren't safe with them. I," he took a deep breath. Let it out. "I could help you."

"No, you can't," I said at once, because it was absolutely true and Mark needed to get that. Helping me could get him killed.

"I could, Lizzie. I mean, I know I'm a low-level worker

here, but I could ask someone, someone might have connections. They could get you out."

Right. If any of the men Mark worked with at the Defence Department caught a look at my face the only thing they'd do is shoot me.

"I'm marked," I told him.

That made him pause.

"I could protect you," he offered at last, a little more hesitantly. "If you... if you were willing to give information, to tell them about what you've witnessed, they'd be lenient. They might even give you a visa. They—"

Inform on Alexander? There was no surer way to end up with a bullet in my brain. And what about Samuel? He hated traitors. Despised them. I never wanted him to look at me the way he'd glared at that man down in the basement. No, I wouldn't do that to him.

"No, Mark."

"Just hear me out—,"

"No." Then, before he could speak again, "I have to go."

I didn't wait for him to say anything back. I pulled the phone from my ear and disconnected the call. Then I shut the thing off and hid it back beneath the magazine.

And I tried very, very hard to put the whole conversation right out of my mind.

CHAPTER TWELVE

"Why are we here?" I asked, craning my neck to look around me. "Are we scouting?"

Three weeks had passed since the bombing and in all that time I'd barely left the Bancroft Road address. Alexander had had no more jobs for me and Samuel had kept well away. I'd unwillingly spent most of my time with Zane, taking stock or helping to update the books in the basement. I had no more contact with Mark, purposefully or just through lack of opportunity I wasn't quite sure. He'd scared me with his offer. Could I...? No – I stopped that thought right there – as I did each time it crossed my mind, which was often.

Then this morning Samuel had come for me, taken me for a ride. We were parked in a residential street in a neighbourhood I'd never been to before. The houses were terraced, little red boxes with tiny front gardens in various states of disrepair. Most of the cars parked against the curb had clear signs of not having moved for a long, long time.

"We're not scouting," Samuel replied.

"Oh." I waited, thinking he would explain. But he didn't.

"Are we making a delivery?" I guessed.

"No."

"Are we picking up?"

"No."

I looked at him, exasperated and amused. "Are we visiting your grandmother?"

He cracked a smile for half a second.

"No."

"Okay," I sat back and stared ahead, watching a cat lick its paws on the roof of a Nissan Micra with four flat tyres and no glass in any of its windows.

"Lizzie, do you ever wonder what we're doing here?"

I looked at him, incredulous. He smirked wryly.

"I don't mean here," he pointed to the street scene outside the windshield. "I mean... what is it we're trying to do?"

I blew out a breath, not sure what to say. We'd never had a real conversation before, not like equals, and I didn't know if I knew him well enough, could trust him enough, to speak the truth.

"Are we chasing a pipe dream? Bombing the wall, the Home Office building... we're snapping at the government's heels like an irritable terrier, but we're not making any actual progress."

Samuel rubbed at his forehead and I snapped my mouth closed, realising I wasn't supposed to contribute, just listen.

"And Alex doesn't really want change. He's making

money hand over fist, cashing in on every dirty deal that just didn't exist before. You know he's trafficking people now, bringing Celt girls into the country, smuggling them in then selling them off to rich English tossers?"

I shook my head. I hadn't known that.

"Sometimes I think I should just get the hell out of here, head back across the border and see what I can make of myself back in Cardiff. I've still got contacts there. Christ knows there's not much keeping me in London. I mean, I thought we were trying to achieve something, but I'm just deluding myself."

He turned to stare at me, green eyes burning into mine, a carbon copy of Alexander's and yet completely different. There was life in Samuel's stare: humanity. Warmth. I held his gaze, my mind reeling. Why was he telling me this, confiding in me? It was dangerous; for all he knew I'd turn round and spill to Alexander, who would not be pleased. He wouldn't want to hear that Samuel was having second thoughts; that he wanted to leave. Nobody left Alexander.

I wouldn't tell – I owed him more than that – but it was a big risk to take.

"You have contacts in Wales?" I asked hesitantly. I'd trained myself not to ask questions – not real ones, personal ones – but I was curious and Samuel had never treated me like his brother did, with his fists. And a churning nausea had cemented itself in my gut at the thought of Samuel leaving. He was my only ally at Bancroft Road; he was... No. He couldn't leave me.

"Cousins," he said quietly, running one hand through his thick brown hair, leaving it tousled and untidy. "They're smugglers, they bring things over from France, sometimes Germany. I reckon they'd set me up, but Alex would—" he broke off.

"Alex would?"

But Samuel didn't finish the thought. He didn't need to – I knew how it ended. Alexander would kill him, and the cousins.

"There's another option," he said on a sigh. "A big player in Cardiff. He's a ruthless son of a bitch, but he knows what it means to be Welsh."

I wasn't quite sure what Samuel meant by this. Did he think Alexander had lost sight of that? I was tempted to ask who the big wig was, but common sense prevailed.

"What's it like there?" I prompted, my voice barely above a whisper. "Wales. Is it like here?" I gestured to the rundown street in front of me that was practically synonymous with the rest of London outside the Zone, "Or is it like... like the north?" Like Scotland. My home. A country ruined, where it was everyone for themselves and survival depended on what you were willing to do. Like steal food from a small child or stab a sleeping man to death for the coat he wore. Like leave your daughter in a cold, empty, damp-stained flat while you searched for something better. I shook my head to chase that memory away and focused on the man beside me.

Would he leave me too?

Samuel sighed. "It's..." He shook his head. "It's a mess.

Cardiff's not too bad, it's being held together by the gangs." My eyes widened. That didn't sound good to me, but then I suppose if you were in one of the gangs... "But outside of the city? Yeah, it's bad. Really bad. People are starving; no one's safe, not even in their own homes. "That," he huffed a laugh, "that was why I came here, you know? I was going to make it better." He shook his head derisively, then fixed his eyes on me. "You should leave too, Lizzie."

"What?" I asked, confused by the sudden change of direction the conversation had taken.

"You should leave, head back to Scotland."

"I can't," I croaked.

There was nothing for me in Scotland. No family, nowhere to go, no one to help me. Only bad memories. And, of course, there was Alexander. I'd been warned often enough what he'd do to me if I ever tried to get away. North of the wall would not be far enough. I doubted Mars would be.

"It would be better for you there," he insisted. "I could help you to get out."

"No," I whispered. It was quiet, but final.

Samuel sighed. "Lizzie, if you don't get out, you're not going to survive much longer."

"What do you mean?"

"Alex's going to kill you."

I gaped at him.

"Don't be..." But my denial died, because it wasn't ridiculous. It was a cosh I'd been living under for so long I'd almost forgotten it was there. Somehow I'd made myself comfortable, balanced on my razor-sharp tightrope. Samuel's words were a rude awakening, a sharp shock of cold water on my face, reminding me of what I'd always known: my life hung on Alexander's say-so. I closed my eyes. "How do you know?"

"Alex wants you do to another job. The kind of job you don't come back from, the martyr kind. I've talked him out of it for now, but you're living on borrowed time, Lizzie." I stared at him, aghast. The words I'd overheard in Alexander's office suddenly took on a new, horrifying meaning. "You were never meant to come back from the border."

A thought occurred to me.

"That's why he sent Cameron instead of you."

Samuel nodded gravely. That was why they'd found us; that was why they'd been ready, snipers in place, dogs in situ. It would have been cleaner, easier, to have the bombers captured – dead, so we couldn't talk – than to risk us making a frantic dash back across the country and leading the GE to Alexander.

My tongue suddenly felt too big for my mouth.

"Did you know?" I asked thickly.

"No." I turned my face away from him, disbelieving, but he grabbed my chin and yanked it back. "No," he repeated.

"Then why did you give me the phone?" I smiled ruefully as his eyes tightened defensively.

"I knew Alex was planning something, but he didn't

tell me what. Lizzie!" He paused, because I'd twisted my head away from him again. Reluctantly I met his gaze. "I'm telling you the truth."

I considered him. His eyes blazed with sincerity, his jaw was clenched. It was a face it was difficult to doubt. But then, I knew Alexander's web of treachery spun many layers.

"Why are you telling me?"

Samuel sighed, reached up to cup my jaw with his hand. My nostrils filled with the scent of his leather jacket and something musky, muted. I waited, but he wasn't going to answer. Instead he stroked my cheek with his thumb, then turned away and started the car. Eyes on the road, he pulled away from the curb. I continued to stare at him, my heart pounding.

"Samuel, if you go to Wales, take me with you." I hadn't meant to speak, but as Samuel accelerated up through the gears, taking us out of this moment, back to reality, panic had risen in my chest until it just spilled out.

He breathed out heavily through his nose then shook his head infinitesimally, eyes on the road. "No, Lizzie."

No? Blackness threatened to swallow me up as my throat constricted. I wanted to reach out for him, grab hold and refuse to let go. Instead, I thrust my hands under my legs and dug my fingers into the scratchy material of the passenger seat. I turned to stare ahead, trying to stay in control.

"Are you taking me back to Alexander?"

He smiled at the windscreen.

"Do you have anywhere else to go?"

No.

"Samuel, am I going to be... safe?"

No.

It was crystal clear on his face.

"Samuel." I said his name as a plea. Then I caught sight of an old-fashioned red telephone box. A thought flashed through my head. "Samuel—"

"I don't know Lizzie—" he began to answer, but I wasn't interested in my question any more.

"No, Samuel. Stop. Stop!"

He pulled over, and the engine whined as it idled. I stared at the phone box, my brain whirling in circles.

"I do have someone I can call," I said at last.

"Who?" his face darkened in suspicion and... jealousy?

"Mark," I breathed.

Was I kidding? Mark, the boy I'd only met a handful of times? Mark, who I barely knew? But the idea had taken hold and I was struggling to push it aside. He'd offered to help me, hadn't he? He said he could get me out, protect me. I squashed down the memory of what he said I might have to do for that protection.

But three long weeks had gone by. Would his offer still stand? I could at least call him. What was the worst he could say? No... or yes.

"Lizzie, no." Samuel shook his head.

"Why not?" I frowned at him.

"Because..." he paused, searching for a reason. "How well do you even know this boy?"

Boy... but the way Samuel said it I knew he meant child. I bristled at the word. Mark was older than me. My hackles rose and I found myself defending him, despite my own doubts.

"I'd be safe with Mark. He's nice. I can trust him, I know I can."

Something about the word 'trust' sent Samuel's mouth twisting into a grimace.

"What, and he's just going to let you move in, is he?" he barked, raising one eyebrow belligerently.

"For a while," I said, the heat draining from my voice.

"And then what?"

I stared into his cynicism, desperately holding on to my plan, unwilling to admit to the trump card I held. The one I didn't want to play. But Samuel was thinking about leaving. Leaving me alone with Alexander. He was forcing my hand. Please, please let me not have to betray him.

Maybe it wouldn't come to that.

"Then... I don't know. I'll figure something out." I stalled. Samuel snorted, unimpressed. "Am I better going back to Alexander? What happens if tonight's the night he decides he's had enough?"

"He won't," Samuel shook his head dismissively.

"How do you know?" I demanded.

"Lizzie—"

"No, Samuel," I snapped at him, my eyes fierce. Then I bit my lip. "Can you lend me some coins for the phone?"

He stared at me for the longest time, his eyes dark,

the corners of his lips turned down, then he reached into his jeans pocket and thrust a handful of change into my waiting palm.

"Thank you," I said, then I got out and shut the door on his disapproval.

In the phone booth I hesitated. I could feel Samuel's unhappy eyes on me. I wasn't sure what his problem was – ten minutes ago he'd been telling me to leave the country – but I felt bad, like I was disappointing him.

"Sorry Samuel," I whispered. Then I fired his money into the slot and closed my eyes, trying to conjure up the scrap of paper with Mark's number on it. With nimble fingers I tapped out the digits as I saw them.

The ringer trilled sharply in my ear, going on for so long I was about to give up, but just as I went to pull the receiver from my ear, the noise cut out and a breathless voice answered.

"Hello?"

"Mark?"

"Lizzie!" He sounded surprised, but pleased. I smiled into the mouthpiece.

"Yeah. Hi."

I waited for him to say something, but then I realised that he was waiting for me to take the lead. Heaving in a deep breath, I forged ahead. Nothing like getting right down to it.

"I was wondering if I could ask you a favour...?"

Blanket silence.

"Remember what we talked about?" I peeked at

Samuel, still watching me broodingly from the car. An uncomfortable weight settled in my chest.

"Go on." He sounded wary.

"I—" I tried to breathe, had to turn my back on Samuel before I could continue. "Things have changed and... I... I want out. Could... could I come and stay with you for a little while? At your flat?"

"Now? As in, today? Er..." His hesitation brought me up short. I realised I was asking a virtual stranger for board and breakfast.

What was I thinking?

"Look, Mark. Never mind. I'm sorry to have asked. Sorry to have bothered you. I'll see you around."

I went to hang up.

"No, wait!" His voice was loud enough to reach me even though my hand was halfway to the hook. I cradled it back into the crook of my neck. "Lizzie? Lizzie, you there?"

Pause.

"I'm here."

"Oh. Great." He blew out a breath. "I'm sorry. I was just startled. Come over. Of course you can stay. Jesus, you're really going to do it? Wow. I'll put in a call with—"

"NO!" I heard a sharp intake of breath as my yelp echoed down the phone. I tried to lower my voice down to a normal level. "Can we just keep this between you and me? For now," I added, a plea in my voice.

"Okay," he sounded full of uncertainty, but I heard him swallow it down. A forced laugh buzzed in my ear.

"I should warn you, I don't have much room."

"You got a sofa?"

He chuckled. "Yeah, I got a sofa. It'll break your back, though."

"Don't worry, I'm not a princess with a pea. You're in Bethnal Green, right?"

"Hackney." He gave me his address. "Where are you? Do you need me to come and get you?"

"No," I looked through the glass door of the booth to the darkened interior of Samuel's car. "I've got a ride."

I knew if I wanted to be safe it would be better to make my own way there, to leave Samuel here and just walk; because if Samuel knew where I was, then Alexander was only a step away from finding out. But I wasn't ready to cut my ties, not just yet. I got back in the car. Samuel took one look at my face, sighed heavily, and put the car in gear.

"Where to?" he asked.

I repeated Mark's address.

We drove there in silence, my guilt a third person in the car. Samuel cut across town like an old-fashioned London cabbie, ignoring the signs, constructing a route from the maps in his head. I didn't recognise any of the streets, not even when we stopped in what must have been Mark's road. It was a lot like the shabby street in Stepney where Alexander had his empire: huge townhouses dissected into flats. The building Samuel parked beside looked in better shape than most, but the paint was peeling on the large front door and the cream sandstone brickwork was black with city smog.

"This is it," he said, looking up at the building and away from me.

"Right," I replied, but I didn't move. There was a lump in my throat. Was this goodbye? It felt like it; but if it was, I didn't know what to say.

Thanks for the memories? Thanks for teaching me how to make bombs? Thanks for not letting your brother kill me?

"What will you tell Alexander?" I asked.

Samuel shrugged. "I'll make something up."

He still didn't look at me, but stared down at the steering wheel. I shifted in my seat, wanting to leave but not wanting to.

"Samuel—"

"You should go," he said. A pain stabbed at me. Suddenly chilled, I shivered. Samuel caught the movement. "Here." Reaching into the backseat he grabbed my jacket – which had laid there since the night he'd rescued me – and thrust it at me. Knowing it wouldn't do much to warm me, I pulled it on anyway and stuck my hands in my jacket pockets. My left hand curled around something I'd forgotten all about. I drew it out, stared at it then up at him. A spark of something that felt like hope ignited in me. "Can I keep this?"

I held up the phone he'd given me; the one that called him, only him.

He thought about it.

"Yeah. Yeah, you can keep that."

"Will it still work?"

"It'll still call me."

I smiled, relieved. That was what I wanted.

I tried again to say something, something like goodbye. "Samuel—"

"Go on," he gestured with his head. "Go. Now. Before I change my mind."

He grabbed the gearstick, forced the car into first.

I blinked, startled to realise there were tears in my eyes. Eager to escape the car before he saw them, I squeezed his hand for the briefest moment, his knuckles hot in my icy palm, then I threw myself out of the car. He almost didn't give me time to shut the door before he'd pulled away.

Alone on the street, I contemplated Mark's building. But I wasn't really looking at the symmetrical spattering of sash windows; I was lost in my own head. I'd just done it: I'd just walked out of Alexander's clutches. So why didn't I feel relief? Joy? The heady giddiness of freedom?

Because I had no money, no visa, and a vivid black tattoo scrawled across my face. Had I just made the biggest mistake of my life? Unsure of the answer, I forced myself up the stone steps and jabbed my finger on Mark's buzzer.

"Hello?" He answered so quickly I knew he'd been waiting for me.

"Mark? It's me."

The intercom buzzed at me as the door came loose in my hand. I swung it open, then took one last, fleeting look at the street before I disappeared inside. The hallway was cavernous and damp, and smelled slightly of mould. I started up a stone staircase, running my fingers gingerly along a grand banister that was chipped and peeling. None of the doors I passed had names on them. They were firmly closed and imposing. I felt trepidation plunge into my stomach. Was this a really bad idea?

As I reached the second floor I heard a soft click and a whoosh as a door was drawn back. Mark's head peeked out, smiling nervously at me.

"Hey," he waved.

I returned his wave half-heartedly. Was there still time to call Samuel before he made it back to Stepney and told Alexander I'd... disappeared?

Probably not.

"Hi Mark. Thanks for, y'know." I squirmed on his doorstep, embarrassed.

"No problem." We faced each other, both smiling a little awkwardly. Mark swung his arms back and forth twice, then crossed them, tucking his hands into his armpits like he didn't know what else to do with them. We were still on the doorstep. I raised my eyebrows, my smile twisting for the first time with any real amusement. Wasn't he going to invite me in?

He cottoned on a second later.

"So... er... come inside."

I moved forward and went to remove my jacket, but stopped halfway. His flat was even colder than the hall, possibly even colder than outside. It was bright, though;

large windows letting in plenty of light to bounce around on walls painted a warm shade of cream. From where I stood in the tiny hallway I could see all the rooms. Dead ahead was a living room, a tired-looking couch just visible through the half-open door. To my left a tiny kitchen, a sink full of bubbles not quite hiding the mountain of dishes. I suppressed a smirk, willing to bet that on the other side of the only closed door I'd find a half-made bed and overflowing laundry basket.

"It's nice," I said lamely, catching sight of his expectant face.

"It's not much," he said. "But it's a start." He looked at my empty hands. "No stuff?"

I gestured to the clothes I was wearing.

"This is pretty much what I have."

There was a very small wardrobe full of outfits back at Alexander's, but other than that I owned almost nothing.

Mark led me into his living room, which I was relieved to find was slightly warmer thanks to the several large, fat candles burning around the room.

"Candles?" I asked. I hoped he wasn't trying to set a mood.

"Yeah, sorry," he grinned impishly. "The pilot light's gone out on the heating, and until I can get it going again we're on old-fashioned flame."

"Oh." I breathed a sigh of relief. "I can probably look at that. If you want." I didn't want to offend his manly sensibilities, but the night-time temperature had been dipping more and more as the summer died away.

Pride, it seemed, was not Mark's sin.

"That'd be great!"

It took me all of five minutes on my back under his boiler to kick the heating into gear. Immediately the pipes started to creak and groan in every room as heat began to flush through the system.

"You're amazing!" Mark admitted with delight, pressing his hands to the side of the radiator. "Man, that feels good."

"How long have you been without heating?" I asked.

"About a week." He was both shamefaced and amused. "I mean, my dad could have come round and fixed it in a second, but, y'know, the whole point of moving out was to be more independent."

"But it's okay to have a girl do it for you?"

"Yeah, well. We'll call it rent."

"Right!" I laughed.

But the incident had broken the ice and I felt much more comfortable as we shared the sofa to watch Mark's tiny television. We watched the EBC News – neither of us commenting on the long feature about the work being done to restore the damage to the wall. Then there was a rerun of a detective show made in the days before budget cuts hacked at the production values of British programming. There were explosions and car smashes galore. It was horribly wasteful, glorious escapism. The kind of thing I hadn't done in, well, almost as long as I could remember.

Late afternoon, as the light began to dim, Mark made

us pasta. The twirls were a little underdone, and I was pretty sure the sauce came from a jar, but I couldn't have told you the last time a person cooked for me. He served the food with a large glass of red wine, swiftly followed by another, then another, so that by the time it was properly dark I was feeling exceptionally comfortable, and giggly, and just a tiny bit sick. Mark seemed to be handling the alcohol a little better than I was, but his cheeks were flushed and he was grinning an awful lot.

"Okay, I really have to go to bed," he said, standing up and swaying slightly. "I have to go to work in the morning."

"Oh." I pouted. It hadn't occurred to me that it was a Sunday and normal people would have to get up early the next day and face the dawn rush hour. Working for Alexander wasn't exactly nine to five.

"I'll try to come home early," he promised. "Maybe I can take a half day."

"You won't tell anyone about me, will you?" I whispered.

He shook his head, smiled at me reassuringly. "I promise."

"And you're sure it's okay if I stay?" I asked for about the tenth time.

"Yes!" he said emphatically. Then he looked around himself, a confused expression on his face. "What was I doing?"

I giggled. Maybe he wasn't handling the alcohol better than me after all.

"Going to bed," I reminded him.

"Right!" he nodded his head, then traipsed out of the room.

He was back a moment later, shirtless, and carrying a huge purple blanket in his arms. A pillow was clenched in his teeth.

"For you," he said, dumping his bundle on the sofa.

"Thanks," I said, trying not to look at the naked expanse of flesh he was displaying. It was hard to miss, though. He wasn't like Alexander, all bulk and overworked muscles. He was thin, but solid-looking, and pale, like his torso had never seen the sun.

"Goodnight," he chirruped. I dragged my eyes away from the light trail of hair leading from his belly button to meet his gaze. He smirked at me smugly, and I felt heat in my cheeks, although that could have been the wine.

"Night," I mumbled.

He shut the door to give me some privacy and I arranged the blanket across the sofa. I shrugged out of my jeans, but left the rest of my clothes on in place of pyjamas. I pounded the pillow into a plumper shape and lay down. I was immediately uncomfortable. The cushions were lumpy, a spring digging into my hip, and the way I had the pillow resting on the arm of the sofa was hurting my neck. I grimaced and twisted round. Alexander's king-size bed was a lot more comfortable – even Samuel's leather sofa was better than this – but at least I was safe, no noose around my neck.

Despite my discomfort, I smiled. Mark was really great for letting me stay. I mean, I was practically a stranger.

Worse than that, I was a Celt, a marked Celt. If he was to believe the news reports running almost nightly on EBC, I should be dangerous, untrustworthy, devious. Certainly not someone you should welcome into your home. I wondered idly if he was sleeping with a knife under his pillow. Then I wondered what he hoped to get out of his generosity. In Alexander's world, my world, nothing was free. Trouble was, I didn't have anything to offer.

Well, I had one thing.

Without stopping to think about it, I slipped from the covers and padded, bare legged and barefoot, out of the room. In the hallway all of the doors were closed. Without knocking, I opened up the one door that had been shut earlier, the door I knew had to lead to Mark's bedroom. I was right. The room was small, dominated by an old iron-frame bed, and bathed in the muted glow from a bedside lamp. He was still awake then.

"Hi," I said softly, slipping inside and closing the door.

He blinked, surprised, then yanked the duvet up to cover his bare chest, forgetting, I guessed, that he'd already paraded in front of me without his top. Or maybe it was just that it was different, in this room.

"Do you need something?" he asked.

"No." I sidled over and sat on the side of the bed.

I saw him visibly swallow, then he shut the magazine he'd been reading and laid it down on the bedside table. I smiled, readjusting myself on the bed until I was lying alongside him, propped up on one elbow. He didn't move, but his eyes watched me warily. I considered him for a moment, then moved in.

"What are you doing?" he asked, just as our lips were about to touch.

I leaned back so that I could see his expression. "What does it look like I'm doing?"

"Well," he gave an embarrassed half smile. "It looks like you're... well, you know."

"That's right," I smiled and inclined my head again, but this time he deliberately pulled away.

"But... why?"

I sat up, then shuffled back towards the edge of the bed, mortification setting my features into a mask.

"Don't you want to?" I asked.

"Well, I... I mean. It's not that I don't want to," he looked distinctly uncomfortable. "But, the thing is. Lizzie... why are you doing this?"

I stared at him, lost. "Well, you've been really great, letting me stay and everything. I just wanted to say thank you."

And right now I just wanted to crawl back to my couch and hide under the thick purple blanket.

He smiled at me, his expression somewhere between pity and understanding. I didn't like it.

"Lizzie, you don't have to pay me by sleeping with me."

I swallowed against a painful lump in my throat. He was making me sound like a prostitute.

"I... not... that's not what I was doing," I said.

"Okay," he agreed quickly, sycophantically.

"I'm tired," I said suddenly, swinging myself up and off the bed. "I'm going to sleep."

He let me walk away, but called out just as I had my hand on the door.

"Lizzie!" I turned. "I really appreciate the—" he stopped short of saying the 'offer', realising, I hoped, how it would sound. "Look, let me take you out tomorrow after work. On a date."

A date? I'd never been on a date. A little bubble of girlish excitement fluttered inside me – something I'd never felt before – but it was mostly snuffed out by my lingering embarrassment. I smiled, though it turned out more like a grimace. "That'd be nice."

Then I fled to my makeshift bed and hid my red-hot face under the protective cover of the blanket.

CHAPTER THIRTEEN

When I woke up in the morning the flat was quiet, peaceful. The sun was up, filtering in through ill-fitting venetian blinds, but the clock on the wall told me that it was still early, not even eight. The door to the lounge was firmly closed, but I had the feeling that I was alone in the flat. I was also sweltering. Tossing the blanket aside I sat up and stretched the kinks out of my back and shoulders, then I tiptoed across the room, peeking out into the tiny hallway.

"Mark?" I called.

No answer.

"Mark, are you in?"

I paused for several seconds, listening for a reply, but there was only silence. I threw the door open and trotted into the bathroom. He'd left out a clean towel for me and I took advantage of the empty flat to have a long, luxurious shower, trying to wash the memory of the night before down the plughole. Unfortunately I'd no option but to put my dirty clothes back on.

Mark had left me a note in the kitchen, propped

up against an ancient coffee machine still half full of steaming dark caffeine:

Didn't want to wake you. Help yourself to anything in the fridge (I apologise in advance!). I'll try and be back early. And for our date tonight - how about going out for dinner?

I smiled, feeling that flutter again at the word 'date', then grimaced as his letter triggered a flashback to my faux pas from the previous night. It was going to be a little awkward when he got back.

Mark hadn't been kidding: there was almost nothing edible in the kitchen. I cobbled together some stale-looking cereal and milk that was definitely on the verge of going off. Taking my bowl back to the lounge, I tossed my blanket off the sofa then settled down, remote in hand. For once I was going to watch what I wanted on the television.

After about twenty minutes, however, the novelty had worn off. There really was nothing on! Since the government had introduced a tax on any programme made outside the UK, half the channels had closed down, and the ones that hadn't had dropped the US shows like they were hot potatoes on babies' fingers. Now morning TV was nothing but antiques shows and reruns of chat shows featuring the very worst dregs of humanity. Hitting the standby button, I killed the image on the screen before the fat girl could push her finger any harder into her pathetic-looking boyfriend's face.

What to do? I drummed my fingers on the arm of the

sofa, kicking my feet against the threadbare carpet. I was restless, itching to get up, to do something. At Alexander's I'd be out on a delivery, or down in the basement sorting out imports, or loitering in a plump white leather chair in the office, listening to things not meant for my ears. Hanging around like this was strangely disconcerting. I'd been in Mark's one-bedroom flat for maybe fourteen hours, and already I had cabin fever. I was not suited, it seemed, for going to ground. Hiding from Alexander was a different proposition than hiding from the GE.

Just for the chance to move about, I wandered into the bathroom, thinking I'd tidy it up or something. I paused in front of the mirror, fussing with my fringe, which had dried at a funny angle. When I looked down at the clutter of shavers and gel and bottles of whatever it is men use in the bathroom, I noticed one topped with a little yellow Post-it. It had my name on. I didn't know how I'd missed it before, but when I picked it up I knew at once what it was. Where did he get it from?

"Thank you, Mark!" I breathed. Then I spun the top under my fingers, revealing a lump of light beige cream. Ultimate concealer. I slathered it on, then gazed at my reflection. Just another nobody. Reaching up, I fingered the blue fringe. I really did like it, but it made me stick out like a sore thumb. It made me memorable. Sighing, I took a firmer grip, picked up a pair of little nail scissors and cut.

Minutes later, I yanked on my shoes and my jacket and snatched up the spare key from where Mark had left it, hooked on a nail just inside the front door. Slamming the heavy door to engage the lock, I tripped down the stairs and out into the muted grey light of another overcast day. I didn't truly breathe until I was on the pavement. There my lungs expanded, drinking in the smog and fumes of an early autumn day in the heart of the city.

Freedom. But where to go? I didn't have any money, and I didn't know the area so it probably wasn't safe to go too far, but a little walk couldn't do any harm. Just enough to clear the haze in my brain, stretch my legs and kill some time. Around the block I noticed a row of shops just a few hundred metres ahead. Fingering the change in my pocket, left over from my phone call to Mark, I tried to think how long it had been since I'd had something as simple as a chocolate bar and a can of fizz. It seemed wasteful – I wasn't really hungry and God knows I didn't have any cash to spare – but the more I thought about it the stronger the craving became. I could almost taste the sweet velvety smoothness, feel the tingling bubbles of pop on my tongue. There'd be no chance of a Coke – that was number one on the government's banned American goods list – but lemonade would be nice.

The shop bell dinged politely as I pushed it open. Inside was empty, except for a bored-looking girl reading a glossy magazine behind a counter heaving with papers.

"Hi," I mumbled, but my hesitant smile died in the face of her frosty welcome. She raised one eyebrow disdainfully, then went back to some story about a has-been footballer and his bit of skirt.

I took my time making my choice, knowing I could only afford one and finding, even in the limited stock retailers were now allowed to display, that there were so many chocolate bars from my childhood that I hadn't even realised were still made. In the end, I eeny-meeny-miny-moed my way to a Caramel. Just as I turned to make for the counter and the unhelpful salesgirl, something outside the shop window caught my eye. It was blurry, moving fast. I squinted, but the large square of glass was mostly covered over with a mixture of government ads and sales promotion posters, and my view was obscured. I was almost certain, though, that I had caught a flash of white-blond.

Zane.

No, don't be ridiculous, I told myself. What the hell would he be doing here? It must have been somebody else, or maybe just my mind playing tricks on me. It couldn't possibly be him. Nonetheless, I paid for my purchases and headed back to Mark's flat quickly, looking over my shoulder every two seconds until I'd let myself in through the reassuringly impenetrable main door. I didn't see the flash of blond again.

Mark came back mid-afternoon. It had been three hours since my jaunt to the shops and I'd spent all of that time trying not to think. Trying not to wonder what Samuel had said to Alexander and whether the elder of the two brothers was looking for me: whether that had been Zane I'd seen, whether I had done the right thing.

When I caught the sound of keys in the door I was so relieved that I was no longer alone with my thoughts that I all but ambushed Mark as he opened the door.

"Hey!" I said, smiling hugely in greeting.

"Hey," he replied.

He was dressed smartly, in grey trousers and a white shirt, tie yanked down a few inches so that it no longer choked at his throat. Even with the top button undone and his jacket tossed untidily over one arm, he looked different, grown up.

"Did you survive on your own?" he asked.

I shrugged, not wanting to confess the muddied doubts that had circled in my head. "Daytime TV is rubbish."

"I wouldn't know," he smirked.

"Right." I shifted my weight from foot to foot, back to being a little uncomfortable with Mark. The wine had smoothed the way last night; without its calming influence I felt awkward.

Suddenly he cocked his head to the side and stared at me. One hand reached out and ran over the hacked bristles along my hairline. It tickled but I didn't move.

"You cut off the blue," he said softly.

"Yeah. Seemed smart." For some reason I had to push the words past a lump in my throat. I shrugged. "It's only hair." So why did I feel like crying?

There was an uncomfortable pause while Mark looked at me and I looked at the floor. I got the sense he wanted to hug me and I hoped he didn't because I had the feeling that then I really would start bawling.

The moment passed.

"So, about that date," Mark tossed his jacket aside and looked at his watch. "Is it too early to go out? I'll buy you something to eat? We can call it *lunner*."

"*Dinch*," I amended. "And it's definitely not too early, I'm starving."

Mark changed into jeans and a light blue V-necked jumper that set off his flint grey eyes, then he took me to a little cafe-cum-restaurant just a few streets away from his flat. It served Anglo-Indian cuisine, more Anglo than Indian now that the government refused to allow anyone to import foreign foods – including spices – but the curried lamb I had was tender and tasty, if a little weird served with mashed potatoes instead of rice. Rice was available, but it was twice the price and I already felt bad that Mark was footing the bill. He had chicken breast and chips coated in a sludgy brown spicy sauce. It looked disgusting, though he said it tasted nice. The restaurant was all but empty, in that lull between lunchtime and the pre-theatre bookings, so we were served in double-quick time and back out on the street before I knew it. Or maybe it was just that the conversation was flowing and I was, for once in my life, having fun. We purposefully avoided discussing anything serious. Who I was running from; whether they'd be chasing me; how long I could stay with Mark. The possibility I could turn traitor, turning informer. Mark was laid-back and naturally cheery, and I managed to forget about my worries as he cracked jokes and entertained me with stories of his childhood, which sounded much rosier than mine.

"So," Mark banged lightly into my shoulder as we began the walk back to his flat, "Did you enjoy your *dinch*?"

"*Lunner*," I corrected.

"You..." he rolled his eyes and smirked.

"Bloody Celt?" I suggested.

"Yes!" he huffed, but the corners of his mouth were twitching. He reached for my hand, fingers curling around mine. Looking down at me, he squeezed gently and I blushed. A strange warmth was zinging through my veins. It felt nice.

We walked close together as we wound our way slowly back to Mark's flat. The schools were just out and the pavement was crowded with teenagers in various different uniforms, mothers dragging along smaller, tired-looking children with Bob the Builder lunch boxes and dirt on their noses. We had to sidestep and weave around the throng, our progress made much harder by the fact that we were joined at the fingers, but I didn't want to let go of Mark's hand, and he, it seemed, did not want to let go of me.

"Good afternoon." Someone stepped in front of us, blocking our way and commanding our complete attention.

Mark was slow to react, but I instantly stiffened. My eyes were level with the man's broad chest and I recognised the distinctive bulky black vest, which was both uniform and lifesaver. If there was any doubt, the GE emblem was emblazoned just below his left shoulder. I stared at it, then, inch by inch, I dragged my gaze up to his face.

Oh my God.

I knew that face. Frantically I wracked my brain, flashing through memories, searching for the time I'd seen him before. It didn't take long – I didn't come into contact with many Government Enforcement officers. It had been at St Paul's. This was the bent officer who I'd delivered Alexander's package of drugs to. What was his name?

Riley. His name was Riley.

"Is there a problem, officer?" Mark asked politely.

Riley had been looking at me, but now he snapped his gaze to Mark's courteously curious face. I was glad he still held on to my hand; I was gripping his now, using it to support my shaking body. If I'd recognised Riley, surely he had recognised me? Why else would he have been staring at me like that?

"I'm following up on reports that a Celt girl has been seen in the area," he said.

"Oh, I see," Mark sounded shocked. "Well," he glanced down at me, "I don't think we've come across anyone like that. What does she look like?"

Riley's eyes glared back down at me.

"Small, thin. Short dark hair with a blue fringe. Scottish accent."

In short, an awful lot like me. I kept my lips pinned closed, aware that I was hardly the master of a convincing English accent.

"Has she been branded?" Mark asked.

"Yes."

The tattoo on my cheek seemed to burn, as if it wanted to melt away the heavy make-up and expose me. I resisted the urge to cover half my face with my hand.

"Well, officer," Mark pulled me to the side as he made to inch around Riley. "If we see her, we shall certainly not hesitate to call in the GE."

"Wait," Riley threw his arm out. "Before you go, I'd like to see your IDs."

No 'please'. It wasn't a request. The badge on his uniform and the gun discreetly holstered at his side was all the authority he needed.

"Certainly," Mark pulled out his wallet and handed over the credit-card sized licence. Riley took it, gave it a cursory glance, then turned to me.

I opened my mouth, but no sound came out.

"Angel?" Mark looked down at me to smile, then his gaze dropped to my free hand and he frowned. "Where's your handbag?" he asked.

I blinked, totally confused. What handbag?

He sighed indulgently. "You haven't forgotten it have you?"

Eh?

His eyes burned into mine, trying to convey a message. I stared back, my brain trying to scramble into gear but stalling instead. Handbag?

Oh. Realisation dawned. God, I was slow.

"I... I must have," I mumbled, trying to keep my voice low to hide the Scottish lilt that I'd never managed to drop.

"Not again!" Mark sounded annoyed.

I tried to look sheepish, a bit embarrassed, but really what I was, was impressed. The lies were tripping easily off Mark's tongue, the fake emotions convincing. Forget officer work, he should be an actor.

But then, I supposed, the danger here was all focused on me.

"Sorry," I whispered.

"Don't worry, we'll just phone the restaurant when we get home, see if anyone's handed it in."

"So you don't have ID?" Riley's eyes narrowed.

I shook my head, trying to look believably innocent. And not frightened. Though I was sure he'd see right through my poor pretence.

Riley pulled a notepad out of his trouser pocket. He flipped it to a blank page then fixed me with penetrating blue eyes.

"Name?" His voice was curt and commanding, officer mode, and it turned on some switch in my brain. I was used to being ordered and sneered at. My terror vanished, and I knew at once who I was going to be.

"Tanya. Tanya Middleton," I said without hesitating, my tongue rolling oddly around an upper class accent.

"Address?"

I gave him a street in Chelsea, one that made his eyebrows ride up his forehead and the first stirring of doubt creep into his expression.

"And what do you do, Miss Middleton?"

Much more polite now. I smiled.

"I'm still at school."

"Which school?"

"King's Court College."

"I see."

He flipped the notebook closed.

The conflicting thoughts were clear on his face. He didn't believe me, I was fairly sure, but the story I'd fed him was making him think twice. If I really was who I claimed to be and he had accused me of being a Celt, he'd be in big, big trouble. I was quite sure little Tanya's dad would be an important enough man to have him fired. Everyone in the street she lived in was somebody – somebody with their fingers in every pie, every government official's pocket.

"Well, Miss Middleton, I, er..." He shifted from foot to foot, deliberating. "I'd make sure you phone that restaurant just as soon as you get in. There are thieves about, you know."

"Thank you, officer," I smiled sweetly.

Then he stepped aside.

The pavement was suddenly clear before us. I took one step, then another, half amazed, half convinced it was a trick and that his hand was going to clamp down on my upper arm and then laugh in my face. But he didn't. Mark and I continued forward, only his grip on my hand stopping me from breaking out into a sprint. We strolled towards the corner, deliberately not looking back, then as soon as a wall hid our backs from Riley's view, we erupted into hysterical laughter. The tears streamed down my face and I clutched at my ribs, trying to rub away the sudden stitch that gripped them. How had we got away with that? The abrupt relief of tension made me light-headed. We were still giggling as we collapsed into the flat.

"Come here," Mark said, grabbing my hand and dragging me to his bedroom. He dropped me on the bed then disappeared back across the hallway into the bathroom. When he returned he clutched the facecloth in his hand. Droplets of water cascaded down to splash silently on the varnished wooden floor.

"What are you doing?" I asked suspiciously as he approached me.

"Taking that stuff off your cheek," he replied, his expression serious now.

He sat beside me and started to rub my face gently.

"But... why?" I couldn't help asking.

He smiled at me, a slow, genuine smile that made the muscles in my lower stomach contract.

"Because you're prettier without it," he said.

His hand on my cheek, Mark leaned in to kiss me. I held completely still, my breath caught in my throat. This was totally different from Alexander. I knew that at any time I could pull back, at any time I could say stop. He was going to kiss me because he wanted to, and I only had to kiss him back because I wanted to. Normality to most people: completely new to me. And empowering. I considered stopping him, just because I could, but I didn't. Because I wanted to feel if his lips were as soft as I thought they'd be; I wanted to have him slide his hand into my short hair, wanted to feel his breath mingling with mine.

Our lips touched just as the sharp drone of the buzzer cut through the air. Mark pulled back and paused, his mouth just millimetres from mine.

"Ignore it," I implored.

He didn't take much persuading. He grinned briefly, then pressed his lips against mine once more. They were warm, tender, pliable. They teased mine, gently opening my mouth so that his tongue could slide inside. My fingers knotted themselves into the front of his shirt, trying to pull him closer to me. Two arms wound around my shoulders, squeezing me, holding me together.

We both jumped as an invisible hand pounded at the door. Five loud thumps shook and rattled the frame; impatient, angry.

We jerked apart and I stared up at Mark, my eyes widening.

"Oh God," I whispered. "Do you think that GE officer followed us?"

Mark shrugged even as his arms tightened around me. Before he could answer, a second hammering filled the air.

"Ignore it." Mark hushed.

Before I had time to open my mouth, the banging started again.

We stared at each other, waiting. There a brief lull, then more banging, louder and faster.

Mark pummelled his pillow in frustration then pushed back off the bed. He stood and looked down at me, his eyes narrowing as the knocking continued in the background. Suddenly his expression changed, he was more wary than annoyed. "Stay here," he ordered, sounding much more like Alexander or Samuel than the happy-go-lucky Mark I was beginning to get to know.

I nodded and drew my knees up to my chest, winding my arms around them. Maybe it was nothing. I hoped whoever it was would go away quickly. I wanted Mark to kiss me again. I wanted that fuzzy warmth that was so different from the cocktail of fear and excitement that gripped me whenever Alexander touched me.

Mark pulled the door to the bedroom almost fully closed as he strolled to the door, readjusting his T-shirt and running his hands over his hair, trying to right the tangled mess I'd created. He stopped to latch on the security chain before opening the door a crack.

"Yes?" I heard him ask tersely.

The response was too low for me to make out, but through the slither of open doorway I saw Mark's face drop in horror and my stomach seemed to plummet through all three floors of the building, right into the basement. I uncoiled from the bed, my body ready to roll upright, to go to his aid, just as Mark tried to slam the door closed. Whoever it was must have had their foot barring the way, however, because the door bounced back towards Mark, halting inches from his face as the chain stretched taut.

"What the hell do you think you're doing?" Mark yelled.

Then it exploded inwards. The chain ripped loose from the doorframe and the edge of the door caught Mark on the chin, sending him tumbling backwards. I froze, hardly daring to breathe.

"Mark?" I mouthed, but there wasn't enough volume in my voice for the word to leave the room.

I tried to move, to get up, to help him, but my muscles had gone into lock down. I could do nothing but watch as Mark gathered himself, hanging onto the wall then pushing off to try once more to close the front door. He only made it a step, however, before some invisible force smashed into his head, kicking it backwards and taking his feet out from under him. The crash his body made as it hit the ground wiped out the gentle pop that preceded it, but in my head the noise reverberated, echoing long after Mark lay still. I knew that sound. God help me, I knew that sound.

My eyes widened as I saw an arm enter the room. With its hand firmly coiled around a shiny, black gun, the barrel unnaturally long. Alexander didn't like to shout, and he didn't like the thundering crack of gunshots. But he did like his gun. The silencer was his idea of a compromise.

CHAPTER FOURTEEN

"Elizabeth?" I heard his voice before I saw his face, but then he glided into view. But only in profile. He stared dead ahead, into the lounge, so I was spared the hypnotic danger of his eyes. "Elizabeth, I know you're in here. Come out. Now."

Quiet. Soothing. Almost melodic.

And the most terrifying sound in my world.

I tried to keep control of my breathing, knowing he would hear if I gave in to the desire to gasp and whimper. If he continued forward, maybe I could sneak past, escape onto the stairwell and then just run for it.

But he was much too smart for that. Alexander lingered in the hall, pushing at the living room door, letting it swing open to reveal the empty room. Then he turned, preparing to give the kitchen the same treatment. In the handkerchief-sized hall, he didn't need to leave the door – the only exit – and he could quite easily check the whole flat. Here, with no witnesses and the silencer to cushion the noise, he wouldn't need to hesitate before he shot me.

I didn't want to die.

Slowly, silently, I began edging backwards, feeling my way around the bed, trying to make my way to the window without taking my eyes off Alexander. The angle of the door was unkind, however, and as soon as I'd taken two steps to the side I lost him. Instead, I saw Mark. He was motionless on the floor, head turned to me, eyes wide open. A hole had been gouged into his forehead. I stared at him, appalled. Mark, poor Mark. Dead, gone. Because of me. A sob would have burst its way out of my chest but I clamped my mouth shut tight enough to send pain ratcheting through my jaw.

If I left him here, how long would it be before someone discovered his lifeless body? Or would he just disappear? Alexander was good at making that happen. I pictured Mark's parents, waiting by a phone, hoping for a call that would never come.

"Don't hide from me, Elizabeth," Alexander sang.

His voice jolted me from my thoughts. I had to go, no matter how much the thought of abandoning Mark burned in my gut. Turning my back on the scene in the hallway, I pushed open the sash window, relieved when it slid up without a sound, and threw myself out through the tiny opening. I didn't look down. Mark's flat was two stories up.

Instead I closed my eyes and reached to my left, grabbing hold of the downpipe whilst my feet scrabbled for purchase against the vertical wall.

The iron piping was rusted and dirty and rough,

scraping the skin off my palms and gouging out a chunk of flesh between two of my fingers. I held on, though, using the drainpipe to hold myself close to the wall as my feet scuttled under me, trying to slow my descent to the ground. But I couldn't compete with gravity. When my boots slammed into the gravel and weeds clogging up the tiny rectangle of outside space behind Mark's block of flats, the shock shot straight up through my ankles, into my knees. The pain drove the breath from my lungs, forced me down into a crouch. To stop myself crying out, I bit down on my lip so hard that I drew blood. I tasted it in my mouth, metallic and warm.

Instinctively I looked up, but it was impossible to tell from here which of the many windows I'd made my escape from. I knew if I lingered, eventually I would see Alexander's angry face glowering down at me; it didn't seem smart to wait for that.

I half ran, half hobbled along the alleyway between the two high blocks of terraced buildings, wincing every step. My ankle hurt badly enough to be broken, but I told myself it was just a sprain. Either way, I couldn't afford to stop. Not unless I wanted to end up like Mark; poor, innocent Mark. I suppressed another sob. Now wasn't the time to grieve for him. Now was the time to survive. I took the tears and shoved them deep down, burying them until I could breathe again.

At the end of the alley I had a choice to make: head left into nowhere, or right into nowhere. I dithered for a few precious seconds, then went left, choosing on nothing more substantial than that it was downhill and I was hurting. As I walked I flipped my hood up and over my head, pulling one side forward to conceal my tattoo. The pavements were empty, though rush hour traffic clogged the road. I shoved my fingers into my jacket pocket, doing a quick inventory. I had a handful of coins, half a pack of mints and the key to Mark's flat, a place I knew I'd never go back to.

And a mobile.

I pulled out the little phone and stared at it for a full minute, letting my feet find their own path. Then I stuffed it back in my pocket.

I looked around, paranoid. There was no sign of anyone behind me, except for a couple of old ladies, and I was fairly certain they were not working for a Welsh gangster. The cars that drove past, too, were innocuous, maintaining a constant speed, the drivers not giving me a glance as they passed by. Nobody peeked out from behind a curtain, phone in hand. But I was nervous. I knew Alexander wouldn't chase me down and shoot me in the street; that wasn't his style. But I also knew that he'd cut his nose off before he'd let me get away. He'd be watching me, waiting, biding his time.

I just had to make sure I saw him before he saw me.

Trying to remain calm, trying not to think about what I'd just seen, I picked up the pace. I memorised all the street signs that I passed, but I'd no idea where I was, or which way I was heading. The buses that drove past had destinations that I'd never heard of written in block capitals across the front. I was tempted to get on one, any one, but it would only take an overzealous bus driver to clock my cheek and radio in for a GE patrol. So instead I kept on walking, letting block after block pass me by.

All the while I was fighting to concentrate, fighting to stay here, in the now. My mind was desperate to rewind the minutes, to drag me back to Mark's flat and force me to relive what had happened, over and over again. He was dead. Mark was dead. A single bullet to the head. Alexander's hand. My fault. All because he'd been foolish enough to try to chat up a schoolgirl on the train. A heavy price for an innocent act.

I'm sorry Mark. I'm sorry, sorry, sorry.

My face closed in on itself as the first tears started to shimmer in my eyes, blurring the world around me, letting a blue car sneak past then jam on its brakes without my seeing. I heard the sound of tyres twisting in a tight circle, but I didn't process the noise. Seconds later it ghosted up alongside me.

"Hello, Elizabeth."

My heart stopped, but my feet kept walking. I refused to look at him, burning a hole into the pavement instead.

"Where are you going?"

His voice was soft, inquisitive. Almost polite. Terrifying. My stomach flipped, but I kept the fear from my face.

"Can I offer you a lift?"

He wasn't asking. It was an order: get in the car.

But if I got in the car, I was dead.

Still refusing to look at him, I shook my head.

"I've been looking for you, Elizabeth. You had me worried. It's lucky Zane saw you. But," his voice chilled, "I had to call on one of my GE contacts to find that boy's flat. I'm not happy about that, sweetheart."

The car crawled along, keeping the driver's window just level with my shoulder. The road was long and straight, double yellow lines painting a path for him to follow me.

"You're not upset about what I had to do to him, are you?" he sounded almost amused. My stomach clenched. "I warned you. I warned you what would happen if you got involved with another man. You should have listened to me, Elizabeth. Now get in the car."

At last his anger broke through the veneer of patience, edging the final command with steel.

I ignored him.

The car revved, pushing forward for a moment so that his face glided into my peripheral vision. I resisted the urge to turn my head away, but I could feel his gaze burning into me. His jaw was set, eyebrows furrowed menacingly.

"I will shoot you right here. You think any of these people are going to stop me? Call the police?"

No, of course they weren't. They were too smart for that. Selective blindness was the first survival tactic parents taught their children these days.

"Lizzie, get in the car."

He spat each word at me, so angry he even shortened my name. Last chance. Do it or die. Do it and die later.

I stopped walking, turned to look at him. Alexander's dark green eyes were hypnotic. His face broke into a smile that was both dazzling and petrifying, an angel-demon.

"Good girl," he crooned.

But I didn't get in the car.

I ran. Across the road and down the next, winding in between cars, twisting round pedestrians. Behind me I heard the squeal of tyres – Alexander's roar of rage. The car accelerated, but I was always one step ahead. I flew through a junction snarled up with traffic; cars all waiting patiently on a red light, pinning him back behind a white van and a rusting Landrover. He slammed his hand on the horn, but the vehicles had nowhere to go. Ahead of them traffic slowly crossed the junction at right angles. Pressing my advantage, I threw myself between them, causing someone – I didn't pause to see the vehicle – to slam on their brakes to avoid breaking both my legs.

Across the junction, I flat-out sprinted, ignoring the agonising protests from my knees and ankles, and zigzagged my way down several blocks, losing myself, trying desperately to lose Alexander. I ran and ran, too frightened of what I'd see to look backwards. People walking hurried to move out of my way as I bolted past them. They stared, shocked and wary, but if they managed to catch a glimpse of my now naked cheek as I hurtled by, I was long gone by the time they processed what was wrong with the picture.

I didn't stop until I hit the river.

It was one of the most familiar things in my world,

certainly more familiar than any of the streets around me, but it shocked me to a halt. It was a barrier, wide and uncrossable. At least for me.

I recognised immediately where I was. Tower Hill. Just in front of me the Tower of London rose magnificently up into the sky, and between its legs wove the bridge. The bridge that marked the gateway into the Central Zone. The bridge controlled by the GE. The bridge I couldn't cross.

I stood there, staring for the longest time, hauling in great lungfuls of air. Then I turned and gazed back the way I'd come. The blue car was nowhere in sight.

Now what?

Slowly, hesitantly, I drew the phone out of my pocket. Without permission, my thumb moved to the power key and held it down until the screen flickered into life. No need to scroll through the contacts list. I hit call, then dragged the phone up to my ear, listening to the shrill ring.

Answer.

Don't answer.

Answer.

Don't answer.

"Hello?"

"Samuel?" I was gasping, though I'd been standing motionless for a full five minutes. The word came out as a mush, twisted and contorted by my strangled throat.

He understood at once who it was, though.

"Hang on." His voice was clipped, businesslike.

I listened to the sounds of him walking quickly, then a door opening and closing, biting my tongue to hold my cries at bay. "Lizzie? Lizzie, what's wrong?" The cold, harsh tones were gone, replaced with a whisper layered in stress, apprehension.

"I'm sorry," I blubbered. "I have no one else to call."

"What's happened? In fact, wait a second—" There was a strange sound over the line, the background noises melting away like he'd put his palm over the receiver. "Zane, do me a favour? Go down and see how they're getting on in the basement. I want to make sure none of it goes missing this time." It was like listening underwater, Samuel's voice muffled and far away. Zane's curt response was even quieter, but it was still enough to make my blood run cold. Samuel was at Bancroft Road, at the house. Unconsciously I started shaking, the phone vibrating against my ear.

"Lizzie? You there?"

I realised I'd tuned out. Had he been speaking to me?

"I'm here," I rasped. My throat felt like I'd been swallowing razor blades.

"What happened? What's wrong?"

"Everything," I exploded. "Alexander's—" but I didn't get any further than that.

"Shhh!" he hissed. "Keep your voice down." I heard more movement, the thump of feet on stairs. "Alex's what?"

I swallowed, trying to get a handle on the adrenaline coursing through my veins, pushing me towards hysteria.

"He found me. At Mark's. He... he... Jesus Christ!" I clamped my hand over my mouth as sobs wracked my frame. The glimpse I'd caught of Mark's prone body, his bloodless face in stark contrast to the streak of red running down his temple, danced in front of my eyes.

"Lizzie!" Samuel's voice dragged me back to the present. "Get it together!" He waited whilst I fought to get my breathing under control. "Now, tell me what happened."

It was a command, and I was so conditioned to obeying that my body automatically reacted. A deadened calm flooded through me, like numbing anaesthetic injected straight into my nervous system.

"Alexander came to Mark's flat. He shot Mark. He was going to shoot me." It didn't sound like me. It didn't even feel like I was saying the words.

"You got away?"

"I climbed out of the window. Then I ran. But he knew I was there. He... he followed me into the street and he... he spoke to me." My voice quavered as the memory of Alexander's words murmured like deadly velvet in the back of my head.

"Where are you now?"

"Samuel, I—" I bit my lip. Was it safe to tell him?

He'd known I was at Mark's; in fact, he'd been the only person who knew I was there. But somehow I felt positive he hadn't told Alexander. Zane had seen me in the shop. From the sounds of it, Riley had been the one to point the way to Mark's flat. If Samuel had told on me, Alexander wouldn't have had to chase me around like that, wouldn't have had to call on any of his 'contacts'. No, it couldn't have been him.

But could I trust him?

Did I have any other choice?

"Lizzie?"

"Uh-huh?" I chewed on my fingernail, still thinking.

"Where are you?"

I hesitated.

"Lizzie?" He sounded almost angry now, frustrated by my dithering.

"I..." I decided. "I'm at the river. At Tower Hill."

I had to trust someone. I wouldn't last until nightfall. Not branded the way I was.

I listened keenly to the silence on the other end of the line.

"Stay there."

He rang off without another word. I took his advice literally, standing motionless and holding the phone tight against my cheek, hiding my face from the shoppers and workers and normal people passing idly by.

Before long, though, I started to get cold feet. My jaw clenched shut against the screams in my throat, I must have looked so weird: waiting there, not talking. My eyes darted back and forth, flickering from black jacket to black jacket, hunting for the GE officers who were bound to be patrolling this close to the Central Zone. It wasn't safe to linger here. But that wasn't what was frightening me.

Was it safe to wait for Samuel?

What if he rolled up with Alexander in the passenger

seat? Or Zane? Or anyone else from Bancroft Road? Even alone, he could overpower me easily, drag me back to face my judgement, face Alexander. I should just cut and run, use the remaining money in my pocket to buy my way out of London, then head north any way I could. I couldn't trust anyone except myself. I definitely shouldn't trust someone so close to the man I absolutely had to stay away from.

Go, I told myself, the last of a hundred times. Disappear down the stairs and get on a train going anywhere.

But I didn't. I stood there, and I watched every vehicle that drove past, hunting for the one that would bring Samuel to me.

CHAPTER FIFTEEN

I assumed he'd come by car, taking one of the many untaxed, uninsured and untraceable motors Alexander used in his complex web of business ventures and criminal escapades, so I concentrated on the busy junction in front of me, only moving back into the shadow of a foul-smelling public toilet when I spotted the shiny emblem of a GE patrol or a police car. So when a hand clamped down on my shoulder I just about jumped out of my skin, yelping and spinning round, wide-eyed.

Samuel frowned at me, shushing me with a finger to his lips. I snapped my teeth together, swallowing back the rest of the scream. Passers-by stared at us curiously.

"Sorry," I whispered, glancing around. Eyes drifted away as soon as they saw me looking back, but I could still feel the heat of Samuel's disapproval.

"Come on," he said, turning from me and heading away from the river, away from the boundary of the Central Zone, back into the maze of London streets and the safety of obscurity.

"You don't have a car?" I asked, jogging to keep up with his long strides.

He shook his head. "Zane would have asked why I needed it."

I made a face.

"What business is it of Zane's if you want to borrow a car?"

"He'd make it his business."

"Oh." I didn't know what to say to that. Besides, I had more pertinent questions. "Where are we going?"

"Islington." Samuel didn't look at me, but continued staring straight ahead, his hands stuffed in his pockets. I felt a bit like a naughty child trotting after an angry parent.

"Right. What's in Islington?"

He didn't answer. I waited for a full minute, just in case, but his lips were pressed together in a thin line.

"Are we walking?"

He gave me a sidelong look, raising one eyebrow, then cut across me into the throng of traffic, weaving between queuing vehicles. I followed, waving apologetically at a white van that beeped angrily at me, anxious to inch forward another two feet. When we reached the pavement opposite, Samuel halted, folding his arms and leaning against the flaking paint of a bus stop pole. His left cheek was to me, and staring at him I could just see the faint outline of black moving under a thick layer of almost imperceptible make-up. I wondered if he had any with him, any for me. My hood was up, but I still felt exposed.

I moved to stand alongside him somewhat apprehensively. He looked annoyed, his mouth turned down and his forehead furrowed. Animosity seemed to roll off him in waves. I hadn't expected him to be angry. I'd thought... I didn't know what I'd thought. That he'd be pleased to see me? That he'd be concerned, or sympathetic? This cold indifference reminded me of the first few jobs we'd done together, before I'd got to know him. It made me want to throw myself at him and ask him to hug me. It made me want to cry.

Curling my fingers into fists, I set my face into a deep scowl and glared at the passing traffic.

It took the bus fifteen minutes to arrive, and for that whole time we didn't speak. Several more people joined us at the stop, most of them in crumpled suits, shoulders hunched against the fatigue of another long day. It was a relief when the double-decker chugged to a stop in front of us, belching out warm smoke as the hydraulics hissed and groaned. I reached into my pocket, prepared to give away the last of my pitiful collection of change, but when Samuel climbed onto the bus just in front of me, I heard him ask for two singles, to a stop I didn't recognise.

The lower deck was mobbed, but Samuel found a free pole halfway down, and managed to carve out enough space for him and me by glowering menacingly at the faces around. We were still squashed in like sardines, though, my nose just inches from Samuel's chest, breathing in the heady scent of his black leather jacket. It was nice, more comforting than staring into the unfriendly darkness of his eyes.

Even though the bus was crowded, it was quiet, subdued. The tinny jingle of a mobile phone ringing cut through the thick atmosphere. Several people around me patted coats or rifled through bags, hunting for their own devices, but the noise was coming from Samuel's waist. I stared down towards the source, then up into his face. He was gazing back down at me.

"Aren't you going to answer that?" a sour-faced, balding man snapped from my right. Samuel silenced him with a look, then slowly drew a small black mobile out of his jacket pocket. He stared down at the screen for a heartbeat, then straight back to me.

"It's Alex," he said, his voice expressionless.

A sharp pain stabbed in my chest as my heart began to thump erratically. It felt like he was here, standing next to me, breathing down my neck. I resisted the urge to turn round and check.

"What are you going to do?" My voice was barely loud enough for me to hear.

Rather than answer me, he lifted the phone to his ear. "Hey."

I clamped down on my lower lip, determined not to make a sound.

"I'm on a bus," Samuel said, raising his voice slightly over the roar of the engine as the double-decker surged forward into a gap in the traffic. I felt myself toppling backwards as the floor moved oddly under me. Samuel's free hand flashed out, grabbed the front of my jacket and jerked me to a stop, bracing his shoulder against the pole.

"Oh," my breath exhaled in a puff. I slapped my hand over my mouth to stifle the noise. Samuel glared at me.

"No, I won't be back till later."

My hand still wrapped protectively over my jaw, I leaned in closer, trying to hear what Alexander was saying. Samuel pushed me back gently but firmly, still gripping a handful of my jacket. He shook his head infinitesimally, ignoring me when I pouted childishly.

"I'm heading to Lewisham. I got a tip about someone who might have seen Lizzie."

My eyes widened. What was he doing?

Lewisham, at least, was in the opposite direction to Islington. Clearly Samuel was trying to lead a false trail, but why bring me up at all?

"Really?"

I heard a layer of surprise in Samuel's voice and I wondered if Alexander was recounting our encounter. Of course, he wasn't supposed to know anything about it.

"Well, it might turn out to be nothing, but I thought I should check it out." His eyes darkened as he listened, nodding subconsciously. "Yeah, I know what to do."

Samuel dropped the phone from his ear and slid it back into his pocket. Then he turned away from me, staring over the heads of other passengers, out of the windshield at the stationary traffic ahead.

"What did you mean?" I whispered.

"Hmmm?" Samuel didn't look at me.

I cleared my throat. "What did you mean when you said you know what to do?"

Samuel dropped his gaze to mine, just for a moment, and let his left eyebrow slide up his forehead. What did I think?

I blanched, understanding. If Samuel came across me, he was supposed to take me out. Either that or drag me back to Alexander's so that he could do it himself.

"Right," I mumbled, but I'd already lost my audience.

The bus had half emptied by the time Samuel indicated to me, with a jerk of his head, that it was time for us to get off. We stepped out onto a narrow pavement, potholes and cracks turning the charcoal-grey asphalt into an obstacle course. There were few pedestrians, but a long line of traffic still trickled nose to tail off into the distance. This place was nothing but a thoroughfare to better things. I noticed, as I passed them, that none of the drivers were pausing to admire the scenery, and glancing around me I couldn't blame them. This main street was grey and depressing, as were all the narrower roads winding off it – dreary, endless rows of terraced houses with peeling paint and yellowing net curtains behind dirty windows. Gardens grew wild, or had been killed with concrete.

I didn't bother asking where we were going again. Samuel was in a reticent mood, the hunch of his shoulders warding off unnecessary questions.

Eventually we stopped at the faded red door of a house no grubbier or nicer than the two on either side.

Samuel produced a key from somewhere and, after a brief struggle with the Yale lock, kicked the door open. There was a low scraping sound as a small mountain of junk mail slithered across a bare wooden floor.

"In," Samuel ordered, holding the door open for me.

I stepped inside, passing through the tiny hallway into a sparsely decorated lounge. There was a sofa and matching armchair, a coffee table and an ancient television in the corner. Along one wall were several bookshelves groaning under rows of dusty volumes.

"You can stay here for now," Samuel said, following me into the dimly lit space. He crossed to the window and yanked the curtains closed before hitting the light switch. A naked bulb flickered to life above my head. "Keep the curtains closed, keep the noise down, and don't go outside. If anyone comes to the door, ignore it. There's some food in the cupboard, tins and the like. Help yourself. I'll be back. Don't phone me."

He didn't look at me once. Instead he turned to head for the door.

"Samuel," I yelped.

"What?" he kept his back to me, but at least he inclined his head.

What? I didn't know what to say, except...

"I'm sorry."

"For what?" His voice was harsh and I cringed.

For a million different things.

"For not listening to you when you told me to get out. For making you take me to Mark's. For getting you to lie to Alexander. For making you piggy in the middle. For calling you."

He swivelled round and took a half step back inside the room. A ghost of a smile warmed his features.

"You didn't make me lie to Alex. And don't be sorry for calling me. I'll be back, I promise."

"When?" I couldn't help asking.

Samuel glanced at his watch.

"Before midnight," he said. "I'll make some excuse."

I nodded gratefully.

"Thanks, Samuel."

He nodded and gave me a quick wink, but the hard, set expression was back on his face by the time he made it to the door.

Then I was on my own. Momentarily at a loss, I plopped down onto the sofa, sending a plume of dust whirling around me. I had to pinch the bridge of my nose to stem the sneezing fit that threatened, not sure if that constituted being noisy. I rubbed my forearms, feeling a shiver of goosebumps though the place wasn't cold, and wondered where I was. It seemed odd that Samuel could have a bolthole that Alexander didn't know about – Alexander made it his business to know about everything.

I was hungry, but the urge wasn't strong enough to rouse me from my stupor on the sofa. Instead I wrapped my arms across my stomach and dropped my head back until it banged lightly off the backrest. I shut my eyes against the depressing seediness of the room and breathed deeply, trying to relax the knot of tension that twisted tightly between my shoulder blades. I was safe, for the moment. But I was in limbo. The ground beneath my feet was less substantial than air. It was laughable, but being with Alexander had been stability. Out of his overprotective shadow, I was freefalling. Mark had not been enough of a cushion to break my fall. I should never have let him try. Putting him in the way, I'd killed him. He was dead, and it was all my fault.

What about Samuel? Was he protection enough?

I rubbed at my temples. My head was pounding. I couldn't believe it, but what I wanted to do more than anything was wind the clock back two, three days. I wanted to be under Alexander's thumb, sitting on his sofa feeling uncomfortable and ignored. I wanted to be in his bed, feeling sick at myself. I wanted my life back, because, as claustrophobic and miserable and terrifying as it had been, it was better than this. I couldn't see a future. When Samuel came back – if Samuel came back – then what? Would his offer still stand to help me get out of the country, back up to Scotland? So that I could do what...? Starve? Steal? Survive, for a while?

Did I have another option? Staying in London, I was much too close to Alexander. How long had it taken him to find me at Mark's? A day and a half? And if he didn't get me, I knew who would. The GE. I'd lasted this long branded as I was, only because Alexander had the power to keep me safe.

Looking for something to drown out the thoughts echoing in my head, I staggered to my feet and plugged in the television that was sitting in the corner. It was coated in dust, edged in a mock wood that was scratched and chipped, but it zapped into life when I pushed the button on the front. There was no remote, but by prodding at four discreet buttons at the side I managed to flick through the channels. I settled on a film. I'd no idea what it was called, didn't recognise any of the actors or actresses, but that didn't really matter; I wasn't going to watch it. I was just going to stare at the movement and the colours, waiting out the seconds and minutes and hours until Samuel came back and told me what to do.

It worked. With my senses occupied, my mind lulled itself into a trance. Hunger pangs came and went, but I was barely aware of them. After a while I gathered up the energy to visit the bathroom, chugging down some tepid water out of a dusty tumbler, but I was moving without conscious thought, gravitating back towards the couch, sinking back into oblivion. I wasn't asleep, but only because my eyes were open.

So I didn't hear the key slip into the lock, or the hand quietly turning the door handle, or the muted tread of feet stepping onto the cheap laminate flooring of the hallway.

"Hey."

Samuel's warm, lilting voice jerked me out of my daze. I blinked, swivelled my head to look at him. He grimaced at me, hovering in the tiny square hall. I watched as he shrugged his way out of his leather jacket and deposited it on the post at the end of the banister.

"What have you been up to?"

I shrugged. "TV."

"Did you eat?" Samuel bypassed me, heading straight for the kitchen. I didn't respond, knowing he'd find the answer in the empty sink, the clean countertops.

A minute later he was back, two tins in his hand.

"Soup, or beans?"

I raised one eyebrow, smiling in spite of myself.

"Is there toast?"

He looked over his shoulder, then back to me.

"No."

"Soup, then."

He nodded and disappeared, and I heard the clatter of a pan banging down onto a stove. He was going to make me dinner? Intrigued and amused, I pulled myself to my feet and wandered through to the kitchen. It was compact, the units beige with ugly brown handles, the oven rusting at the corners but clean enough. Samuel had rolled the sleeves of his green shirt up to his elbows and was stirring a wooden spoon in a dented silver pot.

"It's tomato," he said, looking up to see me loitering in the doorway. "That all right?"

"Yeah," I shook my head, incredulous. I moved forward, reaching for the spoon. "I can do that."

"I got it."

He waved me away, so I sank down on a hard wooden chair, watching him work. He spun round and grabbed two white bowls from a cupboard high up on the wall opposite, rinsing them in the sink before dumping them down beside two spoons. He must have sensed me watching him, because he looked up, smiled. I smiled back. I was glad that the dark mood he'd been in earlier, when he'd dropped me off here, had disappeared.

"What did you tell him?"

"What?"

Samuel went back to stirring the soup, but there was a defensive hunch to his shoulders.

"What did you tell Alexander?"

He shrugged, non-committal. I waited, playing with my tongue between my teeth. Eventually Samuel sighed.

"He thinks I'm seeing Natalie."

Natalie. Samuel's girlfriend. For some reason hearing her name brought the taste of bile to my tongue but I made sure to keep my expression clear.

"What if he finds out you're not?" I asked.

"There's no reason why he should."

But Samuel didn't look at me. He was concentrating on pouring the heated soup into the bowls, focusing on the task like he was assembling a nuclear bomb.

"Samuel... I don't want you to get into trouble. Because of me."

Balancing a brimming bowl in each hand, Samuel strolled over to me, taking the only remaining seat on the other side of a wobbly oval-shaped table.

"Don't worry about me," he said as he placed my meal in front of me.

"But—"

"Lizzie!" he said my name sharply, cutting off my protest. "I said don't worry."

I said nothing, picking up my spoon and needlessly stirring the steaming red liquid before spooning a mouthful to my lips. It blistered my tongue and throat, but my stomach growled gratefully. I studied Samuel as I ate. He seemed relaxed: the hand that wasn't gripping his piece of cutlery curled into a loose fist and resting on the tabletop, his broad shoulders leaning casually against the back of the chair. He didn't look back at me, but stared over my head towards the small window above the sink, a square of inky blackness.

Without thinking, I said the first thing that came into my head.

"Samuel," I paused, and he flicked his gaze to mine. "Why are you nice to me?"

"What?" He grinned, his forehead creasing in confusion.

I blushed, squirming slightly in my chair and half wishing I'd kept my mouth shut, but asked my question again.

"Why are you nice to me? I mean," I rushed on before he could answer, "you lied to Alexander for me; you gave me that phone when I went on the job with Cameron; you talked Alexander out of sending me on a suicide job; you took me to M—Mark's," my voice stuttered over the name, "and here you are. Again. I just... I just wondered why."

Samuel stared at me for a long moment.

"Do you wish I hadn't done all those things?"

"No..."

"Well then," Samuel gave me a tight smile and went back to his soup. I frowned down at the remains of mine, dissatisfied.

CHAPTER SIXTEEN

I made as much noise as I could, clattering the dishes into the sink and sending water gushing down from the mixer tap. There was no washing-up liquid, but I scrubbed noisily at the bowls and the saucepan with a battered-looking scourer. Anything to fill the quiet. Samuel stayed where he was in the chair, watching me. Our positions were reversed, much more like normal, yet I was highly uncomfortable.

It seemed Samuel and I had nothing to say to each other. The polite norms of conversation – the weather, how we'd spent our day, what we thought of the government – just seemed ludicrous in our, my, current predicament. What I really wanted to talk about – what I was going to do, what Samuel thought I should do – was the elephant in the room that I couldn't bring myself to address. And Samuel, well I'd no idea what Samuel was thinking. He seemed content just to sit, quietly thinking, but his eyes were serious, sombre.

I wracked my brain for a safe topic of conversation.

"So, you and Natalie. Is that going well?" I tried to

smile blithely, but I realised as soon as I'd said it that I was treading on dangerous ground. Relationships were something friends might discuss, and whatever Samuel and I had, it wasn't friendship. I bit my lip and waited for him to tell me it was none of my business, for him to put me back in my place.

Instead he sighed.

"Natalie and me?" There was a mocking tone to his voice that made me look up. He was grimacing ruefully. "There is no Natalie and me, not really. Alexander thinks she might be useful. Her father has contacts," he explained. I nodded, trying to look like this was news to me, like I hadn't overheard the conversation Samuel had had with Alexander. "But we're not, I mean... There's nothing there. Nothing real. To be honest, she does my head in."

"Oh." I wasn't sure what else to say. "I'm sorry."

I wasn't. Though I didn't want to admit it, a tiny part of me was pleased to hear the dismissive way Samuel spoke of her.

I'd finished the dishes, but I lingered by the sink, rubbing at imaginary spillages on the countertops. I could only do that for so long, though. Eventually I had to return to where Samuel sat. We eyed each other; him relaxed and solemn, me anxious and on edge. The long seconds drew out, the tinny sound of the television drifting in through the open door.

"Are you going to take off?" I asked at last.

It was the least important but most urgent on my list of questions.

Samuel didn't answer at first. He considered me, his fingers drumming on the tabletop.

"I should," he said slowly. I grimaced. "Do you want me to stay?"

"I don't want to be on my own," I admitted.

"Poor Lizzie." Samuel shook his head and heaved himself to his feet, ruffling my hair as he passed. He moseyed across the kitchen, returning seconds later with two small glasses and a bottle of amber liquid three-quarters full.

"No Coke," he said, slamming the glasses down and half filling them. "You'll have to take it like a man."

I grinned. He'd come by car, I knew. The evidence, a Ford key, lay tossed carelessly on the table before me. If he was drinking, he was staying. My immediate fears temporarily allayed, I took a swig from my glass, then choked. The whisky was cheap, burning my throat, setting my chest on fire. It tasted awful, but it felt good. I gulped the rest down, trying not to let it stay too long on my tongue. The burning moved down to my belly.

"That's nasty," I said, my eyes watering a little.

"It'll get better," Samuel promised as he refilled my glass. He'd downed his own in one.

It did get better. A bit. A very little bit. But I found, as the level sank lower and lower down the label of the bottle until there was only a dribble left, that I really didn't care. The soup in my stomach was no match for the percentage alcohol in my glass. I got drunk. Very drunk. And sleepy. I didn't even notice that I was sitting with my head slumped down on the cool formica until I felt Samuel's hand gripping my upper arms, pulling me from the chair.

"Come on," he whispered in my ear. "Time for bed."

Hanging on to his shoulders, I let him lead me through the living room and up the darkened stairway into one of the upstairs bedrooms. He lowered me gently down onto the bed, then I felt his body heat seep away as he stood up. I didn't like that.

"Where are you going?" I mumbled, tightening my grip.

"Back downstairs," he said, his voice low. "There's only one bed. I'll take the sofa."

"No," I frowned, shaking my head in the dark. "Don't leave me."

I heard him sigh, but he stopped trying to pull out of my grasp.

"Lizzie—"

"I don't want to be on my own," I slurred, no more than semi-conscious.

There was a moment's pause, then I felt the mattress shift as Samuel settled down beside me.

"Thank you," I breathed.

"You're welcome," his voice was a murmur in my ear.

I smiled, and wriggled backwards into the cocoon of his arms. Thanks to the drink-haze I felt comfortable, at ease. Warm, and so, so sleepy.

"Do you want to know why I'm nice to you?" Samuel whispered.

"Mmm?"

But I was gone, and his reply fell on deaf ears.

In the morning I woke up to an empty bed, stark white light, and a blinding hangover. I groaned, rolled over, tried to hide my eyes under the covers, but the movement sent a wave of nausea through my body. My stomach churned uneasily and saliva flooded my mouth. Awareness dawned just in time for me to scramble out from underneath the covers and run to the bathroom. I flung the door wide open and dropped to my knees, sticking my head over the pan just in time for whatever was left of the whisky in my stomach to expel itself from my mouth and nose. I wretched, choking and gagging as it burned my taste buds savagely.

Afterwards I dropped my head down onto the cool plastic of the toilet seat, groaning quietly as the world spun around me. The sickly sweet, acidic fumes floated up and I felt my stomach heave again in protest. Reaching up blindly, I fumbled for the flush, keen to get rid of the evidence.

Unfortunately my raging hangover didn't disappear with the vomit. I rinsed out my mouth at the sink, then used some ancient-looking toothpaste and my finger to try and brush my teeth. There was a battered medicine cabinet on the wall above the sink, but it was empty bar a cheap Bic razor and a pile of plasters. Disappointed, I closed the door to stare at myself in the cracked mirror. I looked horrendous. My skin was pallid, my hair sticking up everywhere. Dark circles ringed my eyes and my mouth was turned down – a result of the twisting in my stomach and the pounding in my head.

Turning away, I stared down the stairs. I could just make out the outline of Samuel's leather jacket at the bottom of the banister. He was still here then. Relief took the edge off my headache, but I hoped he hadn't heard me being sick.

His face when I walked into the living room told me that he had. It was both pitying and amused, but he didn't speak and he held up his hand to silence me. He was on the phone.

I waved, but I didn't move to sit beside him on the sofa. If he was talking to Alexander or Zane, he might not want me to listen in. I remembered how he'd pushed me away on the bus the day before.

"Yeah, yeah I understand," he paused, covered the mouthpiece with the palm of his hand and turned to me. "Make us a cup of tea, will you, Lizzie?"

I gaped at him, but he'd gone back to his conversation.

"What? No, she's nobody. Yeah. So tell me exactly what it is you're looking for."

I moved slowly towards the kitchen, completely confused. Who was Samuel talking to? I wasn't remotely bothered about being referred to as 'nobody' – after all, that was the truth – but I couldn't imagine who would be far enough removed from Alexander's circle for Samuel to casually throw my name out.

By the time I'd made the tea – no milk but I found some clumpy sugar in the cupboard – and returned to the living room, Samuel was wrapping up, saying goodbye and arranging to call again once he'd made the 'preparations'. He rang off and reached for his tea, gracing me with a grateful smile.

"Thanks, Lizzie."

It was on the tip of my tongue to ask who he'd been speaking to, but I knew it was none of my business. Instead I sipped my tea in silence, feeling the sugar and caffeine kickstart my system.

"How are you feeling?" Samuel asked, eyes raking across my pallid face.

I tried to smile. "Okay..."

He smirked, but nodded in acceptance. Embarrassed, I dropped my gaze to the floor, noted that his feet were encased in heavy black boots.

"You have to go," I said. It wasn't a question, and I did a poor job of hiding the trepidation in my voice.

"Yes." Samuel sighed, considered me.

"Can I stay here?"

He nodded, but there was a trace of hesitation in the furrowing of his brow. I knew what he was thinking. Yes, I could stay here for a day, maybe two, a week at an absolute push. But not for ever. Because Samuel couldn't keep disappearing, couldn't keep providing me with food, or money, or clothes. Not without Alexander finding out. This was a temporary fix, not a solution.

Tears stung my eyes.

"Samuel, what am I going to do?"

He didn't give an answer. Either because he didn't have one, or, more frighteningly, because there wasn't one.

I looked down at my hands, clinging to the residual

heat of my empty cup. Samuel's hand drifted into my vision, pulled the cup out of my unresisting fingers, and curled around my knuckles, squeezing gently. His touch was much warmer than the chipped china, but not enough to chase away the chill that had me firmly in its grasp.

"Lizzie, Alex doesn't know where you are. He won't find you here."

Alexander hadn't known I was at Mark's either, but that hadn't stopped him. I trusted Samuel, though. He knew his brother; if anyone could keep me free of Alexander's clutches, it was Samuel.

"I know," I spoke to my knees. "But I can't stay here for ever."

"Come here," Samuel pulled on my hand, tugging me into his side. I let him draw me in, but kept my face firmly cast down. I didn't have the alcohol to numb away my inhibitions any more, and it felt awkward to be tucked in Samuel's embrace. Awkward, but nice.

"It'll be all right," he murmured into my hair. It felt almost like he dropped a kiss onto the top of my head. I didn't move, frightened he'd remember himself and pull away if I so much as shifted on the sofa. "I'll help you," he promised.

"To the Scottish border?" I asked.

"Is that what you want?"

I shook my head. But where else was there to go?

We sat there for ten, maybe fifteen minutes. I stared down at a faded patch on Samuel's knee, and he stroked his fingers absentmindedly through my hair. The couple of times I dared to glance up at him, he was staring off into space, deep in thought. Eventually he sighed.

"I have to go," he said.

He took his arm from my shoulders and stood. Instantly I felt cold.

"Here," Samuel handed me something. It was a plug, with a long snaking wire growing out of one end. "A charger for the phone I gave you," he explained. "Keep the phone switched on. I'll call you later. In the meantime—"

"Stay inside and stay quiet?" I looked up, a ghost of a smile twitching at the corners of my mouth.

"Right," he smiled at me, green eyes crinkling at the corners, warmth I hadn't seen before on his face.

"Where are you going?" I tried to sound innocently curious. I didn't fool him.

"I'm not going to Bancroft Road," he said. "Not this morning, anyway. I'm going to the Zone. There's something I have to pick up. In fact—" He wandered away from me, into the hall where he rooted around in the depths of his jacket pocket. When he came back he held a small tub in the palm of one hand. "Would you help me out?"

He opened the tub and held it out to me. It was half full of thick beige cream. Concealer.

I got up and approached him. Dipping two fingers into the gooey substance, I paused. Samuel's tattoo stood out less than mine, thanks to the slightly darker shade of his skin and the shadow of stubble that grazed his jaw, but it was impossible to miss, now that I was looking at it. Strangely, it was something I didn't usually notice.

It was just part of his face, like the straight black eyebrows that hooded his eyes, or the scar running down his left temple. A handsome face, in a tough, masculine kind of way. A face I'd never touched. My fingers stalled, nervous of reaching out, nervous of Samuel.

I watched him watching me, raising one eyebrow questioningly as I prevaricated.

"Lizzie?"

"Sorry," I shook my head a little, then lifted my hand and smeared the make-up across his left cheek. In three deft strokes I'd hidden the Celtic knot, but I took my time to blend the edges in to the tone of Samuel's skin, enjoying the tiny bristling hairs scratching at the soft skin of my fingertips. When I'd finished he looked just like anybody else. But not like him.

"How do I look?"

"Wrong," I wrinkled my nose. "But passable," I amended, knowing that was what he was looking for.

"That'll do," he said. "Here." He put the top back on the make-up and handed it to me. "Just in case."

I watched him shrug his way into his jacket then head for the door. I was struggling not to pout, or burst into tears. What the hell was wrong with me?

"I'll call you later," he promised, pausing to give me a half smile before he disappeared through the door.

I stood there, not quite sure what to do, but then the hangover that I'd almost forgotten jumped back into the foreground, throbbing and spiking and punishing me. For lack of any better options, I went back to bed.

I don't know if it was the lingering effects of the alcohol, but I had strange dreams. I was in a street I didn't recognise, although I felt that I should, and I was on the phone. It was the mobile that Samuel had given me and his voice was coming through the speaker, but quiet, crackly. It was hard to hear what he said. But I needed to, because he was giving me directions. He was trying to lead me to a door, one of hundreds lining the road. And I had to get the right door, because behind the wrong ones loitered my demons: Alexander; Zane; Mark, with a bullet hole gaping between his eyes; the Wall; a GE officer. I couldn't see any of them, but I knew they were there – waiting to get me if I made one mistake. I was safe only so long as I listened to Samuel, followed every word. But I couldn't quite hear what he was saying. I was panicking, spinning round and round, looking at door after door...

A repetitive, shrill ringing sound broke through the dream, pulling me back to the surface. My eyes snapped open, completely disorientated. It took another few seconds to process that the noise that had rescued me from the nightmare came from the phone, trilling impatiently from the cheap pine bedside table. The phone Samuel had given me. How long had it been ringing?

"Shit!"

I erupted into action, twisting round and clawing my way across the mattress, frantic hands clumsily reaching for the little phone and sending it spinning down onto the floor instead.

"No, no, no. I'm coming, hold on!" I shouted uselessly at the phone as I dived over the side of the bed and stretched across the carpet. My scrabbling fingers finally coaxed it into my palm. I jabbed at the answer button and thrust it against my ear.

"Hello?" I was breathless, my head spinning as the blood rushed through my system.

"Where are you? What took so long?" Samuel's voice was gruff, almost annoyed.

"Sorry," I rubbed at my forehead, "I was asleep."

"Well get up." I jerked upright as I processed his tone. It was short, businesslike. As if we were on a job. "Someone's coming over to the house. I need you to let them in."

"Here?" I hissed, my throat constricting. "Who?"

"His name's Rhys. He probably won't be alone."

"Rhys Davis?" I asked.

There was a pause.

"You pay attention, don't you?"

Was that a compliment or was he scolding me?

"They'll be there in less than an hour, Lizzie."

"And when will you be here?" It was impossible to keep the nervous tremor out of my voice. If Samuel was giving me a heads up, it meant they'd be arriving before him.

"As soon as I can. There's something I have to do. Just... just let them in. And try not to say anything. Especially about Alex. All right?" I couldn't answer. I'd gone cold and clammy. I'd never met Rhys Davis, but I knew he was a man Alexander respected. And someone Alexander respected was a man to be feared.

"Lizzie?"

"Okay," I croaked.

"Good."

Samuel rang off. Still, I didn't lower the phone. I just sat there, half propped up on my knees, staring at nothing.

CHAPTER SEVENTEEN

Five minutes later, I'd given myself a shake and managed to get my head together enough to function. I got up, straightened the bed and did my best to fix my hair and my clothes in the tiny bathroom mirror. I half considered using the make-up Samuel had given me to hide the tattoo on my cheek, but Rhys Davis and his associates were Welsh, they fought for the 'cause'. I decided I'd win myself more favours just as I was: branded.

I tidied the lounge a bit too, using a ripped cloth to wipe away the worst of the dust and forcing the sash window up an inch or so to let some of the stale air out. Then I took a quick inventory of the kitchen, scanning the cupboards to see what sort of provisions Samuel kept there. Not much. As a last touch I switched on the television, turning it to a sports channel showing some football match, thinking that at least the noise from the commentators and the cheering crowd would interrupt the silence.

In truth what I was doing was filling time. Keeping my hands busy stopped me craning my neck every three seconds, hunting for signs of a terrifying stranger walking up to the front door. But when I'd done all I could think of to do, he still wasn't here, and I had to resort to sitting on the sofa, jangling my legs up and down, waiting.

Even though I was listening for it, I still jumped when three short raps rattled the glass panel of the front door. I stood up quickly and faced the hallway. I really didn't want to answer, but if Rhys was anything like Alexander, he wouldn't like to be kept waiting. I forced my feet to walk to the door and, ignoring the security chain, pulled it wide open.

A massive figure stood on the top step, blocking out most of the light from the street. He was dressed in black jeans and a bomber jacket that wouldn't quite shut over his huge barrel chest. Or maybe it was just that he wanted the gun tucked against his hip to be nice and obvious. Either way the effect was intimidating. He scowled at me, looking me up and down, assessing me. I knew at once that this wasn't Rhys Davis. This was his muscle. He had the same aggressive, on-edge alertness that Zane exuded whenever he and Alexander travelled out and about. Once he'd decided I wasn't a threat, he pushed past me and began to check the rooms of the house, both upstairs and down. And I was left face-to-face with his boss.

If I'd ever imagined what an armed robber might look like, Rhys Davis was fairly close to the mark. He was medium height, medium build, and his head was shaved down to a buzz cut, leaving a thick haze of dark-brown bristles, peppered with grey. He wore a checked shirt and black cords. His face was clean-shaven and craggy, both cheeks free of black ink. It was wreathed in lines, although I guessed he was only in his early thirties. His eyes were dark, almost black, and they were both shrewd and amused as they took me in.

"You'll be Lizzie then?"

I nodded and stood aside for him to enter, but he didn't move. I frowned, wondering what he was waiting for, but at that moment his bodyguard came clattering down the stairs.

"Clear," he grunted.

Davis nodded and stepped inside. A thin, sour-faced man that I hadn't noticed before dogged his steps.

I followed them into the living room. Davis and the thin man took the two seats on the sofa, whilst the bigger man stood by the window, twitching the net curtain aside and glaring down the street. I hovered in the doorway, wondering if they expected me to stay in the room or get out of the way. I glanced quickly back towards the door, hoping that Samuel would miraculously appear.

No one spoke. Muscle watched the street, thin man watched Davis, and Davis watched me. I let my eyes dart about the room, never resting on any of the men long enough to make what could be called eye contact.

"Can I get you anything to drink?" I offered, thinking that would allow me to escape to the kitchen for a while.

Davis smiled, although the gesture reminded me a bit of a fox.

"You can get me a cup of tea as well, Lizzie."

As well? I stared at him dumbly for a moment before it clicked. It must have been Davis who Samuel had been speaking to when I'd come downstairs earlier. I'd thought Samuel had given him my name, but maybe he'd just remembered it, assumed I was the same girl, the same nobody. I wondered if he knew I was the person who'd laid the other half of the bomb at the Welsh wall.

"Would anyone else like one?" I spoke to Davis, wary of addressing his henchmen, but the two men shook their heads. "How do you take it?" I asked him. "There's no milk. Sorry."

"Then I guess I take it black."

He winked at me, but like his smile, the action seemed off. I sensed he'd be the sort of man to grin at you even as he fired the bullet that was heading straight for your chest.

I turned on my heel and hid in the other room for the length of time it took the ancient kettle to boil and a teabag to stew in the least chipped mug. Now that I was out of the way, I heard the muted hum of conversation, but the three men were careful to keep their voices low enough that I couldn't make out any of what was said.

I made my way back into the living room just as Davis's muscle pulled out his gun and the front door opened. I froze, eyes popping open at the sight of the sleek, black weapon, but no one was paying any attention to me.

Samuel stood on the threshold, his hands held up

in surrender to the gun pointing at his heart, his eyes on Davis.

"Samuel," Rhys stood up, smiled.

He shot his bodyguard a look and the man slid the gun away.

"Rhys," Samuel stepped forward and shook Davis's outstretched hand. His smile was welcoming, but his eyes were wary. His shoulders were tense, his posture just slightly defensive. My hand shook slightly, making the tea tremble. If Samuel was nervous...

"Danny, how are you?" Samuel addressed the thin man on the sofa, who nodded once in his direction, looking bored. "No Euan?"

Davis smirked.

"No. Euan and I have had a... parting of ways."

"I see," Samuel replied carefully.

Euan was probably buried in a shallow grave somewhere. That was the only way employees left Alexander, especially those close enough to be his personal bodyguards.

"This is Gavin."

Gavin, the muscle, gave a twitch that might have been an attempt at a smile. Then he went back to watching the window.

"Is Lizzie looking after you?" Samuel asked.

Both men looked at me and I took that as my cue to offload the rapidly cooling tea before my shaking hand spilt it all over the floor.

"She's quite adorable," Davis leered as I handed it over, turning from a fox to a wolf, "Is she yours?"

I blinked and turned to Samuel, shocked.

He gave Davis a dark look, and for a moment I saw Alexander shining out from behind his eyes.

"Yes." My stomach clenched at the idea that Samuel was claiming me, the air whooshing from my lungs.

"Shame," Davis mused, his eyes lingering on me.

I blushed and shifted a little closer to Samuel.

"Lizzie," he dropped a possessive hand on the back of my neck. "I'm hungry. Go see what you can dredge out of the kitchen."

I took the hint: he wanted me out of the room. That was okay, because I was desperate to get the hell out from under Davis's stare. Increasingly he was reminding me of a less refined, older version of Alexander.

I'd noticed a couple of frozen pizzas in the bottom tray of the freezer during my earlier inventory and I dragged them out, scraping a thick layer of ice from the cardboard packaging. Goodness only knew how long they'd been in there, but I figured they'd still be edible. I fired up the cooker and stuck the two pizzas on trays, ready for the little orange light to blink off and tell me the oven was ready. Then I settled myself in one of the kitchen chairs, out of sight, but within earshot.

Why was Samuel meeting with Rhys Davis without Alexander's knowledge?

I hardly knew anything about him, except that he operated out of Cardiff and he'd been part of the successful plot to blow a hole in the Welsh wall. Cardiff – the same place Samuel had lived before he'd come to London to join his brother. Did they have a history together? I eased the chair a little closer to the half-closed door and leaned forward, listening. Samuel was talking. He was describing a job, a bombing. I frowned, trying to catch up.

"It was a high-risk operation, a big target. We knew there would be heavy security. When you attempt something like that you have to expect casualties."

What were they talking about?

"The diversion at Monmouth was your idea—"

"Alex's," Samuel corrected.

"Your idea," Davis continued, as if Samuel hadn't spoken. "And the GE seemed to know exactly what time my man would be there. Then both my men at the real target were picked up; my driver shot. And these were skilled men, men I'd sent on countless jobs. Men I valued."

The Wall. They were talking about the bombing at the Welsh border. And Davis, it seemed, was unhappy with the way it had gone. There was an implication behind his words. A suspicion. I could feel Samuel bristling through the wall.

"Our driver was shot as well."

"And your bomber?"

"No."

"How did he get away?"

"She—"

"She?" Davis pounced on the word. "You used a woman?"

There was no response to the question. When Davis spoke again, he sounded incredulous.

"Little Lizzie?"

He laughed, and I imagined that Samuel's face must have confirmed his guess.

"How the hell did that girl make it out of there when three of my men couldn't, when your man couldn't?"

"She has a talent for surviving," Samuel replied dryly.

I grimaced. That wasn't it at all. I'd survived because Samuel had given me a phone, because he'd had a strange inkling that something might go wrong. Had it been more than that? Had he known that Alexander had sold all of us to the GE?

I still didn't understand: why would he choose to save me?

I flicked my gaze back to the cooker, surprised to see the little light had cut off. I tried to stand quietly, hoping the men in the other room had forgotten all about me, but the oven door squeaked noisily as I opened it and the built-in fan whooshed in my ears as it fought to circulate the heat.

There was silence in the living room when I returned to the chair. I rested my knee on the hard wooden seat, but I didn't sit on it. The door had been swung wide open and several pairs of eyes were staring at me, only one of them friendly. The other three ranged from amused to incredulous to utterly disinterested.

"How's the food coming along?" Samuel asked.

"It's in the oven," I replied, my voice dying a little with fright.

He patted the arm of the dusty looking armchair he lounged in.

"Come and sit with me," he said.

I crossed the room self-consciously and perched awkwardly on the hard edge of the chair arm. Samuel very deliberately wound an arm around my waist. I saw Davis register the gesture.

"So you called this meeting. What is it you want?" Davis asked. He sat forward on the sofa, clasped his hands between his knees, suddenly businesslike.

Samuel took his time replying. I couldn't see his face, seated as I was, but I felt him shift his weight, heard a small sigh escape his lips.

"I want to go back to Cardiff."

Surprise lifted Davis's heavy eyebrows, but he quickly smothered the expression. I found it harder. Samuel was serious about leaving then? A dewy sweat formed at the base of my back. If he disappeared, what would happen to me?

Davis considered him shrewdly for a moment. Even the thin man, Danny, looked interested now.

"Why do you need me for that?"

"I need you to get me across the border."

"No you don't," Davis disagreed.

I twisted round so that I could sneak a look at Samuel. He was frowning.

Davis went on, "Not with your connections. Your cousins," he lifted his lips in a facsimile of a grin, "your brother. Alexander has connections everywhere.

He could get you into Wales much more easily than I could."

"I don't want to go through Alex." Samuel spoke with measured calm, as though the words had no importance, no significance, but Davis's mouth curled into a smirk.

"You mean you don't want him to know."

Samuel's silence was taken for assent. Davis laughed. Even Gavin cracked a smile. I didn't. I was frozen, immobile. I felt like I was missing something, but I couldn't catch up fast enough.

"Alexander won't like that," Davis chuckled. That was the understatement of the century. "So what has happened to make you want to break up the mighty Evans Empire?"

Samuel shrugged, his movement rubbing against the thin material of my T-shirt, tickling my skin. His fingers began absent-mindedly to trace the contour of my side. It was something Alexander would have done: a possessive gesture. I didn't feel the usual flutter of fear, though. Just a warm tingling sensation along the trail of his touch.

"We have a difference of opinion. It's time for – what did you call it? – a parting of ways."

"No," Davis smiled wolfishly. "When two brothers have a parting of ways, it's because one of them is in the ground."

"Not this time," Samuel's eyes flashed steel. "Let's just say we want to focus on different things."

Davis considered him, then gave a slight shrug and leaned back against the sofa.

"So, once you get back to Wales, what is it you plan to do?"

Samuel gave a wry smile. "I'll be looking for a job."

There was an astonished pause before Davis cackled, throwing his head back and letting the sound erupt out of his mouth.

"Let me get this right: you want me to sneak you out of England, and then employ you?"

"That's correct."

Davis's laughter died in the face of Samuel's stony expression.

"And why would I do that?" he asked, his eyes narrowing back into seriousness.

"You said yourself you lost some of your best men on the Wall job. I can fill one of those roles."

"Can you?" Davis lifted one eyebrow in question.

"You and I, we want the same thing," Samuel said earnestly. "I know you support the cause. If we want to pull Wales out of the mire, we have to fight for it. You have to fight for it." He sat back and gave Davis a level look. "You could use me."

"Forgive me, Samuel, but I'd always been under the impression that you were more of a logistics man. More planning than wires and putty and boom."

"True. But I have my own field operative who'll be coming with me."

I didn't dare look at Samuel, but my heart started pounding a mile a minute. Was he talking about me?

Davis obviously thought so.

"Little Lizzie?" he asked. "The girl with a talent for surviving. Well, maybe I don't need you. Maybe I just need her."

Samuel's grip tightened around my waist. My heart skipped a beat.

"She goes where I go."

A light gleamed in Davis's eye.

"Is that it? Is that the real reason?"

Samuel scowled. Davis looked amused.

"Alexander's not a man to share," Davis winked at Samuel, whose glower deepened.

I went from face to face, mystified.

"Hope she's worth it," Davis said, scrutinising me keenly. I looked at the floor.

Samuel was willing to walk away from everything he'd built here, walk away from Alexander, just to get me out? Davis seemed to assume that Samuel... wanted me. But I was just useful to him; his operative. His bombmaker. Wasn't I?

There was a long minute of silence. I sensed that things were being decided, could all but see the cogs whirring behind Davis's eyes.

"Look, Samuel," he leaned forward again, fixing Samuel with a piercing stare. "You're asking for a lot here. Getting you across the border is child's play, you're right. And I can always do with a man of your experience, for the cause... and other things. Especially if you're bringing your little explosives expert along. But you're planning to piss off a very dangerous man. And I happen to know for a fact," Davis paused, looking hard at me, "that Alexander's quite partial to that little plaything you intend to disappear with. So if I help you, I'm making a statement. I'm taking a side."

That sounded like no to me, but Samuel didn't look disappointed, just resigned, cautious.

"What do you want?" he asked.

Davis grinned wickedly.

"Alexander," he replied.

CHAPTER EIGHTEEN

The cheese on the pizza had cooled and congealed, but Samuel still hadn't eaten any. He sat with his head in his hands, eyes burning a hole into the carpet. On the low, ugly coffee table in front of him sat a bottle of whisky. The top was off and about a third of the liquid was gone. Without looking up, Samuel fumbled for the neck. his fingers curled around it, then lifted it to his mouth where he took another heavy swig.

I sat across the room, curled into the armchair, my legs drawn up until my chin rested on my knees, watching him.

We hadn't said a word since Davis had left half an hour earlier. The afternoon was bleeding away into evening, and Samuel's mobile had rung three times. He hadn't answered it. We both knew who it would be.

Alexander. That was Davis's price for helping Samuel: for getting him – and me – into Wales; for giving him a fresh start, a chance to focus completely on fighting for his all-important cause. Davis wanted Alexander's cold, dead body, lying in the ashes of his crumbled empire.

Because according to Davis, Alexander had grown just a bit too big for his designer boots, and though he couldn't prove it, he was sure Alexander had sold his operatives down the river on the Wall job, raking in cash or favours for the tip-off.

Samuel was ideally placed to pull the trigger. In fact, he was probably one of the only people – barring Zane, whose loyalty was absolute and unwavering – who could ever get close enough to do it.

But Alexander was his brother. His flesh and blood. Family.

When Rhys Davis had suggested it, I'd expected Samuel to refuse point-blank. I'd thought he would storm and rail and throw Davis and his entourage out. But he didn't. He listened in silence, and when Davis had finished spelling out exactly what he wanted, Samuel's face had been completely impassive. Rhys had left him to think it over.

That's when Samuel had sent me out, face lathered in make-up, for the whisky.

"What do I do, Lizzie?" Samuel asked, his voice mumbled through his hands.

I swallowed audibly, wide-eyed, shocked to be asked my opinion.

Samuel looked up when I didn't answer, green eyes piercing, jaw clenched tight. I shrugged, unwilling to voice the thoughts screaming in my head. Because I wanted Alexander gone. Dead or just far away, it didn't matter. Though I loathed him for treating me as his slave and I could not forgive him for dispatching Mark so coldly, still I owed him my life. If it were not for him, I'd be dead. I had no stomach for revenge, no desire to cause Alexander pain and suffering. I just wanted him to vanish, disappear.

But that was for my own, selfish reasons.

"I don't know," I whispered, feeling a need to fill the thick, suffocating silence.

Samuel dropped his gaze from mine. He pressed his palms together as if he were praying and rested his chin upon his fingertips.

"I'm a bad man, Lizzie," he said at last, sighing heavily.

"No you're—" I tried to disagree but Samuel flicked his stare back up to mine, shaking his head at my denial.

"Yes, I am. I've killed a lot of people, for different reasons, good and bad. I've stolen, I've damaged. I've ruined innocent lives peddling Alex's drugs. I've broken so many laws they could throw a library at me, never mind the book."

I tried to smile, but my mouth wasn't working.

"But can I kill my brother?"

I knew from the way he said it he wasn't talking to me any more. He was asking himself. Really asking.

I watched him take another slug of whisky, then another. There was just over half the bottle left now. The rest he'd chased straight from the neck. Shot after shot. It would have floored me. But, though his eyes were glazed, it didn't seem to be having much effect on Samuel.

"I don't know," he said, rubbing at his temples. "Alex is... Alex is..."

He trailed off, unable to find a phrase to describe his brother.

"A bad man?" I suggested timidly.

Samuel smirked.

"You don't know the half of it," he said. "Some of the things he's done... He deserves to die. But by me? I don't know. Christ, I don't know."

"Could you do it?" I asked.

Samuel stared at me hard for a long moment, and I realised he didn't have an answer. That surprised me. I'd thought the brothers were close. Samuel had come all the way from Cardiff to be with Alexander; and together they'd built up a business, together they'd carved out a sizeable chunk of London as their 'patch'. They spent every day together. Alexander even allowed Samuel to shorten his name, something others had died for, as I knew only too well.

But Samuel had come for a reason: to fight to bring Wales back into the United Kingdom and out of poverty and chaos. Alexander had told him he wanted that too; and maybe he did, but he wanted money and power more.

"Lizzie, you know Alex," he said. "He's a total shit. He'd kill someone as soon as look at them. He doesn't give a crap about anything or anyone, unless they can make him money. He's not who he used to be. He's not the brother I grew up with any more."

I gave a tight smile. It was hard to imagine Alexander as anything other than a cold, ruthless bastard.

"What was he like?" I asked.

"Normal." Samuel twisted his mouth to the side. "He was smart. He didn't do well at school, but he had a head for business, you know?"

I nodded.

"He had plans to set up a restaurant. He was just... normal." Samuel smiled. "I mean, don't get me wrong, he was tough as nails even then. He had a criminal record for assault by the time he was fifteen. But he was nothing like he is now. He was my big brother. Our parents, they weren't... Da was pissed more often than not and my mam, she was a shadow. It was Alex who stepped up to the mark, kept a roof over our heads, stood up to Da when he got mean. He looked after me. Now... I'm not sure there's anyone he wouldn't step on to get what he wanted. Even me."

"What are you going to do?" I asked. We'd come full circle.

Samuel ran his hand through his hair.

"Jesus, I don't know."

The phone rang. It was shrill and piercing, the volume increasing as Samuel pulled it out of his pocket, stared at it and sighed.

"It's Alex," he said.

Of course it was.

"What are you going to do?" The same words, a different question.

Samuel gave me a twisted smile and raised a finger to his lips.

"Hey," he said.

I bit my lip. Could Alexander hear the stress in his voice as easily as I could?

"Yeah, sorry. I couldn't answer. No... nothing's wrong." There was a long pause. "I'm sorry, Alex."

Samuel winced into the phone, probably imagining, as I was, the curdled look on Alexander's face as he poured his quiet outrage into Samuel's ear.

"No, I'm coming back now. Yes. Right," Samuel's eyes flashed to mine. "I understand, Alex."

Samuel hung up and stood in one decisive movement. He stared down at me. Was he swaying, or was it just the blood pumping behind my eyes? I swallowed back the question I most wanted to ask: whether the last part of his terse conversation with Alexander had been about me.

"You have to go?" I asked, my mouth automatically turning down. I sensed another prolonged period of lonely isolation.

"I have to go," Samuel agreed. "Sorry."

I glanced down at the depleted bottle of whisky.

"Are you okay to drive?" I asked quietly. That was easier than telling him I was desperate for him to stay.

"I'll have to be." He shrugged.

He crossed the room in three steps and tucked a finger under my chin, stroking along the length of my jawbone. I kept utterly still and stared at him, trying not to pout, trying not to beg him to stay. It was dark outside and through the dirty net curtains I imagined shadows lurking, just waiting for their chance when I was alone.

"But I've decided," he said, apropos of nothing.

"Decided?" I echoed, yanked temporarily away from my morbid thoughts.

His face turned serious, his eyes seeming to darken in the muted light.

"Davis can have Alex."

Then he turned and marched away from me. I watched him go, saying nothing until he had his hand on the door. Suddenly I jumped up.

"Samuel!"

He paused, twisted his head to face me.

"Why...?" I shook my head, baffled. What had changed in the last two minutes?

Bizarrely he smiled at me, an impish, almost embarrassed expression.

"Isn't it obvious?" he asked. Then he disappeared.

I puzzled over Samuel's strange remark for a while, rolling it round and round in my head, using it as a distraction from the fear I felt in the house on my own. Perhaps I was being incredibly dense, but it wasn't obvious at all. Not to me. The only conclusion that I could come to, which might conceivably make sense, I dismissed out of hand. Because it was ridiculous.

I turned the television on to stop myself tuning in to every tiny bump and creak, and to pass the time I ate cold beans straight from the can, using a fork to pick out one bean at a time, making them last. Because I knew once I got to the end of the can, there would be nothing more to do but sit on the lumpy sofa, stare blankly at the telly, twiddle my thumbs and try not to go insane waiting for Samuel. I was right at the bottom of the can, using the long tines of the fork to force the remaining beans into a smiley face, when two things happened at once: there was a knock at the door and the phone rang.

I launched myself off the sofa so fast it was like I'd been electrocuted. Then I froze, only my head moving, whipping from side to side, staring at the front door, then at the table in the kitchen where my phone sat, then to the door, back to the table. The knock came again, loud, aggressive bangs. Whoever it was sounded impatient. I half turned towards the sound - I wanted to stop the noise - but sense caught up with me before I'd even lifted my foot to take the first step. I'd no idea who was on the other side of the door. I'd closed the thick, dusty curtains over the large window so that no one would be able to see my shadow moving around the room from the street outside, but that also meant I could see nothing beyond the confines of the room. It could be anybody out there.

Whereas, I knew with almost total certainty who was on the other end of the phone.

Ignoring another three powerful raps, I darted to the kitchen table and snatched up the tiny mobile.

"Hello?" I whispered as soon as I had the thing to my ear.

"Lizzie, are you all right?" Samuel's voice was hard to hear over the roar of a car engine.

I opened my mouth, but he didn't wait for my answer. I'd been all right enough to answer the phone and what he had to say couldn't wait.

"Zane knows where you are."

"What?" But I'd mouthed the words. Terror had strangled me. My eyes swivelled of their own volition to stare at the door, just visible across the length of the living room.

"Lizzie?" Samuel's voice was terse, urgent. The engine noise dropped as he changed gears, then revved even louder than before.

"There's someone at the door," I stuttered quietly into the mouthpiece.

"Don't answer," Samuel ordered.

I nodded, too numb with panic to realise that he couldn't see me. Instead I tiptoed back into the living room, my searching fingers fumbling for the off-switch on the television and then the light switch on the wall, whilst my gaze never deviated an inch from the door handle, waiting for it to swivel on its axel, waiting for the door to open.

Even though I'd made it happen, I gasped when the room was doused in darkness. I felt blind and clumsy rather than hidden and, like a moth to a flame, my eyes were even more fixed on the tiny hallway, where a small pool of light slunk in through the frosted-glass pane.

"What's happening?" Samuel dragged me out of my trance.

I was halfway through the word 'nothing', when the

knocks came again, cutting me off. They were so loud this time that even Samuel heard them.

"What do I do?" I hissed.

"Go out the back door."

I obeyed automatically, my feet shuffling backwards so that I could keep the door in sight. My heels connected with the corner of the armchair with a low thud that barely reached my ears, but I winced like I'd sent all the china in the kitchen cupboards crashing to the floor. I edged sideways two paces, then reversed through the kitchen door.

"Are you out?" Samuel asked in my ear.

His words almost drowned out the quiet click of a door opening. I stopped mid-step, my eyes widening, the blood draining from my face. The front door was still fully closed.

Cool air tickled the back of my neck as the backdoor swung silently open just two metres behind me. One heavy foot stepped onto the linoleum, squeaking quietly, the rubber treads wet from the dewy grass. Before the second foot could join it, I ran lightly back across the living room, my thumb hanging up on Samuel, holding down the button to turn the phone off completely. If he'd spoken, if he'd even made a noise on the other end of the line, Zane would know exactly where I was.

I made it to the hallway before my intruder had time to step fully inside the kitchen and close the door. I heard the low scraping of a key turning in the lock, then another noise that could only be the sound of that same key pulling out of the door before it slipped into a pocket. One escape route closed off. For the briefest of moments I paused in the light. Did I have time to get the door open and closed before whoever it was crossed the kitchen and saw me? Maybe.

But maybe wasn't good enough. I heard the snap of a gun being cocked and the noise drove me up the stairs. At the top I went straight for the only door with a lock: the bathroom. But I didn't close the door. I needed to see, needed to hear. I needed to know what he was doing.

Something cut out the light in the hallway, plunging me into a deeper darkness. Suddenly the noise of my breathing seemed incredibly loud, like a beacon. I swallowed and concentrated on slowing down my breaths, pulling the air into my lungs quietly, calmly. Immediately my chest began to burn, demanding oxygen, but I ignored the feeling. I closed my eyes and focused on my ears. What was he doing?

I didn't have to wonder for long, because he decided to announce himself.

"I know you're there."

No whisper. No menacing growl. It was almost conversational; his harsh Northern Irish twang sounded amused. Or delighted. At last he had the go ahead to do what he'd been itching to do to me since the moment we met. I could imagine the broad grin stretched tight across Zane's face.

As his first foot trod lightly on the bottom step, I eased

myself into the bath, pressing against the wall between the patterned glass screen and the old electric shower. A drop of cold water seeped out of the showerhead as my shoulder nudged the coiling steel hose, landing in the middle of my forehead. I bit down on my tongue to quell my startled yelp, my teeth coming together so fast they drew blood.

I pressed my lips together tightly, inhaled deeply through my nose. Calming myself; preparing myself. If I could just survive Zane's cursory inspection of the bathroom I might be able to run back down the stairs when he moved on to check the two bedrooms. Surely that's where he'd expect me to be. There were much better places to hide in there: under the bed, in one of the cupboards, in the laundry basket even. I frowned, pushed my ear closer to the glass screen. I couldn't hear anything. Why wasn't he continuing up the stairs?

I got my answer a second later. The bathroom flooded with light, blazing in from the naked bulb in the hallway. I groaned, my face falling. Zane had obviously decided that I wasn't armed. He didn't need to hide from me, and light was his best weapon. It pinned me in the shadows – for as long as the shadows remained. Panicking, I glanced around the room, hunting for something I could use to defend myself, or, better yet, a way out. But there was nothing. A yellowy-white plastic toilet brush and a small blue towel. The window was no use either. The larger pane was fixed in place, and though I was small, I wasn't small enough to squeeze through the tiny section at the top that opened. I toyed with the idea of locking the door, but decided against it. Zane could easily force it open, by shooting out the lock or just giving the flimsy wooden door a good kick. And in any case, with the door locked, he'd know exactly where I was.

There was nothing for it but to wait and hope to God for an opportunity.

While I waited, I eased the phone into my jeans pocket. There was no point calling Samuel. He couldn't do anything from so far away.

Zane seemed to take forever to ascend the stairs. I couldn't tell if he was drawing it out, enjoying my fear, or if he really wasn't sure that I'd made it up to the first floor and thought I might come tearing out of the living room and head for the front door whilst his back was turned.

"Where are you hiding, you little bitch?"

I flinched. With more grace and silence than I would have thought possible, Zane had made it to the top of the stairs. He was just outside the door. I pressed my back to the tiled surface, in the hope that the wall might swallow me.

The light in the room intensified as Zane pushed the bathroom door open. I squeezed my eyes shut, clenching my hands into fists. I wanted desperately to look, to see what he was doing, but I knew if I moved so much as an inch he would see me.

"Come on, Lizzie. Come on out so that I can shoot you."

He laughed. My stomach clenched, my mouth flooding with saliva as nausea rolled up my throat.

He took a step away from the bathroom. Then another one. My eyes popped open, widened. Surely not? Painstakingly carefully I peeled myself away from the cold slipperiness of the tiles. My feet, encased in worn trainers, inched forward, taking me away from the safety of the wall. Hardly daring to breathe, I slipped out of the bath and crept to the doorway. Zane's back was just disappearing into the first bedroom. His broad shoulders drawn forward, arms locked straight out in front of him, fingers curled around his gun.

I deliberated. I was a big enough target. He could easily swing round and fire off a round, knowing he'd hit me somewhere. The shot might not kill me, but then Zane would like that. I'd be nicely incapacitated and he could take his time.

If I was going to get out, I had to really move. There wouldn't be time to pause at the front door, to fiddle with the latch. And the back was locked. But I had an idea for that. A very bad idea. I took one deep breath. Then another. Now. Now, Lizzie, now.

Zane took one more step forward, crouching down to check under the bed, and I rocketed out of the bathroom. By the time he'd heard me I was at the top of the stairs. As he straightened up and turned, I was freefalling down, concentrating my feet on nothing more than keeping moving. I didn't hear the two steps that took him back to the top of the stairs, but I did register the explosion behind me as he fired off a wildly aimed shot. The bullet slammed into the front door, passing through the space where my shoulder had been just a split second before.

I was already gone, flying through the living room.

"Lizzie!" Zane's bull-like roar followed me the way his bullet never could. Footsteps thundered after, crashing down the hallway.

Too late, Zane.

My eyes were fixed on the back door. The locked back door. The locked glass back door.

I was moving so fast there wasn't time to think about it. I'd made my decision as I'd been waiting in the bathroom. I hadn't stopped to contemplate how it was going to feel; how much it was going to hurt.

As I hit the glass I closed my eyes.

It was like running into a solid brick wall. My pumping arms, my forehead and my knees collided with an immovable barrier. The force of impact sent shock waves of pain ricocheting around my body. I was going nowhere. Then the strangest thing happened. The imaginary bricks disintegrated, fragmenting into a million pieces. The glass had shattered and I was moving again. Cold air tickled my skin as shards of glass rained down.

Was I bleeding? I couldn't tell. I just kept on running.

CHAPTER NINETEEN

"Samuel?"

I was shaking so hard it was difficult to keep the phone pressed to my ear, so I didn't hear his response.

"Samuel I need you!"

My nose was running. I wiped at it, but the back of my hand was wet, slicking a mixture of sweat and blood across my upper lip and cheek.

Laughter to my left made me start. Staring towards the noise, I hunched my shoulders and shrank further into the protective cover of the bushes. The wet leaves tickled the back of my neck, sending droplets sliding down between my shoulder blades. The laughter grew louder, turning into a giggled conversation that reached a peak just in front of me before bleeding away into the night.

I was in a park. I wasn't sure which one, I hadn't paused to look at the sign, I'd just sighed with relief after successfully vaulting the low gate, locked now that it was the middle of the night. I wasn't the only one ignoring the opening hours. It looked like people used the park as a thoroughfare, most of them on their way back from pubs and clubs. I'd jogged past a couple of homeless people stretched out on benches as well.

As soon as I reached the very depths of the wooded area I'd thrown myself off the path, and my trembling hands – shaking with a mixture of fright and cold – had dialled the only number they could; the only number I wanted.

But I was finding it hard to hold a conversation. Why wasn't he saying anything?

"Samuel?" My voice was creeping up in both volume and pitch.

"Lizzie, calm down!"

Samuel's yell exploded out of the earpiece. I realised with shock that he had been talking, I just hadn't heard him. I shut my eyes and tried to quell the panic, the shaking. My legs were quivering, the muscles of my calves close to giving out. I crouched down, putting one hand against the leaf-covered ground to steady me.

"Okay," I breathed. "Okay."

"Are you safe?"

"Yes."

I heard Samuel exhale with relief. The sound warmed a very small part of me.

"Where are you?"

"I don't know." I looked around myself. "I'm in a park."

"Which one?"

"Pass." I spurted a laugh, though there was nothing remotely funny about the situation.

I hadn't run far, maybe fifteen minutes maximum.

I doubted I was more than a mile from Samuel's little bolthole, though I didn't know the area. But I'd been too panicked to watch where my feet were going. Too busy watching behind me for Zane and his shock of hair that glowed even in the darkness. I'd lost him after hurtling through an allotment, the maze of fences and sheds providing me with cover, and tiny gaps that I could squeeze through but he couldn't.

"Lizzie, you need to find me a road. I'm in the area, but I can't drive past the house. It's not safe."

I nodded grimly into the phone, forgetting that Samuel couldn't see me. I didn't want to move from my hiding place, curled up in the bushes. But Samuel would never find me in here. Cautiously, I slunk forward, my legs tight and burning. I emerged onto the path just in front of a pair of girls weaving their way along, arm in arm, high heels clicking against the pebbles inlaid into the compacted dirt. They both started, then one of them lifted her finger to point at me.

"Oh my God, it's a... it's a..."

I turned and ran away from them before the word 'Celt' could form in the girl's mouth and she started screaming for the GE. Emerging from the shrouded cover of the trees lining the edge of the park was trickier. The streetlights seemed blinding after the cosseting darkness of the park, and cars prowled up and down along a nameless street. I slipped out of the gate warily, hunting for pedestrians and brake lights. No sign of Zane, though that meant little. Although he was huge, he had the ability to become invisible when he needed to – just like me.

Directly across from me was a T-junction. I headed over, knowing there would likely be street signs where the two roads intersected. I had to kick away at some trailing ivy, but I found what I was looking for. Aware that the longer I loitered on the street, the more chance I had of bumping into people I didn't want to see – Zane, the GE, Alexander, the police – I trotted back over to the relative safety of the park before I called Samuel.

He answered immediately.

"I'm opposite Hemmingway and Richmond Avenue," I whispered into the receiver.

"Right, okay. I'm just around the corner. Give me a minute. I'm driving a Punto."

In an effort to quell the frantic pounding of my heart as it rattled around in my ribcage, I started to count as I waited. Exactly thirty seconds later, an old-style Punto glided into view. It drew to a halt on the corner of Richmond Avenue. My phone vibrated in my hand.

"I'm here," Samuel said, confirming what I already knew.

The tight knot in my stomach didn't disappear until I'd flung the passenger door open and found myself face-to-face with Samuel. Then it melted, thawed away by a sudden rush of warmth.

"Get in," he ordered, glancing nervously around him.

I smiled at him as I slid inside, giddy with relief and adrenaline, but Samuel didn't so much as look at me. His hands were both clenched into tight fists, one wrapped around the steering wheel, the other clutching the gear-stick so hard I thought the moulded plastic might shatter. His jaw was clamped shut, a muscle twitching in his cheek, right at the heart of his tattoo. I'd never seen him as tense as this, and as soon as I had the door closed – before I'd even had a chance to search for my seat belt – he took off, tyres screeching.

His obvious discomfort and anxiety couldn't pop my bubble of happiness, however. He'd come for me. Again. He'd saved me. Again. He was here with me. Again. As we drove in silence through strange streets, I was content just to stare at him and be thankful.

Eventually Samuel felt the heat of my stare. Either that, or as we drove further from Islington, on towards nowhere, he became more relaxed and dared to look somewhere other than the road in front and behind.

He turned, glanced at me, then back through the windscreen, flicking on the indicator and making a sharp right turn. Back on the straight, he looked at me again, this time with a mouth twitching in amusement.

"What?" he asked. Then he frowned at me, staring, his gaze raking over my face, my arms, flicking his eyes to the road only when he absolutely had to. "Lizzie, you're hurt!"

"Am I?" I was startled. I hadn't been aware of any pain, just the stiffness and cramps from my all-out sprint away from Zane.

"You're covered in blood!" Samuel insisted.

Shocked, I reached up to touch my face. It was wet.

When I pulled my hand away, my fingers were smeared red.

"I ran through the glass in the back door," I told him tonelessly.

Odd, I'd almost forgotten about that. Running from Zane. Hiding out in the park, getting into Samuel's car had pushed it from my mind. Now that I was thinking about it, I was aware of a burning sensation all over my skin. How many cuts did I have? I didn't want to think about it.

"Jesus, Lizzie," Samuel was still staring at me, his expression shocked, concerned.

I grimaced and flushed. How bad did I look?

"We need to get you sorted," he said, turning back to the road at last. "Some of those might need stitches."

"Okay," I bit my lip, looked away from him, out of the windscreen where the tarmac was disappearing under his wheels. "Samuel, where are we going?"

I heard him sigh; out of the corner of my eye, saw him reach up and rub at his jaw, at the fledgling beard that grew there.

"I don't know," he admitted. "We need somewhere to lay low for a bit, to work out what the hell we're going to do."

I nodded, though in truth all I cared about was that he'd started his sentence with 'we'. I was curious, though...

"Samuel, what happened? How did Zane find me, how did he know about the house? What's happening at Bancroft Road? Does... does Alexander know...?" I let my question tail off, knowing Samuel would realise it covered several things.

Did Alexander know I'd been hiding out there?

Did he know it was Samuel's house?

Did he know that Samuel had been helping me?

Did he know that Samuel had met secretly with Davis?

Did he know that his brother was thinking of murdering him?

I was pretty sure the answer would be no to the final one, but the rest, the rest – I had no idea.

Samuel sighed again.

"Alex knows... something," he said, dealing with the most important question first. "He didn't want me to leave tonight. That's why I couldn't beat Zane to the house; I had to be sure I wasn't being followed."

Samuel looked at me apologetically and I tried to mould my face into a smile, though it was more of a grimace.

"And Zane?"

"I don't know how the hell he knew. I was there when he told Alex about the place, said one of his scouts had seen you. It was bull, but I couldn't call him on it. Not in front of my brother. If he saw you, though, he saw me."

I scowled in the darkness. That didn't make any sense.

"Why wouldn't Zane have told on you? Surely he'd love an excuse to drop you in it?"

Samuel shrugged and nodded at the same time.

"I don't know. He's slippery as an eel. Maybe he's biding his time, waiting for the right moment. Whatever he's doing, it might be a good idea if I stay the hell away from Bancroft Road for a while."

"But... won't that make Alexander suspicious?"

"It will, but if Zane's got enough rope to hang me with, I can't just go back there and wait for him to spring a noose around my neck."

Though I could see the consternation in Samuel's eyes, his words were a comfort to me. If he couldn't go back to Alexander's, maybe he'd stay with me. It was only in his company that I actually felt safe.

We stopped at a red light, and Samuel used the opportunity to rifle through his jeans pocket for his phone. I watched him curiously as he typed in a number. He held it up to his ear, steering and changing gears one-handed as the light changed back to green.

"Rhys?"

My eyes widened. He was calling Davis?

"How are you?" He listened for a moment, then, "Look, I've been considering your offer. I think..." he paused, twitched his eyes towards me for the space of a heartbeat, "I think I might be able to make it work. Can we meet up, talk about it?"

He listened intently. So did I, but I could only make out a tinny murmur, no words.

"How about right now?" Another pause. "No, no I'll come to you."

His face grim, Samuel hung up the phone and tossed it onto the dashboard. At the next junction he did a U-turn, taking us back into the heart of the city.

Rhys Davis's London base was in Wandsworth, across the river. We drove beyond the residential streets into an industrial area that seemed to be mostly warehouses and garages. At the end of a long, winding street littered with potholes, we came to a large brick structure that looked as if it had once been a factory. At first glance, it could almost have been disused, but in the darkness the technology gave it away: winking CCTV cameras perched on every corner, a sleek electronic entry system installed beside a flaking garage door. Samuel coasted the Punto to a stop so that the driver's window was level with the console. He rolled the window down a few inches and reached out one arm to push the largest button.

"Yes?" A robotic voice answered immediately.

"I'm here to see Rhys," Samuel said, dropping his voice to a whisper that barely seemed to fill the car never mind reach the speaker on the intercom. He seemed edgy again, his head jerking side to side as he searched the deserted forecourt and peered at the street behind us.

"And you are?"

"It's Samuel."

The garage door opened noiselessly – another clue that this building wasn't what it seemed – and Samuel eased the car forward. I looked around, intrigued. We were in a large underground car park, maybe the size of a swimming pool. There were a variety of vehicles parked in neatly ordered rows: vans, clunkers, and a shiny sports car gleaming under harsh fluorescents.

As soon as the garage door glided shut, someone moved out of the shadows towards us. Samuel indicated that I should get out, then threw his door open and stood to greet the man. It was Danny, the skinny one who'd come with Rhys to Samuel's Islington house. He didn't bother to look at me, but shook Samuel's hand.

"Mr Davis is dealing with a situation just now. He says you can wait, if you want?" Danny spoke with a musical lilt that was not the Welsh accent I'd expected, but something much more northern.

Samuel nodded grimly. "We'll wait." He glanced at me. "Have you got a medical room?"

For the first time, Danny gave me a fleeting look, his eyes flitting across my face.

"Aye, I'll show you where it is." He turned on his heel and began to march away. After shooting me a reassuring smile, Samuel followed suit and I hurried in his wake.

We walked up a staircase. The sterile look of the steel and white-washed walls was ruined by the graffiti proclaiming Celtic rights and threatening the English government. The Welsh dragon featured prominently in the designs, along with the swirls of a Celtic knot that matched the circle on my cheek. At the top of the stairs Danny pushed through a heavy door and led us into a corridor that looked like something out of an office block or a school. Halfway down he stopped and gestured to a doorway on his right.

"You should find everything you need in here," he said. "I'll send someone over to take you to Rhys when you're done. If he's finished with his... little problem."

He gave us a smile completely devoid of warmth and disappeared. Samuel guided me into the room, almost a carbon copy of the mini-hospital in the basement at Bancroft Road. Rhys's men didn't want to put their trust in the government hospitals either, it seemed. A wise move, given that, on admittance, every patient was automatically swabbed and checked against the DNA database.

"Sit up on the bed," Samuel instructed, moving over to a wall of cupboards and raking through their contents. "Take your jacket off, too."

I did as he asked, shivering slightly in the chill of the room. Now that we were underneath the bright lights, I could see the myriad cuts and slices all over my hands and forearms. Blood oozed from a cut in the knee of my jeans, too. I shuddered to think how many holes I'd ripped in my face.

"This is going to sting," Samuel warned, approaching me with a wad of gauze, dampened in some mysterious blue substance.

I watched apprehensively as he came towards me. He started with my hands, wiping away the blood, sweat and dirt. Underneath, my skin was bright pink, the gashes a deep red. Most of them had stopped bleeding and though they nipped in protest, it was more of a dull burning. I'd had much worse. I bit down on my tongue, determined not to complain, as he worked his way steadily up my arm. From there he moved onto my leg, ripping the denim further so that he could reach in and clean my wounds. Despite myself, I sucked in a breath as he daubed the inside of my knee just where it joined the bottom of my thigh.

"Sorry," he murmured. He dropped the gauze and felt around the area with his fingers. His touch was warm against my skin, tickling me and drawing a blush to my cheeks, but then he found what had sent a spike of pain up my leg before, and I tried to jerk myself away from him. "Hold still," he ordered, clamping down on my thigh with his free hand. I winced as he fiddled around the spot, then slowly he drew out a long, thin slither of glass. At least an inch of it was slick with blood. "Dammit, that's really bleeding. Here," he handed the gauze to me. "Hold this against it. Keep it firm."

I took the bloodstained rag from him and reached inside my jeans. I found where the blood was leaking out, warm and wet, and pressed the scrunched-up ball tight against it, squeezing my knees together to increase the pressure.

Samuel returned to me with fresh gauze and started sponging at my neck and face. He stepped in closer this time, leaning forward until he was just a foot away. I dropped my head, a little embarrassed and uncomfortable at the close contact, but that meant he couldn't see the cuts he was trying to clean, so he hooked one finger under my chin and pushed my face gently back up. I flashed him a self-conscious half smile, but Samuel didn't seem to notice. He just continued wiping at the blood, working his way across my forehead and down my temple.

Unable to look into his eyes, I directed my gaze firmly at Samuel's jaw, his mouth. His cheeks were slightly hollowed, his chin blessed with a deep cleft behind a rough centimetre of coarse, dark brown beard. It was his lips that captivated me. Samuel's lips were so like his brother's I felt as though I'd kissed them before. But they were relaxed now, slightly parted, and seemed constantly on the verge of breaking into a smile; I rarely saw Alexander's like that. I wondered, for a wild moment, if I pressed them to mine, whether they'd feel the same.

The thought was both intriguing and discomfiting, so I ripped my eyes back up to Samuel's. It was easier than I thought it'd be to watch him, because he wasn't looking into my eyes, but was concentrating on my cheek, gently rubbing at the skin to lift the dried-in blood.

"Okay," he said at last, dropping his arm. "I've done the best I can. You've a few deep ones, but nothing that needs stitches."

"How do I look?" I asked, mindful of the fact that I had to face Rhys Davis and all his cronies.

Samuel lifted up half his face into a smile.

"Beautiful," he told me.

I blinked. That hadn't been the sort of response I'd been expecting at all. My cheeks, already burning from whatever chemical Samuel had applied, felt as though they might spontaneously combust. Aside from the occasional, "Good job", Samuel almost never paid me a compliment. And nobody had ever told me that I was beautiful.

"I..." I kept opening and closing my mouth, but nothing more came out. I stopped trying when Samuel took a finger and placed it against my lips.

We gazed at each other: him, serious and intense; me, wary but mesmerised. My mouth was suddenly dry, my heart thumping erratically. I'd seen that look often enough in his brother's face, I knew what it meant. Normally, when I was caught like this, I'd be fighting to keep the fear, aversion and self-loathing from my face. Now...

I waited.

Suddenly Samuel moved forward, closed the space between us. His hand grabbed the back of my neck, pulled me into him, but although I raised my face expectantly, it was my forehead that he pressed to his mouth. He held me there for a moment, then dropped his hold and turned away from me.

"Let's go," he spoke to the doorway, giving me half a second to get myself together and shuffle off the bed before he started to walk away. I was glad – I needed that moment to mask my disappointment. And my shock at my reaction.

CHAPTER TWENTY

We were met outside the room by a skinny, scruffy looking young man whose surly expression told us clearly that he thought this assignment was beneath him. He stalked off as soon as Samuel turned into the corridor, scuffing along like a sulky teenager. Only the gun peeking out of the waistband of his trousers made him seem anything more than a child.

Rhys was apparently ready for us, because we were led up yet another flight of stairs, this time to the very top, to a short landing and large, closed, wooden double doors. The atmosphere was different up here, not least because of the plush carpet beneath our feet. A pair of bodyguards stood, alert, between ourselves and the door: Rhys had to be on the other side. They made no move to stop our escort as he stepped right up to the solid oak panelling and hammered several times. He didn't wait for anyone to answer, but turned on his heel and traipsed away without so much as a nod in our direction.

I swallowed and looked nervously to Samuel. He

seemed relaxed, his expression calm, eyes straight ahead. Unconsciously I edged a little closer to him, tucking myself in behind the safety of his broad shoulders. He noticed the movement, reaching down to rub the back of my hand for a second. He pulled his fingers away as the door swung open, but I still felt the comforting heat of his touch. I covered it with my other hand, trying to hold onto it, like it was my courage. I didn't like Rhys Davis.

Another bodyguard stood on the other side of the door. One that I recognised. Gavin. He didn't speak but, on seeing us, pulled the door open wider, allowing us room to enter, to squeeze past his vast frame.

Alexander's private office was all sleek chrome and pristine white. It was hi-tech, minimalist, modern – full of angles and clean lines. It reflected his personality: he liked things ordered, controlled. Clockwork. Rhys's office was totally different. Dark. Muted yellow lights glowed around the room from lamps and sconces attached to the walls. But heavy deep red wallpaper sucked up the light, along with a plush charcoal grey carpet. The furniture, all huge and antique looking, was in shades of mahogany and ebony. I half expected to see Rhys in an armchair by the fire, stroking a cat like some cartoon villain, but instead he sat to the left, in the grandest of several chairs around a gleaming oval table.

"Samuel," he called, standing up to greet us. "Sorry I had to keep you waiting. There was some... housekeeping to be done."

He twitched a smile, eyes glinting like coals. I knew his

idea of 'housekeeping' was the sort of thing that went on in the special rooms in Alexander's basement, the rooms with drains in the floor. I glanced at Gavin. Whenever Zane had an opportunity to dish out some violence, he glowed with a smug air of satisfaction. The bodyguard's face was blank, impassive. Rhys's on the other hand...

I eyed him apprehensively. Unlike Alexander, Rhys looked like the type who enjoyed getting his hands dirty from time to time.

"It's not a problem," Samuel smiled tightly.

Rhys turned his attention to me. Instinctively I tried to shrink into myself, hunching my shoulders.

"I see you brought little Lizzie," he gave me a wink. I blanched, swallowed, tried my best to keep the grimace off my face.

"She goes where I go," Samuel repeated, putting his hand possessively around the back of my neck.

"I see," Rhys mused. He looked thoughtful for a moment, then he smiled. His fox smile. "So you wanted to talk," he held out his arm, indicated the table. "Let's talk."

I wasn't sure I'd be welcome at the meeting – Alexander would have banished me from the room or, more likely, to his bed; another chance to humiliate me, to put me in my place – but Samuel, with his hand on my neck, guided me forward. He pushed me into a chair, then sat beside me, directly opposite Davis. Gavin came and stood discreetly behind his boss; Danny settled himself in between Samuel and Rhys, right in my line of vision.

Samuel leaned his elbows on the table, propped his

fingers into a steeple and rested his chin on them. He sighed.

"Alex."

Rhys gave an evil grin.

"Alexander."

"I can give you his body, but not the man."

"What's the difference?" Rhys raised one eyebrow scathingly.

"My conscience," Samuel's tone was sour. "I have no intention of handing him over to you so that you can exact whatever payback you have planned, slowly and painfully. He is my brother."

"Ha!" Rhys guffawed, showing off a row of blackened, misshapen teeth. "So that's how far the bonds of brotherly love extend?"

He waited, and, after a long moment, Samuel nodded.

"And what if that is not enough?"

Samuel stood. "Then we don't have a deal."

We were leaving? I half raised myself, but stopped when Rhys waved Samuel back down.

"Don't be hasty!" he said, his expression placating. Slowly, Samuel eased himself back into his chair. I dropped into my seat, my eyes swivelling between both men.

"Dead, or not at all," Samuel repeated.

"Dead's not enough. No, wait!" He held up his hand, because Samuel's expression had curdled and once again he looked set to leave. "You take out Alexander and what's to stop his second in command from jumping into the role?"

"I'm his second in command," Samuel said firmly.

Rhys made a dismissive noise. "You won't be, not for much longer. I'm talking about the Irish boy. What's he called?" Rhys clicked his fingers impatiently.

"Zane."

A shiver ran through me at the mention of his name. Zane. Ambitious, ruthless and a thug. The thought of him in charge of the Evans empire was perhaps even more frightening than it was already, with Alexander at the helm. Perhaps.

"That's right, Zane. He needs to go as well."

I allowed myself a brief smile as Samuel shrugged. Zane's demise I would not mourn.

"That's not a problem."

"And I want fanfare."

"What?" Samuel's eyebrows drew forward in confusion. As did mine. Fanfare?

"A song and dance. A spectacle. I don't just want the two of them to disappear into obscurity."

"You want the world to know they're dead?"

Rhys smiled. "Just London will do. And if London knows, the word will trickle out."

"Why?"

Rhys didn't answer the question, but took a deep slug from the tumbler he'd been toying with, half full of golden liquid. He sniffed.

"I'm starting to like London," he said, looking around the room as if it were the city. "I always thought it was a cesspit of scum housing the dregs of society, but the place is growing on me. It's amazing the things you can lay your hands on here, stuff that Cardiff hasn't seen in over a year. And the dodgy deals that are going on. Seems to me that with the right leverage, the right currency, you can get into bed with anyone. Even the prime minister. I can make a difference here. And if not, I can definitely make some money."

He smiled at Samuel. I looked from man to man, totally bemused. Clearly I was missing something, because Samuel's eyes had narrowed in understanding.

"So you want to step into Alex's shoes and—"

"No!" Rhys slammed his hand down on the table. A sharp crack reverberated around the room. "I stand in nobody's shoes. Especially not Alexander Evans's."

He curled his lip in disgust.

"Okay," Samuel held one hand up in surrender. "You want to expand your business ventures in London, shall we say?"

"You could put it like that."

"And with Alex out of the way there'd be a nice little opening. But you don't need a big commotion to achieve that."

"Your brother," Rhys leaned forward; I leaned back but Samuel didn't budge an inch, "is responsible for the deaths of several of my operatives."

"That's not it," Samuel smiled wryly. I held my breath, my tongue trapped between my teeth. I wasn't at all sure that it was wise to disagree with Rhys Davis. "You want revenge for that, take out some of his men—"

"Like Lizzie?" Danny interrupted.

"No," Samuel paused to shoot him a look. "Lizzie's mine now, not Alex's." I squirmed in my seat with a perverse mixture of pleasure and embarrassment; I didn't want to feature in this discussion. Samuel turned back to Rhys. "You want to send a message, get yourself a reputation. Get the right people's attention."

Rhys spread his hands in mock supplication. "We all have our pride, Samuel. But the reason behind it doesn't matter. It's what I want."

Samuel sat back in his chair, thinking.

"What sort of... spectacle did you have in mind?"

"Oh, I don't know," Rhys slanted his eyes left, towards me. "Something explosive."

There wasn't much to say after that. Without a word from his boss, Danny stood and motioned that we should leave. Once again, Samuel claimed me, clamping an arm firmly on my shoulder this time. I was glad. The meeting had been tense and my legs were shaking. Without his firm grip I wasn't convinced I'd still be standing.

Back outside the double doors, Danny halted.

"Are you planning to head back to Bancroft Road?"

I turned to Samuel, my heart beginning to hammer once again. Was he? I couldn't go there. Not if I wanted to stay alive. Samuel's protection would mean nothing face-to-face with Alexander.

"No," Samuel shook his head.

"You need somewhere to..." Danny's eyes flickered

to my face then away again. "Lay low?"

Samuel, too, glanced at me.

"Might be an idea."

Danny nodded and started to walk, jogging lightly down the stairs. We followed.

"There's a hotel on the other side of the industrial estate. It's called The Scelter." Samuel snorted. "It's one of our... investments. The night manager's called Rutlin. Tell him I sent you. He'll sort you out."

Samuel grunted in thanks. We walked the rest of the way in silence, Danny escorting us until we reached the underground garage.

"Come by again tomorrow," he said. "We'll talk some more."

Samuel nodded curtly and stalked away, leaving me standing there awkwardly for half a second before I darted after him.

"Are we going to the hotel," I asked quietly as he started the Punto.

"It's as good a place as any," Samuel replied. "And probably safer than most. Alex has connections in places even I don't know about. At least if we're in one of Davis's premises we should be away from prying eyes. Should be," he repeated.

The Scelter turned out to be a modest-looking building that seemed to skirt the line between hotel and bed and breakfast. I doubted it had more than fifteen rooms, but it boasted a wide reception, manned even at this late time of night. Samuel approached the desk cautiously, with me a step behind him. I saw the night porter clock both of our cheeks, but he didn't seem fazed by the sight of two marked Celts wandering in after midnight.

"We're looking for a room," Samuel told him. "Danny sent us."

Understanding dawned at once. The man nodded and turned to a row of keys on a board behind him. There was no mention of ID cards or payment.

"This is our best room," he said, turning round and sliding a key attached to a large circular fob across the counter. "Top floor."

Samuel grabbed the key and turned away from the porter, without pausing to offer a thank you. Shrugging out of his jacket, he made his way across the small foyer to the stairwell entrance – no lift – and held the door open for me. I blushed, I wasn't used to courtesy, and scuttled through.

We found our room at the top of four flights. It was the only one on that level. Samuel jangled the key in the lock, then pushed his way in. The room was large, housing a wide bed, probably a kingsize, a desk and two winged chairs. There was a dresser and a pair of bedside tables, and a half-closed door through which I caught a glimpse of white porcelain. A large flat-screen television hung on the wall.

"You want to take a shower?" Samuel asked, pointing towards the bathroom.

I blanched, instantly insecure – did I smell? – but then it dawned on me that he probably just wanted some privacy. His phone was already in his hand. Who did he want to call?

I nodded silently and, kicking off my shoes, padded across the carpet into the tiled expanse of the en suite.

"I'll call down, see if I can get pyjamas or something for you," he said, just as I was shutting the door. "Give you a chance to wash your stuff."

I smiled gratefully, cheered by the prospect of fresh underwear and the opportunity to clean the blood stains from my hoodie and jeans.

The shower was heavenly. I stayed under the scalding spray for an age, long after I'd washed off the remains of dirt and blood, letting the spikes of hot water sting my scalp and shoulders, making my cuts and grazes throb. I tried not to use up all the cheap hotel shower gel and shampoo, aware that I had to share, but it calmed me down to concentrate on something so ordinary as soaping, massaging the aches out of my muscles. Eventually I shut off the water, folding myself inside a huge white towel. I vacillated over whether to put my grubby clothes back on, uncomfortable at the thought of entering the bedroom half dressed, but they really were grimy and I hoped Samuel would have made good on his promise to get me something to change into.

Unsure, I picked up my top and sniffed at it. That decided me. I dropped it back to the floor and kicked it – along with the rest of my clothes – into a corner. Then I wrapped the towel around myself as firmly as I could, clamping my elbow to my side to hold it securely, and tiptoed hesitantly out of the door.

I was right to keep quiet. Samuel was on the phone, his back to me as he stared out of the window. He was talking softly, his tone persuasive, pacifying. I wandered over tentatively, straining my ears to catch the words tumbling quietly out of his mouth. Stealthy as I was, Samuel heard my progress. He spun on the spot, his finger rushing up to cover his lips. I understood at once: he was talking to Alexander.

I watched him as he listened intently to whatever Alexander was saying, trying to read his expression, but he kept it veiled. Instead he moved silently over to the bed, picked up a bundle of material and handed it to me. Clothes. He gestured that I should return to the bathroom and I left him and the conversation, pulling the door noiselessly closed. In the steam-filled bathroom I investigated my new outfit. It looked like gym-wear: navy jogging bottoms and a grey T-shirt. Dropping the towel, I pulled them on. They were probably made for a child. The T-shirt was tight against my tiny frame and the trousers stopped halfway up my calves, but they did the job. Aware that I wasn't wanted in the bedroom, I filled up the sink and used the remains of the soap to scrub my clothes. I couldn't do much about my jeans, but I daubed at the worst spots, sponging off the clods of dirt and diluting the bloodstains until they were just darkened smears. Once I'd rung them out as best I could, I hung my clothes on the heated towel rail to dry. Then I tiptoed back out.

My skulking was unnecessary. Samuel was done with his phone calls and was lying across the length of the bed, his arms above him, hands making a pillow for his head.

"Sorry," he said, grimacing at my outfit, "That was the best they could do."

"It's fine," I smiled timidly. Aware that I was bra-less, I crossed my arms over my chest. Not that there was much to hide, but I felt exposed. After a few seconds, however, Samuel returned his gaze to the television. Crossing the room I saw the news was on, though the sound was turned down almost all the way.

"That was Alexander?" I asked.

"Yup."

"And...?" I perched on the end of the bed, gnawing on my lip, eyeing Samuel apprehensively.

He shrugged.

"He's not very pleased with me." Samuel's voice was toneless, but there was an undercurrent in his words.

I stared at him, waiting for more, but he pressed his lips together, eyes fixed on the screen.

"Where did you tell him you were?"

"Natalie's."

I kept my face devoid of emotion, mimicking Samuel's mask, but the mention of his 'girlfriend' unsettled me.

"But I don't think he believed me," Samuel went on, oblivious to my agitation.

"Will he check?"

Samuel blew out a breath.

"Might do. But unless he bursts into her flat to see for himself, there's no way he can really be sure."

That sounded like something Alexander would do, but I swallowed the thought, because there was a more pressing question hovering on my tongue.

"Did he say anything about me?"

Samuel swivelled his head to stare at me. I watched him lick his lips.

"No."

My smile was rueful. Liar.

"How's your leg?" he asked, changing the subject.

"What?"

"Your leg? The cut?"

"Oh." I lifted one shoulder in a nonchalant shrug. I'd all but forgotten about my minor injuries. "It's not bleeding."

"Good," Samuel smiled, warm and reassuring, then he drew one arm out and held it aloft. "Come here."

I blinked. What? But there was nothing ambiguous about the gesture. Feeling suddenly nervous and clumsy, I scooted across the bed and lay down beside him. Samuel put a hand behind my head and pulled me gently onto his chest. Then he wrapped his arm around my shoulders and turned his attention back to the television. His fingers absentmindedly toyed with my hair, still damp from the shower.

I focused on controlling my breathing. This was totally new territory for me. Alexander wanted me, or wanted me the hell out of his way. There was no cuddling, no closeness. I'd become accustomed to his constant blowing hot and cold, accepting that it was my body, not me, that he was after. With Samuel, I was lost. What was he after? What did he expect? The words he'd said in Rhys Davis's office came floating back to me: Lizzie's mine now, not Alexander's.

I waited, waited for his hand to drift down from my hair to my body; waited for him to take charge, take control, take me. But he didn't. He just continued to gaze at the news reporter, turning up the volume so that her clipped English accent filled the room. I tried to listen to the story, but it was hard to hear what she was saying over the pounding of my pulse in my ears.

"Lizzie," Samuel's voice was a whisper in my ear. It sent a frisson of electricity running through me. "Have a rummage in the mini bar. See what you can find to drink."

Relieved – and reluctant – to slide out of his embrace, I wriggled away and squatted down in front of a small cabinet that, when I pulled open the door, revealed itself to be a fridge. I stared at the collection of miniatures. Normally Samuel had whisky, because that's what Alexander drank. But it wasn't what he liked. Not unless he was trying to drink himself into oblivion. Rooting around at the back, I found some Bacardi, then darkened it with cola.

"Oh, good girl," Samuel winked at me, smiling gratefully when I handed him the tumbler. He looked down at my empty hand. "Where's yours?"

"Oh... I," I blushed. "You didn't say."

Samuel gave me a look that was almost pitying, then smiled. "Get yourself a drink, angel."

This time when I returned to the fridge, I was confused, bewildered. I drank whisky too, again because that's what Alexander had. But what did I like? The sad truth was, I didn't know. Just because the bottle was pretty, I pulled out some Tia Maria. It pooled, dark treacle, into the bottom of my glass. I wasn't sure what to dilute it with, so I took it back to the bed still neat, shining and thick.

Samuel had shifted position in my absence, pulling himself up to sit against the headboard.

"Cheers," he smiled, holding his glass out to mine.

I clinked the edge of my tumbler against his and took a sip. The alcohol made me shudder slightly, but after the initial tang of bitterness, it felt smooth and velvety, like cold coffee. It was nice.

"How does it feel?" Samuel asked me suddenly.

"How does what feel?"

"Being free. What's it like?"

I thought about it for a moment. Nothing came.

"Am I free?"

"Well," Samuel gave me a slight shrug, a ghost of a smirk. "You're away from Alex. That must count for something."

"Yeah," I tried to smile at him, took another sip. "I've swapped one Evans brother for another."

His face immediately clouded over, eyes changing from amused to black in an instant.

"Don't say that. Lizzie, it's nothing like that."

His voice was harsh and I was instantly abashed.

"I didn't mean—"

I didn't get any further.

"I'm nothing like Alex, Lizzie. Nothing. You're safe with me. I promise. I'll look after you."

"I know," I smiled, but Samuel kept frowning, his mouth turned down in dissatisfaction.

"Lizzie—"

Without thinking, I put my hand up to his mouth, pressed my fingers to his mouth to stop his words.

"I'm sorry," I said.

His lips didn't feel like Alexander's. They were softer, gentler.

I didn't know where that thought came from. I shook my head infinitesimally, trying to chase it away. Abruptly self-conscious, I tried to draw my hand back, but Samuel gripped my wrist, held me there. I watched as he skimmed his mouth over my hand, kissing my palm then each of my fingertips.

"Lizzie?" he whispered.

It took me a moment to find my voice.

"Yes?"

"Are you afraid of me?"

What a question. I determined to go with the truth.

"Sometimes."

He smiled wryly.

"Now?"

Truth again?

"Yes and no."

The smile morphed into a grin that was swiftly hidden as his kisses trailed downwards to the inside of my wrist. I started to tremble.

"Explain."

I cleared my throat quietly, but the words still seemed to stick.

"I'm scared of what you expect from me. But," I swallowed "But I... I... want it."

He stopped caressing the soft, smooth skin of my forearm with his mouth, fixed me with sparkling green eyes.

"Want what?"

Pause. I dropped my eyes, unable to hold his stare.

"You."

Furiously embarrassed, I let my gaze burn into my knee. I refused to look up, not sure what I would see. I heard the soft rustle of fabric shifting as Samuel moved position on the bed. Seconds later, his warm hand curled around my jaw, tugged with gentle but irresistible pressure until I yielded and let him turn my face towards him. I still didn't look up, this time staring down at the way his T-shirt rumpled against the curve of his half-seated body. Suddenly my view was obscured and there was pressure against my mouth, my lips.

Samuel kissed me with lips that were identical to his brother's. But there, all similarity ended.

CHAPTER TWENTY-ONE

Lying on my back, I stared up at the ceiling. The room was silent except for the quiet breathing of the man beside me. Trailing my eyes down, I gazed at the arm flung across my stomach. The lean muscles rippled in undulating curves beneath the skin, which was patterned with tattoos and several scars. Though Samuel's face was relaxed in deep slumber, his thumb continued to rub soothing circles across my abdomen.

I wondered, if I'd been able to look up into a mirror right then, what expression I'd have seen on my face. Pleasure maybe, or contentment? Certainly something I'd never seen gracing my features before, and I'd have liked to know what it looked like. But maybe I didn't want to see, because there was still a tight knot in my stomach that Samuel's touch, his kisses, hadn't been able to melt away, and I knew it would be visible in my eyes, spoiling the look.

Beside me, Samuel stirred. I turned to watch him, but he didn't open his eyes. Instead he yawned and shifted on the bed. His arm slid further across my stomach, gripped my waist, and he pulled me to him. He kissed my temple, then settled down on his pillow, drifted back to sleep. I let myself smile before I shut my eyes, revelled in the warmth, the safety. The peace.

I was woken by the smell of fresh coffee wafting across the room. When I opened my eyes again the bed was empty. I lifted my head, gazed about me. The room was empty, too. Immediately my mouth went dry, my chest tightened. Where was he?

"Samuel?" I called his name like I thought he'd jump out from behind the dresser or under the bed.

I swallowed, trying to force my heart back down my throat. Don't panic, I thought. He wouldn't leave you. He promised.

But I was panicking. I scuttled out from under the heavy duvet, stopping for a frantic second to pull my borrowed clothes back on, and stared around me, eyes wide with fright. Then I saw his shoes, kicked haphazardly across the floor, his jacket draped over one of the matching winged chairs. I focused on the supple black leather, willed my breathing to slow down. Gradually reason returned, and it was then I heard the soft sound of rain coming from the bathroom. He was taking a shower.

A little giddy with relief, I laughed at myself. Trying to shake away the last wisps of fear, I moved towards the coffee machine, thinking I'd get Samuel a drink ready for when he came out of the shower. I stopped dead after two paces. Two mugs were already laid out on the counter: one half drunk, the other full to the brim and steaming gently. Hesitantly I picked up the full cup, took a sip. It was exactly how I liked it: no milk, but loads of sugar.

I had to put it back down, because my hand was shaking and tears were smarting in my eyes. What the hell was wrong with me? It was just that I wasn't used to anyone taking care of me. It was just that... he'd noticed how I took my coffee.

How pathetic.

I started to make the bed when I heard Samuel shut the water off, so that I wouldn't have to look at him. I was feeling a bit nervous, a bit awkward. I wasn't sure what to say or how to act. My relationship with Alexander was completely dysfunctional, but it was all I knew. I didn't know how to play any other role.

"Leave that," Samuel told me, erupting from the bathroom with a billow of steam.

"I don't mind," I mumbled, focusing intently on tucking the edges of the sheets into perfect square corners.

A hand reached down and covered mine.

"Leave it."

"Okay," I pulled my hand away, straightened up. Faced him.

Rather than make eye contact, I stared forward, my gaze level with his chest. He hadn't put his shirt on and his torso was still damp, the soft black hairs coating sinewy muscles. Below his right clavicle was a roaring red dragon that I'd never noticed before. He was much thinner than Alexander, much more natural. Wiry, but strong.

Attractive. That didn't help my awkwardness.

"Your clothes are dry," he told me. "You've got time for a quick shower, then I want to get out of here."

"Are we going back to Rhys's?" I asked.

Samuel nodded, the gesture just registering on the periphery of my vision.

"Yeah. There are some details to be ironed out, some gear I'm going to need."

This time the factory was much more active. Men loitered in the forecourt, talking, but they eyed us warily as Samuel drove in slowly through the gate. The garage was open, but a man wearing a bomber jacket and a mean expression stepped out to block our path. Samuel wound down the window and looked out. As soon as he saw who it was, the security guard moved aside and waved us through.

Danny raised a hand casually to us as we parked and climbed out of the car. He was standing by the rear of a rusting Mini, speaking quietly to a bedraggled-looking man with a beard and ponytail. Danny was pointing into the boot and he seemed angry. I stood on my tiptoes to try and see in, but all I caught was a flash of black plastic before Danny turned away from the lackey and caught me watching. Instantly I pretended I'd lost all interest, turning round to stare into the empty back seat of the Punto.

"Samuel," Danny ignored me, greeting Samuel as if I didn't exist.

"Danny. Where's Rhys?"

"Mr Davis isn't here." There was a moment's awkward pause. "But he's given me specific instructions to arrange whatever you need."

Danny smiled thinly. Samuel's expression had curdled, but he nodded in acceptance.

"Let's go somewhere where we can talk, shall we?" Danny reached out and put his hand on Samuel's shoulder, guiding him towards a discreet door at the back of the garage, clearly excluding me. Not unfamiliar with this sort of treatment, I stayed where I was, watching Samuel disappear with a mixture of fear and resignation. Aware of the casual grouping of unpleasant men around me, I edged backwards towards the Punto, my searching fingers reaching for the door handle. I'd just lock myself in until he came back, crank the window open a touch and mope like a discarded puppy.

But at the doorway Samuel broke away from Danny's steering hand, his eyes hunting for me. He caught sight of me loitering nervously by the car.

"Lizzie!" he waved me over and I bounded across to him, relieved. Danny looked disgruntled, but I didn't care. I was just thankful that he wasn't going to abandon me here, in a place where it was just possible someone would recognise me.

This time we didn't go up to Davis's plush office, but wound our way through a long, windowless hallway. We passed by various doors, some open, some firmly locked. Through one doorway I caught a glimpse of an ominous cement floor with an inlaid drain, and in another, a series of unmarked boxes. It was the equivalent of Alexander's basement. Danny, I was starting to realise, was something like Zane. This was his domain, his slice of the Davis empire. Subconsciously, I sped up so that I was all but tripping over Samuel's heels. Without turning round, Samuel reached back and grabbed my arm, pulling me in close to his side. He looked completely at ease, but I couldn't help wondering how he really felt.

"So," Danny walked to the very end of the corridor and threw open the final door to reveal a medium-sized office. "Have a seat."

This space was much more clinical than the office upstairs. There was a cheap desk, a few filing cabinets, a large, impregnable-looking safe and yet more boxes. The walls were white, the only light a fluorescent strip that flashed intermittently, irritating my eyes. Danny didn't share the luxury that his boss enjoyed. That pleased me for some bizarre reason.

There was only one chair across from Danny's desk, but a faded beige futon was tucked in along the back wall between two bookshelves that towered with files and office storage boxes. I folded myself unobtrusively onto the futon whilst Samuel settled himself down to face Danny.

"Right," Danny leaned forward on the desk, fixed Samuel with a piercing look. "Tell me what you need."

"No," Samuel leaned back in the chair, his posture relaxed. I could just see the slight lift of his cheek as he smiled serenely at Davis's number two. "You tell me how you're going to get Lizzie and me out of London. Then, if I'm satisfied, I'll tell you how we can deal with my brother."

I waited, my breath held, as Danny stared at Samuel and Samuel gazed calmly back at him. I sensed a power struggle playing out in the air between the two men: how much Samuel wanted out of England versus how much Rhys Davis wanted Alexander dead.

Danny folded first.

"Boat," he said, dropping eye contact and fumbling down at a drawer in the desk. He drew out a map and slapped it on the table with poor grace. "It's an operation we've run a hundred times. There's an old port a few miles out of the city." He jabbed his finger at the paper but I was too low down to see where he was pointing. "A boat will pick you up there, then skirt the channel and dock at Aberystwyth."

Samuel made a disgusted noise.

"I want to go back to Cardiff, not bloody Aberystwyth."

"We'll give you a car," Danny replied, deliberately not reacting to Samuel's scathing tone. "And an escort," he added, because Samuel had opened his mouth to interrupt him again.

I raised my eyebrows. An escort? Why would we need that?

I'd just have to wonder, though, because whilst I was in the room, I wasn't 'at' the meeting, and after all my time with Alexander I knew my place here.

"And then?"

"Mr Davis will set you up with a flat, and we can discuss what sort of a role there might be for you and your operative" – a glance at me – "with us."

"That'll be a conversation I'll want to have with Rhys," Samuel replied.

Danny smiled wryly and dipped his head, acknowledging the slight.

"Of course. But after things in London have been... resolved."

I felt the atmosphere in the room change. Samuel adjusted himself in the chair, sitting up straighter. I could see the tension in the way he held his shoulders. Subconsciously I curled myself into a tighter ball, reacting to the stress.

"London," Samuel prompted. He folded his arms, muscles bulging. I could see he didn't want to take the lead. Danny eyed him shrewdly, picking up on his caginess.

"Mr Davis would like to know what your plans are..." Danny tailed off, opening his hands to indicate that Samuel should fill the silence.

He did, with a derisive snort.

"I'm sure he would," he said.

Danny waited.

I listened to Samuel sigh. I was interested, too. What did Samuel have in mind?

"He wants something explosive, I can give him something explosive."

"A spectacle," Danny reminded him.

"I can guarantee him five minutes on the news."

Danny smiled. "Mr Davis would like that."

There was another snort from Samuel, but Danny's expression didn't change.

"I'll need certain items to make this work."

"Name them." Danny was definitely paying attention now.

"A car. Nondescript and empty, keys in the ignition, parked far enough away from the headquarters to stay under the radar."

"Fine." Danny nodded.

"And I'll need a gun—"

I blinked, confused. Samuel had a gun. It was heavy and mean looking. It had spent the night on the dresser, muzzle pointing at us.

"Anything specific?"

"Something light, accurate. With a silencer. Decent power but low trigger poundage."

"I see," Danny paused. "And who's this for?"

An understanding passed between the two men. A second later it found its way to me. I gasped, earning a filthy look from Danny and a warning glance from Samuel. I bit my lip, abashed.

"What else?"

"C4, enough to split into four blocks. Two half-kilo slabs will probably be enough. And timers. Nothing fancy, no radio controls or anything. Plus enough copper wire to set up four devices."

"And?"

Samuel spread his arms out, palms upturned.

"That's it."

"No muscle? Back up?"

"No." Samuel shook his head slowly. "The best way to do this is stealth. Go storming in and you'll end up in a bloodbath that won't be finished by the time the GE turn up. We go in – quietly – plant, then disappear. Get far enough to make sure your little... commotion happens."

"Okay. When do you need it for?"

Samuel checked his watch.

"About six o'clock."

Danny barked out a laugh but Samuel wasn't smiling.

"You can't be serious?" Danny looked at Samuel incredulously. He just shrugged. "There's no way! I mean, the car and the gun I can do. But it takes time to lay my hands on C4. I haven't just got some lying around out back!"

"Yes, you have."

This time Samuel did smile and I watched Danny's eyes narrow to snakelike slits.

"Samuel—"

"I want to be on a boat, on my way to Cardiff, by the time the sun comes up tomorrow. That's the deal, Danny."

"Why the rush?" Danny demanded.

Samuel took the time to look behind him, to where I was watching the exchange with my mouth gaping open.

"It's not safe to stay any longer than that. If I'm getting out, it's now."

Danny sighed heavily and ran his fingers through his thinning hair. He looked ruffled.

"I'll see what I can do."

Samuel stood up, kicked his chair back.

"Call me when you have everything ready."

Then he turned to me and jerked his head, indicating that we were leaving.

A little surprised at the abrupt end to the meeting, I was clumsy as I stumbled to my feet. Danny, too, seemed taken aback. He didn't rise out of his chair, but watched us disappear from his office, with a grim expression on his face.

While we waited for Danny to get Samuel's list of gear together, we went back to the hotel, The Scelter, to the same room we'd had the night before. There Samuel finally revealed his plan to me.

It was terrifying. He planned to return to Bancroft Road. He'd been away so much over the last few days that not to do so would arouse suspicion, and he worried that, if he didn't reappear, Alexander or Zane would go out looking for him rather than being where we needed them to be: in bed. Then, once all was quiet, he wanted to bring me in with my bombs. I'd sneak around like a cat burglar, planting the four explosive devices at strategic points around the building. I was having palpitations just at the thought of that, but Samuel had one more bombshell for me.

"There can't be any mistakes," he told me, wrapping the warmth of his hand around mine, squeezing to emphasise the importance of his words. "We need to be absolutely sure that Alex and Zane don't walk away from this."

I was no expert, but I was fairly sure that the amount of C4 we were talking about would be sufficient to take care of that problem. It wasn't enough for Samuel, though.

"Have you ever fired a gun before?" he asked me quietly.

"No," I shook my head, eyes wide. Though I'd been surrounded by violence, and guns were an everyday part of my world, I'd never held one. Alexander had seen to that. Not that he thought I would do anything foolish like fire it. No, it was just another way to control me, to keep me under the thumb.

"It's fairly straightforward," he reached behind him, taking out his own gun. I wanted to look down at it, but Samuel held my stare, green eyes burning into mine. He turned my hand over so that it was palm up and I felt the cool weight of moulded steel drop into the cradle of my fingers. "Do you know how to hold it?"

I shook my head again, still watching him, and saw as his face softened into a reassuring smile.

"It's easy. Here, stand up."

I did as he said and he pulled me across the room to stand in front of a full-length mirror.

"Okay, curl your hand around it like this," he bent my fingers to his will, wrapping three of them around the grip, hooking one over the trigger.

"Won't it..." My voice was tremulous, my arm shaking.

I didn't like the feel of the thing in my hands.

"Go off?" he smiled at me in the mirror. "No, the safety's on."

"Oh." I shifted my feet, a bit embarrassed.

"Stand like this," he kicked at my left foot until I moved it. "That's it, shoulder width apart. You need to balance or you won't aim right. Now—" He moved over a bit so that he was standing right behind me. He was broad enough to wrap both arms easily around mine. "Hold it in both hands, your second one will keep it steady. Then you pull down on this – don't touch the trigger now though!" he warned me, drawing what I now realised was the safety catch down with his thumb. "And then all you have to do is squeeze."

He knocked my finger off the trigger – just in case – but let my hands go so that I was holding it myself, pointing at my own reflection. I stared forward, taking in the image. I looked frightening – and frightened. I could see the slight vibration in my shoulders where my muscles were shaking.

"It's heavy!" I complained.

Samuel smiled and reached for the gun, easily taking it out of my grip and sliding the safety catch back on before dropping it with a clatter on the sideboard.

"This is heavy. What I've asked Danny for is much lighter, but you'll still feel the kick when you pull the trigger."

I sat down slowly on the bed, rubbing my clammy hands against the duvet cover.

"And why do I need one?"

"I told you, Lizzie. We've got to be totally sure. If I have to take out the man on the door, and then Alex and Zane, the alarm'll be raised long before you've had a chance to lay the bombs."

I felt the blood drain from my face.

"You want me to shoot someone?"

Samuel sat down beside me on the bed, close enough for me to feel the heat of his skin.

"You're going to have to plant one of the devices in Alex's office anyway," he told me gently.

"Alexander?" I squeaked.

"Would you rather it was Zane? I'll give you the choice Lizzie."

I thought about that. I supposed it didn't matter either way. And I could understand why Samuel would prefer not to have to murder his brother whilst he slept, defenceless and unaware. Besides, I'd never been in Zane's flat before, didn't know the layout.

But the thought of having to get that close to Alexander...

"Why can't we just let the bombs do the job?" I asked quietly.

"We have to be sure. Alex will never let us go, either of us, while there's still a breath in his body. I don't want to spend the rest of my life looking over my shoulder." He sighed. "I hate asking this of you, sweetheart. But if we want a clean getaway, this is what we have to do. Can you?"

I stared up at him silently.

"Yes," I whispered finally. We were doing all this to get away. We needed to get away. "Okay. I can do it." I swallowed, made my voice stronger. "Alexander. I'll take Alexander."

"Are you sure?"

After a long moment, I nodded. Samuel sensed my fear – it must have been clear on my face – and lifted a hand, pressed it to my cheek.

"It'll be fine," he promised me. "It will be."

Then he drew me forward and pressed his mouth to mine.

CHAPTER TWENTY-TWO

The phone call came at seven minutes to six. We were lounging across the bed. The television was on, but we weren't really watching it. Instead I was lying on my back, my arms by my sides, my fingers clenched into fists. My cheeks were on fire, and I was keeping my legs still by crossing and uncrossing my feet, holding down one ankle, then the other.

"You," said Samuel, dropping his head to land a kiss on the soft skin of my inner elbow, "need to start letting people be nice to you."

He hadn't let me move for the past twenty minutes. We'd been eating dinner, a takeaway pizza brought up to us by the receptionist. Afterwards I'd tried to clean up, binning the grease-smeared box and washing down the stained dresser top with a tissue and soap. Then, without being asked, I'd gone to fix Samuel a drink from the mini bar. That's when he'd got annoyed.

"Will you stop running around after me?"

I paused, a small bottle of Bacardi clutched in my hand.

"But—"

"I mean it. Put that down. Come here."

I obeyed and he pulled me onto the bed, forcing me down until I was lying there, staring up at him.

"Samuel, I—"

He put a finger to my lips, and smiled.

"No. It's your turn to be looked after."

Then he pinned me down with his eyes and his smile, and ran his fingers over every inch of my skin until I was tingling all over.

When the phone rang, I was both relieved and frustrated. I went to sit up, startled by the noise, but Samuel pinned me with one elbow and reached across to the bedside table where his phone rested. The screen lit up and the phone vibrated gently against the satin smoothness of the wood. He glanced quickly at the caller ID before hitting one of the buttons on the tiny keypad and raising it to his ear.

"Danny. Have you got everything?"

I couldn't hear what Danny said on the other end of the line, but I saw Samuel's eyes narrow with grim satisfaction.

"No. No, bring it here."

A second later he hung up, stared solemnly at me.

"It's time?" I whispered.

Samuel opened his mouth to answer, but the phone in his hand lit up again and started to buzz. A second later the shrill ringing sounded out, tinny, the speaker half-muffled by his hand. Samuel looked down at the caller

ID again, then up at me. I didn't have to ask who it was.

He curled off the bed and turned his back on me, facing the window, before he answered.

"Yeah?" I could hear the tension layering his voice, making it gruffer, harsh.

Cautiously I eased off the bed, stepped silently up behind him. Though I loathed the idea of hearing his voice, I wanted to know what Alexander was saying. I took another pace, then another. A loose floorboard creaked under my foot. I froze as Samuel whirled around. He raised an eyebrow at me, exactly as his brother might have done, but grabbed me round the shoulder and drew me into his chest, tucking my head under his jaw. From there, I could just about hear what Alexander said.

"...need you here. For the past damned week I've hardly seen hide nor hair of you. I'm getting tired of it, Samuel."

I was right: I didn't want to hear his voice. It was soft, lilting, gentle. Deadly. It struck a bolt of terror and hate shooting down into the pit of my belly. My mouth filled with saliva as nausea rolled in my gut, and I had to swallow against the urge to vomit.

"I told you, I've been with Natalie," Samuel's reply was soothing, apologetic. And guilt-laden.

Alexander heard it at once.

"Don't lie to me!" Not a shout, but clipped and cold. A warning.

"Alex, it's the truth—"

Samuel's denial was half-hearted.

"No, it's not. I swear to God, Samuel, if you weren't my brother..." He let that hang there, the threat floating out of the handset and coiling round Samuel's throat. My throat. Suddenly it was hard to breath. "I want you here. Now. No excuses."

Samuel swallowed quietly. His grip on me tightened.

"Give me an hour."

We left the hotel as soon as one of Davis's men arrived with a discreet black rucksack that was heavy despite its lack of bulk. Samuel drove whilst I sat in the back seat, trying to assemble four small timer-circuits and splice two bricks of cold grey putty into identical chunks. They were simple devices, but the ruts and bumps of the road made my hands clumsy and I knew there was no room to make mistakes. It was dangerous, too. Samuel had to skirt the edges of the Central Zone and in the late rush hour the traffic was sluggish. All we needed was for the wrong person to look in at the wrong moment, for a GE patrol to take an interest in us, and Bancroft Road would be the least of our worries.

But Samuel hadn't wanted to keep Alexander waiting.

By the time we reached the outskirts of Stepney, I had assembled four blocks roughly half the size of a brick and wired up my triggers. All that was left now was to put two and two together and make fire. I didn't want to do that until the last minute, though. Just in case.

"Right," Samuel pulled into a deserted street lined with closed-down industrial units and turned to face me. His eyes raked over the jumble of wires and C4, now organised and set up. "Are you ready for this, Lizzie?"

I nodded and started stuffing everything back into the bag, my expression disgruntled. I did not like Samuel's plan for getting me back inside the walls of Bancroft Road, although admittedly I didn't have any better ideas.

He got out of the car and lifted his seat forward so that I could crawl clumsily out of the back. Then he walked to the rear of the vehicle and, reluctantly, I followed. He opened the boot, stepped back and looked at me sympathetically.

"I'm sorry," he offered. "I'll try and drive as smoothly as possible."

I made a face, though it wasn't the bumps and jerking of the vehicle that I was worried about. It was the tightness of the space. It was the darkness. It was the thought that something could happen to Samuel and I'd be left in there, trapped, with a kilo of explosives.

But Samuel knew all of these arguments. And he was sorry, I could see that. There simply wasn't another option.

With a sigh, I dropped the bag into the boot and shimmied onto the bumper. I swung one leg in, then the other. Giving Samuel one last, frightened glance, I lowered myself gently into the space. He waited until I was as comfortable as I could ever be in there, then closed the door on me. The click of the latch was loud in my ears, locking me in.

"Can you hear me? Are you okay in there?"

I wasn't. I was already fighting the urge to hyperventilate. Samuel had promised me I wouldn't suffocate, but the darkness was thick and penetrating. It was exactly how I imagined it would feel to be buried alive.

"Yes," I called back, but there was no volume to my voice and I don't know if he heard me.

I could hear him, however, though it was muffled, like listening underwater. I listened to the sound of his footsteps walking away from me, then the door opening and the slam as he pulled it shut. I winced as the noise echoed around the closed-in boot. A few seconds later he started the car, and the ground beneath me began to vibrate. I tried to wriggle about, hoping to find a more comfortable position, but the floor of the boot was rock hard and no matter how I lay, something dug into me painfully. I gritted my teeth, hoping the journey wouldn't last long; at the same time, hoping it would last for ever. Because when it was over, I would be much closer to Alexander than I wanted to be.

I tried to keep a map in my head, following Samuel's progress as he turned left and right, weaving his way across Stepney, but I got lost after a series of confusing turns where it felt as if we were doubling back, and I was sure that wasn't right. I gave up after that, and concentrated on trying to keep myself steady and prevent the equipment in my bag from being jostled or bashed. I knew Samuel would be doing his best, but I was aching after less than a mile and I was sure my skin was going to be covered in yet more bruises. A small price to pay, though, if that was the worst that would come my way over the next few hours.

Though I'd lost my bearings, I knew exactly when we hit Bancroft Road. The car wheels trembled as they traversed the short section of uneven patterned brickwork, put in years before as a traffic-calming measure. Now it was Alexander's malevolent aura that kept vehicles away from this street, unless they'd good cause to be there. I held my breath as the car slowed, picturing Samuel pausing in front of the main door, then accelerating gently away. A pair of sharp left-hand turns pushed me to the back of the boot as he manoeuvred into the alleyway and then down into the garages. Unlike Davis's set-up, they were open to the sky, although an eight-foot wall kept out prying eyes.

A series of clicks followed as Samuel yanked up the handbrake, then came the sound of the car door opening and closing, a slight movement of the car as Samuel's weight eased off the seat. Then nothing. I heard him call out to someone, take one, two, three steps. I waited, breath held. Samuel?

At last came the noise I was listening for: the simultaneous beep as he engaged the remote central locking and disengaged the boot lock in the same swift motion. The door in front of me opened a crack, just enough for a slither of yellow light to glimmer around the outline, not enough for anyone to notice. If they weren't looking too closely...

I hadn't been short of air in my moving coffin,

but when the fresh air found its way in, little puffs of cold, fragranced with the heavy scent of car oil and petrol, I drank it in gratefully

Now I just had to wait it out.

On a normal night, I could expect Alexander to join me in his giant bed anywhere between midnight and 1 a.m. Zane was a night owl, but Samuel – having his flat on the same floor as the Irishman – reliably informed me that he, too, was usually asleep not long after one. We'd agreed – or rather, Samuel had told me – that 2 a.m. was the best time to strike. It gave them plenty of opportunity to drift into unconsciousness, and it was late enough that the muscle on the door should be starting to get sleepy, starting to lose focus. Which gave me... I checked my watch in the darkness, grateful for the luminous dials. Quarter past seven. I blew out a breath. That gave me a long time.

A long, long time. Midnight came and went. I tried to sleep, thinking it would pass the time, but I was too uncomfortable and too nervous of missing my moment, of waking up to the blinking light of morning with some very nasty people standing over me. I spent a lot of time unsuccessfully trying not to think. I wondered what my life would have been like if I'd just stayed up in Scotland after I'd been branded. Short, was the likely answer. I thought about the long months I'd spent as Alexander's little pet, trying to focus on the times he'd made me feel sick at myself, useless, worthless, doing my best not to remember the inexplicable times when he'd been kind and gentle, sweet even. I thought of Mark, poor Mark, and wondered what had happened to him, whether Alexander had left him to be found. I tried to convince myself that was all Alexander's fault, another sin to lay at his feet, another reason to pull the trigger on him. I didn't succeed there, either. I knew where the blame lay, but there wasn't room for it in the boot with me; I'd suffocate under the weight of the guilt if I let myself really feel it.

I didn't think about Samuel, because I was too scared to hope...

Just before one, I started to get nervous. Though it was freezing in the car, my clothes were sticking to me, sweat gathering at the base of my back and under my arms. My hands were clammy, moistening up no matter how many times I rubbed them agitatedly against the thighs of my jeans. I was nauseous, too, though that might have been from hunger as the hours ticked further away from the slice and a half of pizza I'd eaten mid-afternoon. I was spared the torment of thirst: my mouth kept filling with saliva that I'd nowhere to spit away.

I was tempted to lift the boot a little, to peek up at the rear of the building. I knew I'd be able to see Alexander's office, and I could probably work out which window belonged to Zane, too. I'd be able to see if the lights were off yet, maybe get a head start on my task. I fingered the phone in my pocket, wondering whether to call Samuel and suggest it. I was eager to get this over with as quickly as possible, not least because every muscle in my body was cramped and aching. But I decided against it. Samuel had a plan. If I went meddling, messed it up... And in any case, there was no guarantee, if I rang Samuel, that he'd be the one to answer.

In fact I'd no guarantee Alexander hadn't already done something to punish his brother that would ruin the whole operation before we'd even started.

That thought sent another wave of palpitations through my already panicked system.

At two exactly, I silently eased open the hatchback door of the Punto, making a gap just big enough for me to squeeze myself through. I crawled out, then dropped to the ground, pulling my rucksack with me. As soon as I felt the rough gravel of the uneven parking area, I scuttled backwards under the car and peered about me. It was empty. That didn't mean anything, though. There were cameras covering almost every inch of the place. Almost every inch. Scooting further back, I felt my foot connect with the wall. I squirmed around until I was lying flat alongside it, the bumper just above my head; then slowly, carefully, cautiously, I stood up.

My back to the wall, I scanned the area. My first assessment had been right: deserted. As long as I stayed here, tucked right up against the brickwork, I should be able to sidle over to the building. Out of sight. Out of the ever-alert lens of Alexander's state-of-the-art security system. At least, that's what Samuel had assured me. Still, I was on tenterhooks, waiting for the shout or the blaze of the floodlights that would tell me I'd been discovered.

I should have had more faith in Samuel. All was still quiet when I touched both hands to the back wall of Alexander's headquarters. I took a moment to inhale a few breaths of relief, then adjusted the rucksack, making sure it was firmly in place over both my shoulders. Then I took three steps to the left and wrapped my hands around the thick iron guttering that twisted, snakelike, across the wall. Taking a firm hold, I lifted one shoe onto the crumbling stone, tried to feel the grip. I was going to have to move fast here; as soon as I was more than six feet off the ground, I'd be easily visible. I looked up before I started, postponing the inevitable, and saw the open window three floors up. Samuel's flat.

The sight was reassuring: Samuel had made it this far in the plan, at least. That put paid to the very worst of my fears.

But I was still standing there. Still motionless. Still scared.

"Go!" I told myself, louder than I meant to.

Bracing my arms, I took my second foot of the ground and started to climb.

It was hard going, and twice I nearly fell, but eventually I made it, my fingertips curling around the lip of the windowsill. One more heave and I'd be up.

Out of nowhere, two hands grabbed my arms, hauled at me. I yelped, startled, as I was twisted around and tugged backwards through the opening, and a hand clamped down over my mouth. That frightened me. I clawed at the hand, struggled, tried to wriggle my way free. A second arm wound round my middle, squeezed me so tight the air was forced from my lungs. I tried to scream, but the hand was so big it covered my nose as well as my mouth, and I didn't have the breath. I didn't stop fighting, though, knowing I'd resist until unconsciousness claimed me.

"Lizzie, stop! Stop!"

I stopped. At once the hands let me go and I whirled to face Samuel.

"You scared me!" I accused in a low voice.

"Sorry," Samuel pulled me into a hug and spoke low into my ear. "When you squealed I was worried someone would hear you."

I let myself luxuriate in the warmth of his embrace, but all too soon Samuel released me.

"Are you ready for this?" he asked me, stroking my cheeks with both his hands. He let his right hand linger, running around the curves of my tattoo.

Feeling the heat of his scrutiny, I nodded. Though I wasn't sure at all.

"What did Alexander say?" I asked, stalling.

Samuel smiled, seeing straight through me.

"Doesn't matter."

"But—"

He shook his head, shushing me.

"In less than an hour, nothing Alex's said or done will matter," he told me. He had a point. "You remember what you have to do?"

I chewed on my lip.

"Yeah."

"Tell me."

I smiled. Typical, thorough Samuel. Everything checked and double-checked.

"Four charges: here, office, ground floor storeroom, basement. Five minutes apart, ten minutes from the final charge. So that's twenty-five minutes here, twenty in the office, fifteen on the ground."

"And?" Samuel raised an eyebrow.

I looked at him, confused. That was it. Everything.

"I..." Oh. "One in the chest, one in the head."

Samuel watched me steadily.

"Are you going to be able to do this, Lizzie?"

I took a deep breath. Thought once again of all the ways Alexander had ever hurt me, humiliated me. Pushed down the memories of when I'd caught a glimpse of another, softer side of him; what I owed him.

"Yeah. Yeah, I can do it."

"Good. Where's the gun?"

He looked down at my empty hands like he expected it to miraculously appear.

"In my bag."

Samuel huffed a laugh, but there was no humour in it.

"In your bag? Lizzie, it's not going to do any damned good in there!"

"Oh, right."

Feeling clumsy and foolish, I slipped the rucksack off my shoulders and rooted through it until my fingers curled around cold metal. I drew out the small semi-automatic, the sleek length of silencer already attached to the muzzle.

"You remember how to use it?" Samuel asked me.

I nodded, though I didn't lift my head to meet his gaze. I couldn't take my eyes off the weapon. Was I really going to do this?

I thought about what might happen if I didn't, and felt steely resolution solidify in my gut.

"Lizzie?" I raised my head. Samuel gave me a shifty smile. "Waiting on you..."

Wordless, I dropped to my knees. I pulled out one of the heavy blocks of C4 and a timer-circuit. With hands that shook only slightly, I finished turning the components into something that would give Davis his spectacle, then held it out to Samuel.

"Where do you want this?"

He looked around the flat. A last look, I realised. He wouldn't be coming back here. If all went to plan, there'd be nothing to come back to.

"Will it fit under the sofa?"

As he spoke he checked the large handgun he held in his hand. I looked up and my breath caught as I realised how... dangerous he looked. Though he was a saint next to his brother, I knew his hands had ended the lives of more people than I wanted to know about, sometimes for good reasons, sometimes not. Which was this?

At that moment it hit home to me just what it was costing Samuel to go through with this.

And that he was doing it, in large part, for me.

"Yeah." I thrust the contraption under the leather two-seater until it was all but out of sight, then smiled at him as I sat back on my heels, trying to put all of my gratitude into the gesture.

"Okay, should I set the timer?"

Samuel checked his watch.

"Do it."

I reached down and flicked the switch. A tiny red LED light immediately began flashing. It seemed an anti-climax after all the tension, and Samuel and I grinned at each other for the briefest of moments. Our expressions didn't last long, though. I lifted myself to my feet and, sombre faced, we turned towards the door.

Samuel moved first, crossing the room, then pausing with his hand on the doorknob.

"I'll deal with Zane, then head down to the front door," he whispered. "Downstairs should be clear by the time you're done in Alex's."

He didn't give me time to respond, but swung the door open and gestured me out. He waited until I'd started to ghost down the stairs before he crossed the tiny landing, his thoughts on nothing but what lay within the flat opposite.

CHAPTER TWENTY-THREE

Though my legs felt as if they didn't belong to me, I somehow made it down the short flight of stairs. The clock was ticking and I didn't have time for fear, but I had to stop for a second. My stomach was churning so much I thought I was going to throw up. Every nerve in my body was screaming at me to run in the opposite direction, to get the hell away from there. Instead, I reached forward, grabbed the doorknob, and turned.

It swung open silently. Inside was absolutely black. Alexander couldn't sleep if there was so much as a chink of light sneaking its way under the blackout blinds he'd had installed over the huge windows. Though the hall was dark, I knew shafts of grey would penetrate, giving me away if Alexander was anything but deeply asleep, so I slipped quickly inside and pulled the door shut behind me.

Breathe, I told myself. Just breathe. The darkness was disorientating, but I knew from experience that my eyes would adjust, that there would be just enough grey to turn the room into a world of shadows. Right now, though, I was blind.

I shut my eyes – they were useless anyway – and mapped out the room in my head. With trembling legs I took four steps forward, then turned away from the direction of the bed, heading towards the office. Behind the safety of the desk I hunkered down. Stuffed the gun in the waistband of my jeans, right at the centre of my back, and, with incredible caution, one tooth at a time, unzipped the rucksack. It seemed like the sound filled the room, but there was nothing else I could do. When at last I'd made a big enough hole to slide my hand in, and the C4 out, I paused, listened. Was that Alexander's breathing I could hear, closer than it should be? Was I just imagining it?

Was that cold sweat on the back of my neck, or the cool metal of Alexander's gun?

I shook my head, trying to chase away my irrational thoughts before I lost it entirely. I put the second device together, checked my watch. I was early, by a minute. Time to wait? That didn't appeal. But I heard a voice inside my head, a strange mixture of Alexander and Samuel: *Clockwork.*

I made myself hide there as sixty seconds ticked by. Then I set the bomb, let the tiny LED bathe me in bloody light. It seemed fitting. Sliding it behind a filing cabinet to hide the glow, I turned my attention to my next... task.

Alexander.

I'd been right, I could see enough now to make out the large rectangle of the pool table, the reflective surfaces of the kitchenette. The curves of the sofas, the sharp edges of the coffee table. And there, at the far end of the room, the bed. A step at a time, I glided closer. I didn't need to look down, to check my path. My feet knew this route like my lungs knew how to breathe, although they weren't doing a very good job of it right now. Each gasp was too loud, too shallow.

I was maybe ten feet from the bed before my eyes could turn the white blob into sheets, a headboard, a mattress. For the first time I wondered if Alexander would be alone. A flashback to the buxom blonde, the girl who'd never had the chance to come down from her high. That stopped me, stopped me cold. It was one thing to put a bullet in Alexander – I'd reason enough for that. But if he wasn't alone, I'd have to pull the trigger twice, because surely – silencer or no – no one could sleep through a murder? On the other hand, if the bullet didn't kill them, the bomb would do it anyway.

I hadn't planned to murder anyone, not in cold blood. I wasn't sure there was room for that on my conscience.

My eyes raked over the surface of the bed, struggling to turn it into identifiable shapes. Slowly, painfully slowly, the picture materialised: a dark circle that could only be a head of closely cropped brown hair; the width of muscular shoulders just beneath it, arms splayed, holding onto an empty bed. I sighed with relief. He was alone.

Reaching back, I grabbed the gun, pulled it round. Though lighter than Samuel's, it still felt heavy. Maybe it was the weight of guilt, of responsibility. Still, I lifted it, planting my feet like Samuel had told me. My thumb pushed down the safety, my finger found the trigger.

Do it, Lizzie. Pull. Squeeze. Tug. Do it.

Five seconds passed. Then five more. I just stood there. The gun got heavier and heavier, but I didn't lower it. And I didn't shoot.

I wasn't in the room. I was back in time, almost a year. Slumped in the passenger seat of a car, crying my eyes out but not making a sound, because the man sitting beside me had shut me up, not with his hand, but with a single look.

"Name?" he'd asked, voice barely carrying over the silent purr of an expensive car.

"Lizzie," I'd croaked.

He turned the force of his eyes on me for a heartbeat and my blood froze.

"I didn't ask what people called you. I asked for your name."

I tried again. "Elizabeth."

That satisfied him. He nodded once, curtly.

"My name is Alexander."

Now that he wasn't looking at me, I felt the need to fill the awkward quiet.

"Thank you," I stuttered. "Thank you for saving me."

He lifted up half a cheek in a mirthless smile.

"Is that what I did?"

I didn't know what to say to that, so we spent the rest of the journey in silence.

Fast forward an hour, maybe two. My feet were in this spot, this exact spot. Alexander was on my left, talking to a white-blond man whose name I didn't yet know. He paused in his conversation to address me.

"Take off your clothes."

I gaped at him, gobsmacked.

"But—"

His lips twitched, eyes gleamed. Beside him, Zane made an amused face that I only saw out of the corner of my eye, because I couldn't look at him.

"Take. Off. Your. Clothes." Still quiet, still softly spoken. But the message was very clear: Alexander wasn't used to repeating himself, and if I made him do it again I'd be very sorry.

I didn't want to. I really didn't want to. But I'd just learned my first lesson at Bancroft Road. You didn't say no to Alexander. Slowly, tremulously, burning with humiliation, I took off my clothes.

The memories were vivid, and they sent a confusing surge of gratitude and hate oozing through my veins like acid. Alexander deserved to die. I was in absolutely no doubt about that. But he had saved my life. Whatever his reasons, he'd done it.

He deserved to die. But not by my hands.

Just by my handiwork.

A compromise. Samuel would not be happy. But then, he hadn't wanted to pull the trigger either. That's why I was standing there, drowning in a sea of doubt.

"Dammit!" I hissed, far too low to reach Alexander's slumbering ears.

There wasn't time to debate it any longer. Two clocks

were tick-tick-ticking at the back of my head. I backed away, unwilling to take my eyes off him in case he opened his. Even when I was far enough away that I could no longer make out the back of his head, the powerful arms, I didn't turn until I felt the pressure of the doorknob digging into my back.

On the other side of the door, I slumped against the wall, breathing hard like I'd been running. Already I was having second thoughts, but it was too late. There wasn't time go back in there, to stand in front of him and do it properly this time. No, the bombs would do their job. They would. Alexander would be dead, and my conscience would be clear. Clearer. Clear enough to live with myself.

Aware that I was running behind after my hesitation, I ran down the stairs, making more noise than was smart. I had to hope that Samuel had taken care of the doorman. At the base of the stairs I found no sign of him, so I took reassurance from that. I turned, heading for the storeroom at the back, my mind firmly on device number three, when a hand clamped down on my shoulder.

This time I didn't panic, because at the same time a familiar Welsh accent breathed "Lizzie!" in my ear.

"What is it?"

Samuel pushed me back into the shadow of the grand banister. His body was radiating tension, his grip on my arm almost painful.

"Zane wasn't in his flat," he whispered. "I can't find him."

I stared into the darkness of his face, just making out two shining eyes.

"What do we do?"

"Carry on. He must have gone out. Davis will have to take care of him later. Have you done the device in here?" He jerked with his head towards the storeroom.

"No."

I saw Samuel check his watch, make a face. I grimaced. How long had I been upstairs?

"Give it to me," he urged. "You sort the one in the basement. I don't want to still be here when the floors start falling on our head."

He gave a strained chuckle, but my face couldn't so much as smile in response.

"Here," I shoved the gun in the bag and thrust both at him. "I'll just take the device down."

I made to slide out from where he had me pinned against the wooden panelling of the hall, but he held me firm a second longer, dropped his head to land a rough kiss on my temple. Then he disappeared into the darkness and I felt my way down the final set of stairs, my hands full of C4.

We hadn't planned a specific room in the basement to leave the final device. It didn't really matter – the fabric of the building would be so destabilised by the other three explosions that a rumble just about anywhere down here would send the place crashing down like a house of cards. Aware of time, then, I darted into the first open door that I saw. It was a storage and records room.

The same room, in fact, where Zane had had me memorise the list of names before he'd sent me to meet Riley and collect schoolgirls' debts for Alexander. I wondered if the girls I'd met would see sense, now. If they'd give up their naughty little habits when they no longer had the handsome Zane persuading them, with his muscles and his smile and his white powder. Probably not, I realised. They'd just drift over to Rhys Davis and buy from Danny instead.

I dropped the C4 down onto the table that sat in the centre of the room and started preparing the electronics. Enough moonlight filtered through a high-up window for me to see what I was doing. Enough to cast shadows across the room, some that moved and some that didn't. Enough to warn me, if I'd been paying attention.

I wasn't. I was focused on the task in hand. On everything working like clockwork. I didn't see the shadow shift into position, didn't hear the low hiss of quiet breathing, hidden beneath my own. Didn't feel the hate-filled stare burning into the back of my neck.

I didn't realise anything was wrong until I heard the laugh.

It was low, and deep, and filled with pleasure.

"Oh, I was so hoping I'd get to be the one to kill you."

I froze, my fingers hovering above the putty, ready to flick the final switch.

"You shouldn't have come back here, Lizzie. I thought you were smarter than that."

"Zane," I greeted him tonelessly.

"What are you doing here?" he asked, stepping forward until the length of his body pinned me in place against the table. It was hot, except for the ice cold of something that wasn't flesh, jabbing at my ribcage. "Come to steal?"

"No," I licked my lips, swallowed.

Silence fell between us.

Say something, Lizzie. Keep him talking. If he's talking he's not shooting you. But my mind was blank.

"Turn around," he hissed.

I did as I was told – with some difficulty, as he didn't move back to give me space.

He was tall, and I had to tilt my head at an awkward angle to look up at him. The light filtering through bounced off his hair, making it glow like an angel's halo.

"I have no idea why Alexander decided to keep you," he murmured, "but thank Christ I don't have to put up with you any longer. He'll be annoyed – he wanted to choke the life out of you himself – but since I've got you here..."

I tried not to listen, tried to block his words out, knowing that fear would probably incapacitate me if I gave in to the idea that I was going to die.

"Zane, you could just let me go?" I whimpered.

He laughed; I knew he would. I'd meant him to. It was enough distraction for me to slip my hands behind me, grab the device. Flip the switch.

I hoped my body would conceal the light from the bomb long enough to blow the smarmy shit to smithereens. If I could just keep myself alive long enough.

"No. No, no, no. Don't think so, Lizzie. Not when it would give me so much pleasure to take your head off." His accent grew stronger in his excitement. It was harsh, jarring. I grimaced, more at the sound of it than the words he was spitting at me.

I wondered, while I stood there waiting for him to shoot me, whether I'd have been able to pull the trigger this time. If I would have been able to send a bullet flying through the air into Zane's brain.

A pointless thought, as the gun was safe upstairs in the bag with Samuel. But I smiled to myself as I realised yes, I would. I had no reason to feel anything but loathing for Zane.

He still hadn't done it – still hadn't shot me, though.

Was he really worried about what Alexander would say if he stole this moment from him? Or was he just revelling in the satisfaction? In the dark it was hard to read the answer in his face.

How much longer did the bomb have? Two minutes? Three?

Longer than I did, I was sure.

I was focused on Zane's face: his eyes, his smile. I was focused on the feel of the gun, pushing hard enough into my side to bruise. So for the second time I didn't hear the stealthy footsteps; see the shadow moving slowly across the room; feel the slight tremor of feet inching their way across aged floorboards.

Not until the last second did I realise that Zane and I were not alone. Not until I saw the gun, racing into my vision from the right, just above my eye level. Pressing lightly against Zane's temple, like the kiss of a lover.

I didn't see the finger squeeze. Didn't hear the pop of a silenced gunshot. But I felt it. The shockwave that Zane's head couldn't withstand; the heat of something wet that coated my face in a fine spray; the gun dropping from my side; the hand trying to grab onto me with the last seconds of life.

I watched as Zane fell to the ground, Samuel's bullet in his brain.

Then, madness. The world rushed back into motion. Samuel was at my side, urging me out of my temporary trance.

"Lizzie, move!"

With one rough hand he seized my hoodie, yanked it, forced my feet to work. Out of the room, up the stairs, out of the door. Fresh air slapped me awake, but my legs couldn't catch up with Samuel's pace as he dragged me along behind him. I stumbled in his wake, nearly fell flat on my face.

A man in a car parked across the road watched us burst out of the door and down the steps with curious eyes. Was he Alexander's? Davis's? The police? It was impossible to tell. Whoever he was, he let us pass.

We hit the street and Samuel instantly started striding away, pulling me along with him. He didn't look back, not once, just kept staring forward, eyes intent, focused.

The world was rent apart before we made it to the corner. I had my back to it, but the explosion still lifted me off my feet, throwing me forward into Samuel, who did his best to catch me before the hard concrete took my teeth. The noise came a split second after. It was immense, dizzying. I heard it ringing in my ears long after silence returned. Next came heat, and with it the acrid, burning, choking taste of smoke.

We'd done it.

I wanted to stop. To witness my handiwork: Rhys's 'spectacle'. I wanted to see a gaping hole where Alexander's empire had been, but Samuel was tugging on me desperately.

"Lizzie, come on. We have to move. This place will be crawling with police and GE in a minute. We can't be caught here."

I didn't even get to look.

Samuel all but carried me round the corner, hauling me down the road until he slung me against the side of a car, letting me slump there whilst he yanked open the driver's side door. Was this the vehicle Danny had provided? Over the tops of the houses in front of me I saw the orange sky, the spirals of smoke. I didn't hunt for souls flying heavenward. I knew there wouldn't be any.

My ears were ringing from the blast, my pulse pounding, but beneath this I thought I caught the sound of feet thumping against pavement. As I stared dead ahead, eyes on the corner, the bleary dark of the street changed. I was so disorientated from the adrenaline rush and the impact of the bomb that it took me a few seconds to realise the strangely shifting shadows in front of me were silhouettes. Running silhouettes. Two of them, maybe three.

Who was it? Survivors?

No, no one could have walked away from that.

Still, someone was coming for us. I turned to warn Samuel, but he was already facing me, one hand reaching out to grab at my hand.

"Get in." He manhandled me into the car, shoving me until I was over the gear lever, in the passenger seat, and he could slip in beside me. I glimpsed the key waiting in the ignition before Samuel grabbed it and twisted hard. The car coughed and stuttered before the engine caught.

"Yes!" I heard him hiss.

In the rear-view mirror I caught a quick glance of whoever it was, drawing closer, but a moment later we were moving; lights and streets and houses flashing by me. Away from the scene. Away from Bancroft Road. Away from Alexander.

We'd done it. Still shocked, I couldn't take it in.

Surely I was still back there, trapped in the basement with Zane? Surely any second now I was going to feel the agony of metal ripping through muscle and bone? This could not be real. Samuel had asked me before how it felt to be free and I'd had no answer for him, because I hadn't really been free. It'd been a temporary reprieve; something that, I knew from my time with Mark, could be ripped away in one swift, terrifying moment. But now Alexander was gone. Dead. Blown into a million tiny pieces. So was I free?

And how did it feel?

I couldn't tell. I felt... numb. Stunned. Too much, too fast. Too deliciously close to something like happiness to trust it.

Beside me, Samuel didn't speak. Minutes and miles passed as he hunkered over the wheel, eyes fixed dead ahead or gazing behind in the rearview mirror. He pushed the car hard, ignoring the noisy protests as it chugged and whined, rollicking over the uneven road surface, smashing into deep potholes.

Watching the world go by so quickly was making me sick, so I took to watching him, trying to convince myself that this was actually happening. That we had survived – succeeded.

Almost. Because we were still in London. Still in England. Still marked.

But we were close – so very, very close.

The further away we got from Stepney, the nearer we got to the port Davis had told Samuel about, the more relaxed he became. He leaned back, eased off the gas, loosened his grip on the steering wheel. He became more aware of his surroundings, flicking on the heater, adjusting the seat so he wasn't hunched up, much too close to the windscreen. He became aware of me.

"Are you all right?" he asked.

I dipped my head in an awkward nod. I wasn't really, but I was getting there.

"Are you hurt?" He flipped the overhead light on for a moment, appraised me.

"No," I shook my head.

"You're bleeding," his brow furrowed with concern.

I reached up and felt my skin. It was wet. Pulling my fingers away, I saw the vivid red; I remembered the horror of the moment.

"It's not mine," I whispered. "It's Zane's."

Suddenly repulsed, I pulled my sleeve over my hand and scraped vigorously at my face, trying to get it all off.

"But you're all right?" he repeated, looking me over again, eyebrows raised like he couldn't believe it.

"I'm fine," I promised, my voice stronger.

He grinned at me before dousing us back into darkness. The interior of the car stayed black for only a heartbeat before powerful white lights blazed into us from behind. I gasped, tensed, twisted round to watch a set of full beams bear down on us with frightening speed. I saw them come close, close, closer. Then, just as it seemed they'd climb right over the back of us, the brightness so intense it burned my eyeballs, whoever was driving the car whipped it to the left in a move that made the vehicle seem to careen dangerously to the side before it rocketed away.

"Arse," Samuel commented, his gaze fixed on the rear view. But his voice was tense. Had he thought the same as me, that someone had found us? The GE coming to arrest us; someone out for retribution for Bancroft Road; a double-cross by Davis? All these fears had flooded my brain and even after the car was long gone I continued to stare back at the empty road for endless moments, waiting for those lights to return and truly engulf us this time. To bring us to account.

They didn't.

After that we saw very little traffic. Samuel drove for what seemed an eternity. It was late, the clock on the dash said almost four in the morning, but sleep had never been further from my mind, despite the hot air wafting out at me through the vents. My eyes were wide pools, drinking in the unfamiliar roads as we raced down them. When he pulled up in an empty car park, instantly killing the headlights, I stared about me. I had no idea where we were.

"Is this it?" I whispered. "Are we here?"

Samuel nodded.

"Come on," he grabbed my hand, pulling me across the seats so that I got out his side. It was awkward: he stood less than a foot from the opening. I was about to ask him to move over a bit, when I realised he was shielding me. I stayed hidden behind his protective bulk, but stood up on my tiptoes, trying to see over his shoulder.

"You made it!" A Scots accent called to us out of the darkness. A second later Danny appeared out of thin air. "How was it?"

Samuel shrugged, his expression hard.

Danny smiled apologetically, as if he realised how it'd sounded.

"I have to tell you, Mr Davis is very pleased. Very pleased indeed. It's already plastered all over the news.

They're calling it gang warfare. Which, I suppose, it is." He smirked.

"Where's the boat?" Samuel asked shortly.

Danny gave him a look which plainly said he didn't appreciate Samuel's tone, but he turned and gestured with his hand.

"It's waiting for you. Direct route to Wales."

He started to walk and Samuel followed, one hand wrapped firmly around mine.

It was a small tug, bobbing lightly on the surface of the Thames. There was no plank to climb, but the rim swayed just a foot or so from a warped wooden jetty. There was a small wheelhouse where I could see a pair of shadows moving.

"Jump on, Lizzie," Samuel said.

I did as he asked, lumbering across the space. It was harder than it looked: the constant movement of the boat made it hard to find somewhere to plant my feet.

"Send me a postcard, won't you?" Danny winked as Samuel joined me. "Let me know how you're enjoying your new life in Wales."

There was something off about his comment that I couldn't place. Samuel didn't react, though.

"It'll be fine," he grunted. "I know what I'm walking into. You're staying here?"

"Mr Davis wants me to oversee the... er, takeover of some businesses. Make sure our expansion goes as planned. I'll be seeing you soon, though, I'm sure."

There was no further goodbye than that. Danny stepped

backwards several paces until the night swallowed him, and the quiet hum of the boat's engines grew louder. One of the men I'd seen in the wheelhouse skirted in front of us and unhooked a thick length of rope, which fell with a loud splash into the water before he hauled it back onto the deck. A few seconds later I realised we were moving, cutting through the gently lapping water. As we picked up speed, wind whipped at my face, tossing my hair around. I couldn't see anything, the driver kept the lights off, probably to avoid any prying eyes.

I wasn't sorry. I wasn't keen to see any more of London, to say farewell. There would be no love lost.

A bright flare of light behind us made me spin round to stare over Samuel's shoulder. Danny – his car turning a wide circle as he drove away, lights reaching far out into the darkness.

Just as the beams swept from the water to the road, I caught a glimpse of something. A shape. But I blinked and it was gone.

I stared at the spot, cloaked again now in inky black, as if it would reveal itself. It didn't.

It's nothing, I told myself. A tree, or a bin. Nothing.

So why did I get the feeling that it was staring back at me? Why did I imagine two green, cat like eyes peering at me, watching, quietly furious?

No. It was nothing.

I turned my face away, back into the wind, letting the slightly damp air cleanse the blood, the hate, the fear away. I smiled as two arms curled their way round my waist and a head dropped onto my shoulder.

"We made it, Lizzie," Samuel whispered in my ear. "You're free."

Free. Was I?

Alexander was gone. I was leaving London, probably never to return. And Samuel was with me. I had what I wanted, but was I free?

I wasn't so sure. It seemed to me that we'd swapped one terrifying gangster for another in Rhys Davis. I didn't trust him. He was as much a criminal as he was a freedom-fighter. Was life in Wales going to be any better than Alexander's London? Yes, the cause was noble, but it was Samuel's fight. Not mine. But then, at least I had Samuel.

The future seemed as murky as the black water sliding by beneath us. I held on tight to Samuel's arms and stared into the uncertain dark.

ACKNOWLEDGEMENTS

Thank-you, thank-you, thank-you to the following folks who made *Bombmaker* happen:

Firstly, my gratitude to everyone at Templar, in particular Helen Boyle for her help, patience, and for looking after me, and to Will Steele for another awesome cover. Thanks to my agent Ben Illis at the BIA for seeing the book's potential in the first place.

Cheers m'dears to Ruth and Clare for being my guinea pigs and my cheerleaders. To Chris, my gorgeous, handsome husband, thank-you for playing so many video games so I wouldn't feel guilty about ignoring you while I wrote...

And as promised, HELLO to all my pupils at Peebles High School. Yes, you are my favourite class...

ABOUT THE AUTHOR

Photograph by Alex Hewitt

Claire McFall grew up just south of Glasgow and is now an English teacher at a high school in the Scottish Borders, where she lives.

As a child, creative writing was always Claire's favourite subject, and she would write short stories on her typewriter. She also loved to read, and firmly believes that, "if you want to write, you need to read".

It was when Claire started commuting to work that ideas for novels began to form in her mind, and now she writes every day. She is currently working on her third book, to be published by Templar in 2015.

WWW.CLAIREMCFALL.CO.UK

Don't miss Claire McFall's first book, *Ferryman*:

When Dylan emerges from the wreckage of a train crash onto
a bleak Scottish hillside, she meets a strange boy who seems
to be waiting for her.

But Tristan is no ordinary teenage boy, and the journey across the
desolate, wraith-infested wasteland is no ordinary journey.

Life, death, love – which will Dylan choose?

'Probably one of the best Young Adult
romance books I have ever read.'
Lovereading.co.uk

ISBN 978-1-84877-963-1   £6.99